S0-BBZ-502

Michael Innes is the pseudonym of J. I. M.
Stewart, who was a Student of Christ Church,
Oxford, from 1949 until his retirement in
1973. He was born in 1906 and was educated at
Edinburgh Academy and Oriel College, Oxford.
He was lecturer in English at the University of
Leeds from 1930 to 1935, and spent the
succeeding ten years as Jury Professor of English
in the University of Adelaide, South Australia.

He has published twelve novels and two
volumes of short stories under his own name, as
well as many detective stories and broadcast
scripts under the pseudonym of Michael Innes.
His *Eight Modern Writers* appeared in 1963 as
the final volume of *The Oxford History of
English Literature*. Michael Innes is married
and has five children.

Michael Innes

What Happened at Hazelwood

Penguin Books

Penguin Books Ltd, Harmondsworth,
Middlesex, England
Penguin Books, 625 Madison Avenue,
New York, New York 10022, U.S.A.
Penguin Books Australia Ltd, Ringwood,
Victoria, Australia
Penguin Books Canada Limited, 2801 John Street,
Markham, Ontario, Canada L3R 1B4
Penguin Books (N.Z.) Ltd, 182–190 Wairau Road,
Auckland 10, New Zealand

First published by Victor Gollancz 1946
Published in Penguin Books 1968
Reprinted 1970, 1976, 1977, 1979

Printed in the United States of America by
George Banta Co., Inc., Harrisonburg, Virginia
Set in Intertype Baskerville

Contents

Part One: Nicolette

I

Nobody could have predicted just what has happened at Hazelwood, and at the moment it appears as if nobody can elucidate it either. That something would occur many have believed – or will afterwards imagine they believed – and indeed the Simneys are eminently the sort of folk of whom one might expect a scandal. Their history, it has to be admitted, is dubious. And their household is dubious too.

George Simney had gone to Australia as a young man and was believed to have engaged in agricultural pursuits there until the baronetcy fell to him. Of course various classes of men may travel with perfect propriety to the antipodes and even sojourn in them for indefinite periods. But this does not hold of the sons of baronets; Victorian fiction established an enduring convention on the point; and everybody realized that Sir George must have been a never-do-well and a bad hat. Very likely he had killed a fellow-prospector on the gold diggings or drowned in a billabong some rival in a lewd love; very likely he would be hunted down one day by the vengeance of a gang of bush-ranging associates whom he had betrayed.

Something of the sort would explain the fact that the master of Hazelwood slept with a shot-gun at his side; that he made his domestics go to church but never thought of going himself; that he had brought back to England a one-eyed butler who looked much more like a retired pirate than a respectable upper servant; that there had been a time when he kept mistresses in Hazelwood Hall instead of discreetly in cottages or the local market-town; that he had

7

caused all ordinary baths to be removed from the house as insanitary and had installed showers instead. Yes, it was to be expected that something would happen to Sir George. But who could have guessed what?

His end has been sudden, unaccountable and violent. He himself, moreover, must have found its approaches extremely surprising, since the features of the corpse displayed that expression of astounded and incredulous terror only assumed by persons who see that they are about to be murdered in the most pronouncedly bizarre way.

In fact this bad baronet has died true to the traditions of his kind – mysteriously in his library, at midnight, while a great deal of snow was falling in the park outside.

It may be said then that in his death Sir George Simney has displayed – even if involuntarily – a sense of style. And people are obscurely grateful. This holds not merely of the police, who look to the affair to bring promotion, and of the journalists, who see in it the makings of a first-rate sensation. It holds of the neighbourhood in general, which has dimly hoped for something of the sort and would have been disappointed had Sir George simply taken to his bed, sent for old Dr Humberstone, weakened, rallied, weakened again and passed away under an oxygen tent. The human mind is avid of evidences of artistry in the frame of things, and has constructed a great deal of philosophy and theology as a result.

Nevertheless it is a theologian – I am told – who constitutes the opposition in this matter. Perhaps the only person who altogether disapproves the fact and manner of Sir George's end is the Reverend Adrian Deamer, the vicar of Hazelwood. This is partly, no doubt, because Mr Deamer believes it to be particularly undesirable that a bad man should very suddenly die. But it is also because Mr Deamer feels that the affair holds depths which he is impelled to fathom. And this distracts him from his proper business of visiting old women, of moderating by various persuasions

8

the incidence of illegitimacy in the parish (his chief occupation), and of preparing a weekly sermon which should pass muster with the more intelligent children in his congregation ... What *happened* at Hazelwood? Mr Deamer feels that he can never really be easy until he knows.

Of course, a number of other people feel the same – and with more evident reason. In a community, mysterious homicide is a sensation, and, perhaps, an intellectual irritant inviting the more active-minded to scratch. But within a household such a calamity is felt chiefly in terms of suspense. It is like the presence of illness of an unknown degree of dangerousness – and there is the same badgering of authority to make pronouncements more definite than authority cares to make. The Hazelwood household wants to know what has *happened*. The police – local constables at first, but now grey-haired men like family solicitors – are extremely close and discreet. They rather resemble those eminent physicians, called down from London at several guineas a mile, who eventually pronounce that unless the patient goes on much as before he is almost sure to get either better or worse. In point of emotional reassurance (which is the relevant point) the local doctor proves the better bargain, after all. And at Hazelwood there are several who already regret the homely Sergeant Laffer, who confidently opined that the vagrant responsible for the deed would before long be picked up in a casual-ward or asleep under a haystack.

And, indeed, does it not look like that? At any one of a dozen kitchen doors in the district the merest tramp might learn of fabled riches in Sir George Simney's study; he might mark the window and note the feasible climb. The light had been low, and therefore very probably indistinguishable through the curtain; so might he not have broken in, expecting the place to himself – and when surprised have killed his challenger in just this way? For Sir George was hit on the head with a blunt instrument – such is the undeniable truth of the matter – and an assault so little

9

refined seems to match with a passing tramp well enough.

But then again – and here is the trouble – it matches with certain Simneys too; you have only to look at some of them to see not only that they could readily scale a trellised wall but also that a blunt instrument would be their choice every time. There is, of course, the fact that Sir George was hit from behind, whereas if you visualize yourself being bludgeoned by a Simney your mind's eye will certainly discern him as coming at you from straight ahead. But this is a point probably too refined for a policeman, even one who looked like a solicitor; and thus the reputation for violence which Simneys in general bear, and of which by and at large they are rather proud, now has its distinctly embarrassing side.

But there is more than this to the fact that Sir George was taken from the rear. There is a prior point – and one so obvious that it was even spotted immediately by Sir George's butler, the retired pirate. One is obliged to say 'even' because this worthy, Alfred Owdon by name, is widely reputed to be devoid of anything distinguishing the human intelligence, and to equate indeed with the equine rather than the canine in mental rating ... However this may be, Owdon it was who pointed out that a man suddenly hit on the head from behind ought not to look as Sir George looked.

Theoretically it is no doubt possible that the last confused scurryings of sensation about the stricken brain of a murdered man may fortuitously imprint upon the features an expression conventionally associated with almost any emotional state. He may, for instance, simply look enormously pleased. But with no one does this abstract view survive the concrete reality of a glance at the dead man as he now lies in his coffin awaiting the pompous oblivion of the Simney family vault. Sir George, one knows, saw something ranging between the extraordinary and the preternatural; and then he was immediately hit on the head – from behind.

There seems to be very little sense in that. But even at this one is not done with the bothersomeness of the blow having come from the back. Such an approach – the grey-haired police detectives call it the *a tergo* approach, so evidently they are learned men – such an approach almost rules out the notion that the assailant struck out hastily upon being surprised. The direction of the stroke power-fully suggests a deliberate assault upon an unsuspecting man. And yet (once more) there is his expression . . .

It has become clear that the police like the case. It gives them something to chew on. They show no signs of going home. If they were asked to describe what has *happened* their answer – it is possible to suspect – would be *Quite a lot*. And, somehow, nobody relishes this. The notion that operating that single definite impact upon a human skull has been, so to speak, an engine or contrivance in which revolved wheels within wheels proves altogether disagree-able. Of course one knows whether one has, or has not, committed a specific crime of violence. And yet as the investigation becomes complicated – and it has become that – it is difficult for any of those concerned to abide confidently even in this absolute security. The complications are like so many hazards on a pin-table. The ball – obscurely visioned as the future verdict of a judge and jury – comes rattling down. And the Simneys, however their individual knowledge and conscience stand, all feel like so many final goals, holes or pockets which may at any moment feel the fatal *plop*.

I know, because I am one of them. I did not kill George. Indeed – and unlike most members of the family – I don't believe I ever even wanted to do so. But I feel like one of those pockets, all the same. Perhaps it is to ease a little of the tension that I am writing these notes.

2

I am glad I have an *alibi*.

This is rational enough. But I am also glad that almost nobody else has, and here there is no possibility of defending myself. To harbour such a sentiment is thoroughly base. But then we are the most ghastly people: that had better be got clear at once. If the eminent Victorian who closed Dowden's *Life of Shelley* murmuring *What a set!* had only lived to make the acquaintance of the Simneys, he would infallibly have exclaimed *What a god-awful crowd!* Whether he would also have thought of any of us as an ineffectual angel beating in the void his luminous wings in vain (which is, I rather fancy, how Mervyn sees himself), I don't at all know. But anyway Matthew Arnold died in 1888 while chasing a bus, and it was left to the grey-haired police detectives to weigh in with a verdict.

I have no doubt as to what their verdict on us has been, nor that the detectives are thoroughly satisfied to arrive at it. They had only to size us up – the whole lot of us, from Lucy to Owdon – to see that the affair was a sleuth's dream come true. And not only because of the baronetcy and the snow and the library and the midnight hour – though the coming together of all these (and, of course, of the blunt instrument, which I would have you remember) must have been very pleasing too. Chiefly their satisfaction must have lain in the observation that we were all so patently ghastly. *It might have been any of them* was what they doubtless whispered together. And – once more – they liked it. They could settle in and get down to a nice, thorough job on each of us in turn.

I fancy the life of the higher constabulary is rather nomadic. They are called in; they glance round; and their superior science and intelligence instantly penetrate whatever uncouth mystification has been practised. One thinks of battle-ships which bear in their bowels machines solving at lightning speed the most intricate problems of gunnery. The calculation is made, the annihilating broadside fired, and the great ship lumbers on. So with these higher eluci-dators of crime: a single comprehensive deductive opera-tion and the next case calls them forward. But it is different with the show we are putting up. And they quite like settling down for a change to a bit of steady blockade.

I dare say that if you want to get on with the business of Sir George you find all this about Shelley and battle-ships pretty intolerable. But artistry, I assure you, is at work. Here is simply a bit of the atmosphere of the Simneys being laid on right at the start. Here is one facet – the showing-off facet. Gerard (so recently arrived from Austra-lia) calls it their fondness for showing their grudge. The Simneys are grudgy. A most extraordinary phrase, but not inexpressive: what is implied is showing off not with the simple aim of gratifying one's own vanity but with some deliberate intention of irritating. And I can think of another epithet that fits. When I was at Oxford carefully spoken undergraduates, I discovered, used the word *bloody* (so omnibus a word with the world at large) in a very pre-cise way. To call a man *bloody*, it seemed, was to ascribe to him a very specific quality of intolerableness – one not easy to define but perfectly well understood in that society. Well, in this sense the Simneys are *bloody*. Are they – or is one of them – *bloody* in another sense?

> Now does he feel
> His secret murders sticking on his hands ...

Is one of them like that? Those grey-haired men propose to find out.

And now I ought to give you first a genealogical account of the Simneys (illustrated by one of those family trees that Galsworthy popularized among novelists) and second a chronological and topographical description of the actual fatality (with a regular crime-story plan: *x* marks the Spot).

Somehow or other all this will have to come, but it seems to me that I had better begin with at least a short scene of greater animation. For I want to gain your interest in this George Simney affair. It interests me.

So consider dinner-time on the Monday. There is a natural starting place there. And if you will unpack your bag, so to speak, for a week's visit to Hazelwood beginning on that day you will have a reasonable opportunity of getting acquainted with us before the thing actually happens and a chance of receiving the final solution just as the car comes round to take you to the station on the following Sunday evening. I don't say that you will find this week at Hazelwood wholly edifying or exactly comfortable. Some rather improper things will happen, numerous meals will be completely upset and it is likely that on several mornings the agitated servants will quite neglect to bring you your hot water or your tea. Still, it will be tolerably lively most of the time.

Moreover you won't be the only visitor. For that was what happened at dinner-time on the Monday. Another couple of Simneys turned up, and one of them brought a wife as well. They turned up without warning from twelve thousand miles away, loudly declaring that George had in some way cheated or defrauded them. This, of course, was likely enough. But we felt that they might well have left these business issues till next morning – particularly as in brief inarticulate intervals they put away so much of that dinner that there was very little left for anybody else. No doubt this was just their rude colonial health. They looked healthy – and Joyleen excessively so: she has the physical perfection that comes of living in sun and surf and idleness. She is also sexy in a thoroughly vulgar way, like the girls in advertisements for swim-suits. She caught George's eye from the first.

But why start with Joyleen? There's no logic in that.

Notice to begin with, then, that this dinner would have been quite notable even if those antipodean cousins hadn't turned up. It would probably have been quite uncomfortable too. George never really got on with his younger brother, Bevis – this, perhaps, because of their long separation in youth – and nothing brought them together except the ritual business of shooting over each other's land. But now here was Bevis staying at Hazelwood, and with him was his son, Willoughby. George was fifty-four, Bevis is fifty-three, and Willoughby is twenty. I can't see how to avoid these bald slabs of information in starting a family chronicle like this. And I warn you that you have to remember them – more or less.

These were the visitors. The permanents were George's widowed sister, Lucy Cockayne, and her son, Mervyn. Lucy is two years younger than Bevis, and Mervyn a year younger than Willoughby – which is symmetrical enough. Then there was George's younger sister, Grace, who is thirty-eight and unmarried. Or at least she is thought to be unmarried. Once you get among baronets and blunt instruments you can never be quite sure of little matters like that, can you?

Oh – and, of course, there was me.

I seem to have started with the genealogy after all, and let the animated scene wait. Still, it's coming. And as for the genealogy, there are vital bits missing still. Don't forget that.

For instance, Timmy. A vital part of his genealogy is notoriously missing. On that evening it didn't seem greatly to matter. You don't need a genealogy to hand soup.

'Timmy,' said George abruptly, 'do you like doing this sort of thing?'

And Timmy Owdon glided behind his father and set down a plate quietly. He wasn't going to let clumsiness express his feelings, as if those feelings came to no more than sulkiness. Timmy Owdon set down a plate and before replying to his master's question reached for another. Old Owdon stood behind George's chair, his one eye impassive

and unwinking. If Timmy's insolence penetrated to his
torpid mental processes he gave no sign. Timmy set the
second plate. Then he said:

'No, sir.'

'That so? Pity. Reckoned as promotion, I'm told.' George,
with the frown of a short-sighted but also of a saturnine
man, peered up the table. 'Lucy, Grace, you look quite
glum. Have a glass of sherry. Or let Owdon pour the claret
now.'

Neither Lucy nor Grace replied. Owdon remained immobile in his place. Timmy glanced slowly round the table,
but his gaze passed some eighteen inches too high for empty
plates. He was taking a good look at us – and very plainly
consigning most of us to the nethermost pit.

Bevis took a glance at the boy, flushed, dropped his eyes.
'George –' he began, and stopped.

'Yes, Bevis?'

Bevis compressed his lips and absorbed himself with the
Simney crest on his spoon. There was a silence. George laid
his little finger on a glass. Owdon poured sherry.

It pleased George to have Timmy Owdon in the room. In
order to achieve this he had contrived (by simple means) to
drive one of the parlour-maids from the house. Timmy was
to have her place. I believe there was a time when footmen
were like game – never provided except in twos or
multiples of two. But now here was this solitary youth in a
sort of livery, which his father had fished out from somewhere and which by no means fitted him. An uncouth lad
would have been a scarecrow. With Timmy you didn't
notice. He would have looked beautiful in anything. And
now in his deep smouldering anger at having been taken
away from the horses and turned into an indoor servant
like his father he looked like a stripling cherub, a fallen
angel with all his brightness still about him.

And yet if there had been an artist in that dining-room
(and, oddly enough, Bevis's boy, Willoughby, is shaping
that way) Timmy Owdon would not have stood alone in

the limelight. For there was Mervyn Cockayne, George's nephew and Lucy's son. Mervyn too was like an angel. In fact, he was like the same angel.

In that lay George's little joke. His butler's boy and his sister's were equally Simneys. You had only to look at them to see that there could be no doubt of it.

So already, you see, the plot begins to thicken. To no lady of feasible age and of the Simney blood could this clamant genetic fact be palatable. And few country gentlemen whose butler has thus obscurely distinguished himself among his womenfolk will first continue to employ the man and then, some sixteen years on, bring the natural child to his table as a footman. But George liked that sort of thing. Hitherto Timmy had lived unobtrusively in the stables. This was the first occasion on which George had chosen to show him off as the family scandal. Or as one of the family scandals. There are a good many more, some of which will presently come in.

'Owdon,' said George, 'how old is your boy?'

George's butler turned abruptly and made a sign to the remaining parlour-maid. He was an unbeautiful creature – in some fray, piratical or otherwise, he had got his face messed up as well as losing that eye – and I used to fancy that an unexpected sensitiveness sometimes made him veer away like this when any general attention was directed on him.

'Sixteen, sir,' said Owdon.

'Is that so?' And George looked up the table. 'Only a couple of years younger than Mervyn. But quite a different type. I mean, quite a different psychological type. Although both, I should say, are intelligent. Owdon, you would agree that Mr Mervyn is intelligent?'

'Certainly, sir.'

And Owdon moved off along the table – rather a silent table. George, of course, could give a wholly adequate rendering of the country gentleman able at any time to converse familiarly with his servants. And somehow this added an extra flavour of nastiness to his atrocious behaviour.

The only person who did not appear upset was young Mervyn Cockayne himself. He looked appraisingly at Timmy, and as if by some instinctive sympathy his angelic features took on momentarily the same sultry look. I think their eyes met – in which case the sensation must have been just that of looking into a mirror. But when he spoke it was altogether sedately.

'It is very respectable' – Mervyn has a high-pitched voice which instantly commanded the table – 'to derive one's retainers from the same family generation by generation. Owdon is to be congratulated for having forwarded so pleasantly feudal a disposition of things.' Mervyn looked round the table and affected to be much struck by an array of frozen faces. 'Mama,' he cried – and his voice rose to a parody of an anxious squeak – 'is it possible that I can have said something *gauche*?'

Lucy Cockayne looked vague, which was her refuge on such occasions. George looked delighted. Of all his relations it was this little toad alone whom he at all tolerated. Indeed, he made a favourite of Mervyn. It was generally agreed that he would leave him the greater part of what it was his to dispose of: a personal fortune of very considerable extent.

'And now it is for Timmy to carry on the tradition.' Mervyn was off again with the largest innocence. His eyes travelled once more round the table – an inquiring and speculative eye. It rested for a moment on his aunt Grace and passed on to the accompaniment of the faintest possible shake of the head. 'Willoughby,' he said suddenly – and much as if an altogether different topic of conversation had struck him – 'did you ever feel, as I have done, that it is a pity not to have a sister?'

Willoughby Simney might have replied to his cousin – only his father forestalled him. 'Lucy' – Bevis had gone a brick red and addressed his sister abruptly – 'your boy ought to be birched. Eighteen or not, he ought to be birched.'

'Whereas if I did have a sister' – and with a skilful pause Mervyn swept in the attention of the whole company again – 'she would have to be churched A less painful experience, but equally embarrassing.'

'Church?' said Lucy absently. Whether she at all understood this indecent talk in which her brat was indulging I don't know. 'That reminds me. Wasn't Mr Deamer here this afternoon?'

'Deamer?' said George sharply. 'Fellow has no business coming about the place.' He spoke much as if the vicar of Hazelwood was a dishonest gamekeeper whom he had turned away. 'Unless to call on a sick servant and leave a tract. Owdon, are any of your people sick?'

'No, sir.'

Grace Simney, who had so far not spoken during the meal, put down her spoon and looked directly at her brother. 'George,' she said, 'the tract was meant for you.'

'Was it indeed, now?' And George sipped his sherry.

'Yes it was!' Grace's voice was suddenly shrill. She was staring at Timmy with a sort of fascinated repulsion, and it was plain that her mind was swinging agitatedly between this ancient family scandal and some revelation of the afternoon. Looking at her one could see why Mervyn had shaken his head. She had not at all the appearance of one likely to become inadvertently the mother of a fresh generation of Hazelwood retainers. Grace is blanched and angular and faded. Intellectually able and full of nervous force, she became in her later twenties headmistress of a girls' school. She is that still. But for years now she has regularly devoted her holidays to mild nervous illness. This always brings her back to Hazelwood – and her brother. And she was looking at him now with features drawn in anger. 'Yes it was,' she repeated. 'Some girl in the village –'

Bevis, who had glanced round the room and seen that

the parlour-maid was still present, abruptly interrupted. 'Willoughby,' he said, 'I didn't like the way you were hunching your shoulders this afternoon. It contracts the chest, my boy, and that means that you have to hold your breath or the aim goes nowhere. And you were having binocular trouble, too. Continuity of glance –'

'A very *young* girl –'

'– and uniformity of movement . . .'

Bevis is all for decency – which doesn't mean that he is any more estimable than other members of the family. I would call him bluff, obtuse and unscrupulous; and he is secret where it is the Simney habit to be open. I don't know that he much improved matters by starting this shouting match with Grace.

But at least he diverted Mervyn.

'To me,' said Mervyn, 'Willoughby appeared to shoot well. But uncle George, too, it seems, can bring down his bird. Mama, let us listen to aunt Grace and plan for the moral regeneration of the village. Let us set up a Vigilance Society at the Hall and have uncle George and Owdon as joint patrons. And our excellent Willoughby shall be beadle.'

'Be what?' said Willoughby.

'The rascally beadle who shall flagellate the fallen daughters of the peasantry. Just your line. And no doubt your papa will lend you a birch. As for aunt Grace –'

Willoughby lifted his sherry glass and pitched it in Mervyn's face. Lucy ridiculously sprang to her feet as if to protect her darling boy, and her chair went over backwards. Grace had now lost all control of herself and was hurling at George whatever it was that Mr Deamer had come cautiously to insinuate. Bevis for some reason was bellowing angrily. And at the whole silly and disordered spectacle George was laughing heartily, as if he were an eighteenth-century backwoods squire in some rough-and-tumble novel by Smollett.

It was at this moment that Owdon, who had left the

dining-room a few minutes previously came in again. It was plain that something had happened. The man was ashen — and a mere vulgar family rumpus would by no means have taken him that way.

'Your Ladyship,' he said, 'Mr Hippias has arrived, and Mr and Mrs Gerard with him.'

You had almost forgotten me, Gentle Reader, had you not? And I don't think you realized that I am a woman — and Lady Simney?

3

But there it is; it is the widow of the late baronet who is telling the story — the unfinished and painful story which lies around me as I write. My name is Nicolette and I am twenty-eight — which means that I was twenty-six years younger than my husband.

You will wonder how I came to marry him. Or perhaps you won't. After all as yet you know nothing about me. And you may be more interested at the moment in Hippias and Gerard and Joyleen, the antipodean cousins who are out there waiting in the hall while Owdon, strangely discomposed, mumbles to me of their arrival at that displeasing dinner table.

But if *you* are not disposed to wonder how I came to marry George I think I may say that Joyleen was thoroughly curious straight away. She is an ignorant little thing and as outlandish as her name. If you asked her to list the Seven Wonders of the World she would undoubtedly begin with Sydney Harbour Bridge and then get no farther. And if she wondered why I had married George I certainly wondered why Gerard had married her — or had been allowed by his father, Hippias, to do so. For I had gathered that the Australian Simneys were folk of the severest social sense.

They were, in fact, pastoralists – a word which suggests robed and bearded persons living in tents, but which (it seems) is simply synonymous with gentry and applied to exclusively-minded folk living retired lives amid millions and millions of sheep. Hippias Simney of Hazelwood Park, New South Wales, was understood to be like that, as had been his father, Guy Simney, before him. And presumably young Gerard had been brought up in the same ovine environment. Perhaps in Joyleen he had been constrained to marry money. Or perhaps it was simply that she had got Gerard on the strength of her charms. She might be accurately described as the sort of girl who would be attractive to most men for a month or two before and a week or two after. I am bound to admit that I disliked her from the first – and you will notice how I tend to go off after her before she ought really to come in. Frankly, she was a bit of a last straw as far as I was concerned.

But don't get me wrong. I'm not at all like George's virgin sister Grace, inept at and condemnatory of the whole odd and inescapable business of the sexes. Joyleen didn't wonder why George married me. She wondered why I married George. She saw that George was of the week-or-two sort – her own sort. And she saw that I wasn't; Perhaps you will presently see it too. At any rate, don't be misled by this hard-boiled style. It just seems the only possible medium for such a narrative as this.

And now where have I got to? George has had Timmy Owdon, whose mother is a sixteen-year-old question-mark, in to wait at table. This has offended both his brother Bevis and his sisters Lucy and Grace. It has given Lucy's beastly little son Mervyn an occasion for his nauseous wit and moved Mervyn's cousin Willoughby to pitch a glass of excellent sherry at him. Grace, too, has been prompted to declaim in a loud voice about certain supposed performances of George's in the village. Hard upon that has come the arrival of these Australians. And now they are going to cool their heels – the whole stupid scene is going to freeze into tableau – while I tell you, quite briefly, how I came to marry the middle-aged Sir George Simney.

My people have been actors and actresses for generations; indeed, since the eighteenth century they have been quite a substantial part of the history of the English legitimate stage. I was always proud of all this. Yet at sixteen, and looking at the stage, I somehow didn't think much of it. It was all temperament and no brains, and there always seemed to be one emotional mess or another round the corner. I hate scenes, and scandals, and people who are everlastingly watching themselves in an invisible mirror. This took me away from the traditional family paths and landed me at Oxford.

But somehow after a time I didn't think much of Oxford. I was the wrong sex for what goes on there. Young women who could get tense on cocoa and whose diet was a muddied amalgam of precocious pedantry and belated crushes just didn't turn out to be my cup of tea any more than the little Emma Bovarys who were hopeful of careers on the London stage. I know that to view my college chiefly in this light was to miss the gracious and important part of it. Still, I just couldn't see past all that. And I don't pretend. At least I didn't in those days.

I didn't pretend about Christopher Hoodless. I acknowledged to myself that I loved him from the first day we met. How these things come about I don't know. It is said that an enduring and exclusive passion may be born of the fact that the shade or texture of a young man's jacket unconsciously reminds one of some rug or blanket one used to suck in one's cot. And certainly falling in love is irrational, and love itself is impersonal – impersonal even though in no other human relationship is it so certain that one particular individual is utterly indispensable and the other just as utterly out of court. This falling in love with Christopher is the chief thing that has happened to me, and the best. And yet I don't understand it at all. As you will pres-

23

ently see, I oughtn't to have done it. Instinctively, I ought to have sheered off. But there it was.

Christopher talked anthropology mostly, and how the University had never really acknowledged it as a science, and how the old descriptive anthropologies were not a great deal of good, and how it was futile to trace cultural affiliations about the globe looking for the Ark or the Garden of Eden. Only something called configurational anthropology (which I came to understand pretty well) was really getting anywhere, and there he himself hoped one day to do this and that. Christopher's talk was on those lines. He was twenty-three, and had some sort of junior Fellowship or research scholarship, and was living half among undergraduates and half in a common-room with a lot of old men. It was in going from one to the other, so to speak, that he caught a glimpse of me and stopped for a good stare. That stare went on for some weeks. I saw that Christopher was very shy.

Christopher was shy and intellectual. He was also something not easy to express, but I think it might best be called the flower of courtesy – that in the most substantial sense the phrase will bear. He was all gentleness and strength. An obligation was absolute with him. For anything in which he believed in the sphere of social justice he would have dropped configurational anthropology in the waste-paper basket and stood and died in his tracks. If I had actors and actresses behind me he had a long line of aristocratic eccentrics and philosophic radicals. We got on well. It looked to me like a marriage made in heaven. I look back and it is a sort of dream: Christopher disengaging himself from mobs of young men and knots of old ones; Christopher anxiously choosing wine at the George; Christopher absently punting up stream from Magdalen Bridge and talking of the Mundugumor and the Tchambuli and the mountain-dwelling Arapesh. The Cher became the Markham or the Sepek as he spoke. He had been living for his first substantial piece of field-work. And that was what happened. One vac there was a letter. Christopher had gone to New Guinea.

Well, that was that. Christopher was not one to let you down. He would not have let down a beggar-woman for all the Mundugumor who ever hollowed out a canoe. He had decided that he didn't measure up to me and walked straight out.

I walked straight out too. Within a week I was doing dramatic art. And if anyone had there and then wanted a young and rather beautiful woman to play the part of Death I just wouldn't have needed any training at all. But of course it wore off – in a way. I had a great deal of hard work and one love-affair. The love-affair was bad – commonplace but bad, so that I don't think I could so much as bear to commit a note of it to a private diary. But oblivion does in a sense take such things. I pushed along. In four years I was playing Cleopatra in a rather arty production of Shakespeare at a coterie theatre. That was quite silly, of course. But it caught the eye of what I must call an intelligent producer. There was to be a *Troilus and Cressida* built up round me for the West End. And I saw at once that there was nothing silly about that. It was my chance to join the family and shake hands with Kemble and Garrick. The play was running and an assured success when Christopher turned up. He had been at the theatre every night. And eventually he walked in on me and asked me to marry him.

By this time Christopher Hoodless was somebody too. When people talked of Franz Boas and Ruth Benedict and Margaret Mead they sometimes mentioned him as well. Well, it seemed perfectly sensible. Brilliant young anthropologists do marry talented legitimate actresses. It is quite the sort of thing that happens. And in addition to being sensible it was delirious. All that. Dull sublunary lovers' love didn't seem to come in. And I just didn't see anything sinister about this. I'd had enough of hasty sexuality in that one love-affair.

Christopher still stared – and sometimes from so far

away that I felt it was a good thing that distance lends enchantment to a view. He might have been the poet Grey meditating his Ode on a Distant Prospect of Eton College. When one gets to this point in a story there's nothing like a little joke.

He got quieter – and then quieter still. One evening about a week before we were to be married we dined in a little place in Gerard Street that is all mirrors round the walls. Christopher said nothing at all. And then I saw him gazing at my reflection six depths of mirror away, and there was naked horror on his face. It was tough. I wanted Christopher, I wanted him so much that I would have taken him on any terms. But I knew he wouldn't look at that. It was the simple truth that he wasn't the sort who marry, he was the sort who go through a high window the night before.

Well, I had a job getting Christopher out of where he'd got. Particularly as I wanted him. But I did manage it and he went back to his islands. Then I bolted to the country. I never guessed there could be such comfort in an old cocoa-drinking, puppy-raising, Girl-Guiding friend.

We went riding and met Sir George Simney. He had a lad with him – it was Timmy – and from his features I thought it must be his son. 'My groom,' he said, and looked me straight in the eye. Well, of course I hadn't been told that the Simney blood was there through the distaff side, and I supposed that he was boldly taking the air with his own illegitimate boy. There is nothing pretty about this, I'm afraid. But he looked at me, and somehow it was so much *not* Christopher –

Anyway, that's how I came to marry George.

4

And now to get back to these new Simneys – the ones from Australia waiting in the hall. It's a very comfortable hall, with an enormous fire blazing in a great stone fireplace. Still, it will be civil to hurry out and make their acquaintance.

Hippias Simney, his son Gerard, and Gerard's wife Joyleen ... I see that in trying to get a flying start with this chronicle I have landed myself with rather a crowded stage at the start. Perhaps it would be better to begin again and have all the characters drop in one by one for a drink, as they do in well-made West End plays. But, no, I'm not going back. I want to go right through with this and have done.

I went out and George followed me. Owdon made as if to come after us; then he hesitated and motioned to Timmy to come instead. Something had taken Owdon. He looked much as if he was to be made to walk the plank there and then. And I remembered that George had picked up this unsightly retainer in Australia. Perhaps Owdon had once relieved cousin Hippias of a watch and chain? It would amuse George to take and cherish a butler who had first contacted the family in that way. And yet that watch and chain would have been a good seventeen years ago, and if backed up by George the ruffian was unlikely to go to gaol for it now. Perhaps Owdon's Australian past held some secret altogether more considerable.

Hippias was a great florid man about George's age and he was standing beside the fire with an ulster thrown back upon loosely-worn tweeds. When he spoke it was with the accent of a man who might have stepped out of a replica of Hazelwood in the next county. Only his mouth had gone tight and thin in some chronic refusal to be stopped with dust. There was something which I took to be typically colonial, too, about the focus of his eyes; he was looking at George as if with effort now; it was only a glance and then his gaze passed on further — rather, I thought, as if he were accustomed to converse with some blue pencil-line of hills on a vast horizon.

'My cousin Hippias,' said George. 'Hippias, my wife, Lady Simney.'

This was formal enough, and there followed such constrained greetings as might pass between in-laws in a grocer's parlour. Not that Joyleen was not an exception, for she started making her passes at George straight away. I suppose she had never met a baronet and thought of him as some terrific great lord of whom the best must at once be made. And George responded. It is difficult to compress what must be called a libidinous look into a split second; but that was what he gave Joyleen now — and then paid no more attention to her throughout the evening. And Joyleen was satisfied. She knew all the moves in her own silly game.

'Hippias,' said George — and his eye took in a pile of suit-cases by the staircase — 'we had no notice of this.' He hesitated. 'You're welcome, of course.'

I was a little surprised at George welcoming anybody (unless, indeed, it was on the strength of their bringing Joyleen) and I was very surprised indeed at something else. That fractional hesitation on George's part — it was just like Owdon's a few minutes before — was something altogether unfamiliar to me. Had George too filched a watch and chain? Well, Hippias's next words pretty well implied that he had.

'Notice?' he said. 'I don't know that it runs in the family. We had none that you proposed to take up Dismal Swamp.'

'Dismal Swamp?' George looked momentarily blank and then burst out laughing. 'There can't really be a place called Dismal Swamp. And how could one take it up if there were? I can imagine sinking into Dismal Swamp. But not, my dear fellow, taking it up. And is this your boy? I remember him in his first riding-breeches.'

This was rather a long speech for George – and the speech of a man who was thinking something out. But the turning attention to Gerard Simney was deft enough. For Gerard was angry; he saw nothing odd in a place being called Dismal Swamp and resented this laughter; and now having an eye coolly turned on him he blushed like a fool. Joyleen looked at him and was plainly thinking him a fool; equally plainly she was making the important discovery that to live in the neighbourhood of a Dismal Swamp is socially disadvantageous. For my own part, I thought it might be possible to like Gerard as well as merely sympathize with him. He was older than his wife – something about my own age – but looked as if he still found life a matter of rather boyish bewilderment. I guessed that for some reason he must have had all his education in his own country and that being pitched into this older Hazelwood had rather got him guessing. And George was perhaps not altogether his idea of an English country gentleman. Certainly he was looking at his titled kinsman suspiciously as well as angrily. Had he noticed that swift glance of George's at his wife? How often had I asked myself questions rather like that!

Meanwhile I was giving orders to Timmy and making a few decent remarks to Joyleen. After all, these people were welcome enough in a way. Even if they were just another dose of Simneys the mere fact that they were comparative strangers was something. They could scarcely be plunged straight into such unedifying scenes as our dining-room had just witnessed ... I hate rows. And they would surely put some brake on them.

Of course I was wrong. Indeed when I turned back from Joyleen I realized that I was. For George and Hippias were at it hammer and tongs about Dismal Swamp. I may as well say now that I have not yet really got the hang of it. Something called reticulation was always cropping up, and I suppose that this must be a method of irrigating large areas of land. My final impression was that the Australian Simneys had given George during his sojourn out there confidential intelligence of some development-scheme in which they were proposing to get rather shadily in on the ground floor. They had information they ought not to have possessed and were about to exploit it by buying potentially valuable land on the cheap. Whereupon George, knowing that they couldn't afford to make an open row, had teamed up with some syndicate or other and done the buying first. This had rankled – it is apparently not the sort of thing the Australian landed gentry do – and now here were Hippias and Gerard proposing to make themselves belatedly nasty about it while digging well in to George's cellar and larder. The situation was drear.

Joyleen, naturally, was not much interested in this old family dispute. She was taking off her coat and at the same time looking at me defensively, much as if my eye was searching for traces of primeval slime about her person. She came from Bondi, she explained – and I gathered that this must be some dressy Sydney suburb. As for Dismal Swamp – and she glanced at her father-in-law and George, who were still slinging mud at each other in more senses than one – she had never so much as set eyes on it.

'But,' I said (for I wanted to get them washed and in to our interrupted dinner, and I was feeling rather cross), 'if a place is like that, why ever should one not call it so? Would you prefer to call it Paradise, or Eden, or Windsor Park?'

This just didn't register on Joyleen. But Gerard spoke up at once. 'Quite right,' he said. 'There were three ways of giving names in Australia. One was to stick to the native ones. Some are quite pleasant, like Yankalilla and Paringa and Mallala. Even the grotesque ones, like Mudamuckla and Cobdogla and Nunjikompita –'

'I like Nunjikompita,' I said.

'It's not bad. And I rather relish Pompoota and Muloo-wurtie. They fit the places, somehow – and nobody remembers that quite a lot of them have surprisingly indelicate meanings. Well, that was one way, and quite a good one. The second was to remember the old folks at home. That gives Hazelwood Park. And it gives names like Clapham and Aldgate and Brighton and Edinburgh to little groups of shacks in the middle of nowhere. A sentimental method, and of course, after a time the effect isn't even sentimental but just silly. The third method was the best. It was just to notice what a place looked like, or remember something that had happened there, or even just acknowledge what it felt like. That gives the real Australian names – the white ones to set over against the marvellous dark ones of the aborigines. Lone Gum, Emu Downs, Wattle Flat, Policeman's Point, Cape Catastrophe, Wild Horse Plains, Mount Despair, Watchman, Disaster Bay, Dismal Swamp. Yes, these are the real ones. Our home – Hazelwood Park – is quite a mature old place in its way, and the furniture is English and must have been a bit old-fashioned in the time of Queen Anne. But is all that right? I can't say that I'm sure it is. The house should be called Claypans or Stringies. And the furniture should be in some decent colonial style that can cope with our hardwoods.' Gerard paused and nodded. 'Yes,' he said, 'it's very satisfactory to have a place called Watchman.'

Gerard, then, despite being a Simney, an Australian, and the husband of Joyleen, was a tolerably civilized human being – and, I thought, definitely nice as well. It was true that he seemed quite willing to be not less aggressive than his father in the matter of George's ancient double-dealing. But I didn't like him any the less for being prepared to square up to my husband. And here I come to something which shows that Hazelwood had of late rather been getting me down. Almost straight away I quite opened up to Gerard on some more or less tacit and instinctive plane. After all, he wasn't a mere boy. And it didn't occur to me to stop and reflect that his acquaintance with women was probably pretty limited – extending perhaps to no more than his pastoral neighbours, the frequenters of some sleepy Government House, and whatever contacts with Bondi had brought him his wife. It didn't occur to me to remember that he had no sort of inoculation against those to whom has been given the doubtful gift of taking Cressida in their stride. Probably his perceptions and categories in the way of women were quite primitive: he saw them as necessarily either bedworthy and brainless or brainy but less bedworthy than a bedstead. Anything that cut across the categories would be an upset, naturally enough.

But this is to run ahead (and is utterly beastly too). Meanwhile I took Joyleen to my room and was going to leave her with my maid while she tidied up. The probability of there being no more soup, the possibility of raising some from tins, the likely state of the fish after this sizable interruption: these were matters a little on my mind. But Joyleen seemed anxious not to let me go – I fancy Martin's respectfully appraising eye scared her rather – and so I stood by the fire and watched her open an expensive leather case and begin to fish ineptly among a great array of cosmetics all labelled *Paris* in letters as big as would go on. Martin watched too, first with interest and then with pain, so that presently I thought it best to pack her off in search of sheets and pillow-cases and towels. We seldom have spare rooms ready and waiting at Hazelwood, and this meant that in the next couple of hours there would be quite a job of work: coals to carry and dust-sheets to take off. And we are the sort of betwixt and between establishment in which that sort of thing ought to happen at a word, but in fact never does. So I daresay I was looking rather absent when Joyleen said abruptly: 'Is this place very old?'

She contrived to suggest that in the answer might lie an explanation of something that was troubling her. It was rather as if after being puzzled for some time one should say: 'Is it possible that there may be something wrong with the drains?'

'It was built during the Protectorate,' I said.

For a moment Joyleen looked blank. Then her expression became at once comprehending and defensive. 'We have protectorates too,' she announced. 'New Guinea's one – and I think some islands in the Pacific. They taught us about them at school.'

'I hope,' I said, 'that you had a good voyage?'

'Beaut.' Joyleen spoke with sudden sincere pleasure, and her expression was both childlike and wholly without innocence. 'There was –' She stopped abruptly and once more looked blank. Presumably she had been on the verge of some indiscreet revelation.

Well, I didn't want that, so I took up the telephone and spoke to cook. When I turned back it was to find Joyleen staring in frank astonishment at a picture over the fire-place. It was a large Munnings – which was much more George's idea of bedroom furniture than mine. 'Horses!' she said.

'Why, yes – or a stockbroker's dream of them.'

Joyleen continued to stare. She wrinkled her pretty, silly little nose. Here, seemingly, was a problem indeed. Then, quite suddenly, she solved it.

'I suppose,' said Joyleen, 'that you got this picture from Australia?'

5

For my new cousin, then, Houyhnhnms were a biological phenomenon to be met with only down under, and the Old World was given over wholly to Yahoos and motor-cars. I said something about hoping to be able to mount her next day, and I don't doubt that I succeeded in being horribly patronizing where I meant to be moderately friendly.

And on this we went downstairs again. The position had not greatly changed. George, Hippias and Gerard were back in the hall, waiting for us; and the rest of the family, with the exception of Mervyn, seemed still to be in a state of suspended animation in the dining-room. Mervyn had emerged in search of diversion, and he was looking at the newcomers with a quite unnecessary expression of urbane wonder, rather as a sophisticated Elizabethan gentleman, not himself given to extensive voyaging, might have regarded a brace of painted savages imported by Sir Francis Drake or Sir Walter Raleigh. Moreover he had summoned Timmy to him and on the pretext of making friendly offers to help with the luggage was keeping the sullen youth at his side – thereby designing, I don't doubt, to exhibit a beguiling little genealogical problem as prominently as possible to any new kinsman inclined to comment or research. Like Bevis, I was all for birching Mervyn, and if somebody had held the young beast down I believe I could have done it with considerable satisfaction myself. But it is necessary to admit that Mervyn's particular brand of offensiveness nearly always displays finish. I don't think this is because he is particularly clever; rather, and in some devious fashion, it has something to do with his being particularly beautiful. I used to hate Mervyn's beauty, although the same thing never at all worried me in Timmy. But that is by the way.

Now Mervyn was staring at Joyleen as we came downstairs. Joyleen, I should imagine, was accustomed to stares and relished them even from puppies of eighteen. But this stare of Mervyn's was rather different. It was admiring. It was even politely admiring. At the same time it contrived to suggest that the girl had put something on inside-out, or had forgotten to put something on, or ought to take something off. Joyleen didn't like it. And then Mervyn suddenly turned on his heel, clapped his hands and ran back into the dining-room. 'Mama, mama,' he cried in an idiotic falsetto, 'there is a young gentlewoman too!'

This brought Lucy out and Mervyn came back with her; I think that after the business of the sherry he didn't much trust himself with Bevis and young Willoughby. Lucy had been thinking up a line, and now she embarked on it heavily. 'Hippias!' she cried. 'Dear uncle Guy's boy! Welcome, and welcome again to Hazelwood.'

Dear uncle Guy's boy received this effusive greeting coolly. 'How d'ye do,' he said. 'But dashed if I didn't think I'd met George's wife ten minutes ago. Slip of a girl. Still, you look more out of his stable. About ages too.'

Lucy was greatly offended. 'I am George's sister Lucy,' she said, 'who married the late Richard Cockayne. And this' – she put her arm round Mervyn – 'is my darling boy.'

'Is that so?' Hippias looked appraisingly at the mother and son. 'Well, I should say that the late Richard Cockayne was well out of it. And don't come bustling round as if you owned the place. Confusing to a stranger. And thought I was right about George's wife. Not quite in the best fleece, but a deuced beautiful woman all the same. What's become of her?' And Hippias started to look round the hall. Then he paused and sniffed. 'Damned hungry,' he said. 'Knew better than to eat roast shoe-leather and boiled grass on a bally awful English train.'

Hippias, I think, may be called Edwardian. His chief acquaintance with the Mother Country must have been at the tail end of that era, and it is to be presumed that he formed his manners upon those of some rag-tag and bob-tail set which had then received him. Hippias is raffish and rude. It was plain that Mervyn was delighted with him; his brisk bludgeoning of the absurd Lucy was perfectly agreeable to the little beast's peculiar filial feelings. 'Cousin Hippias,' he said amiably, 'is a gastronome. Not for him the atrocious lamb which his countrymen disingenuously father upon Canterbury, New Zealand. He comes too from a land of noble wines. Bid Owdon bring up the Chateau Lafite '24 and let it stand its trial at last.' With this Mervyn led the way into the dining-room and began gesticulating at the table. 'These are knives,' he said, 'and those are forks. The little scoops with handles are called spoons; you will use them first. Just follow our lead and all awkwardness will be avoided. Only mark well that Willoughby is an exception. With sherry he has a private ritual of his own which it would be a solecism to imitate. His morals, however are exemplary and such as you may follow blindly. Willoughby's heart is pure – which is why his length is as the length of ten and his wrists stick out so many inches from the sleeves of his dinner-jacket.'

'Mervyn,' said Lucy mildly, 'you are talking a little more than becomes you.' Having been roundly driven from her rôle of gushing chatelaine Lucy had retreated again upon vagueness.

'And here' – for Mervyn was merely stirred to further volubility by this – 'is uncle Bevis. He is a world authority on the History of the Rod, and has written on the subject a monograph of curious interest, available to private subscribers only.' And as he advanced this grotesque flight of fancy Mervyn politely handed Joyleen to a chair on George's right. 'But I must add that much of the material was collected by aunt Grace, the lady who is behaving like a chafing-dish at the far end of the room.'

Grace was certainly simmering – I suspect because the new arrivals had cut short what was to have been quite a major denunciation of George passed on from the Reverend Mr Deamer. It was (it subsequently turned out) the blacksmith's daughter who was in question; and for my own part I would have welcomed quite a covey of Joyleens in order to be spared Grace on a theme like that. After all, nobody was going to reform George – and indeed George as a reformed rake would have been rather more intolerable than George just as he was. So why fuss? The answer in Grace's case was just jealousy. All unknown to herself, she had some infantile fixation on her big bad brother and couldn't bear him to be naughty anywhere outside the old familiar nursery. George knew this – he was far from stupid, and knew most things – and sometimes I had been constrained to believe that a certain unnecessary obtrusiveness in his irregular courses was simply a means he took to diverting himself by tormenting his sister. It was even possible to think that one day he might go too far, and drive Grace into some frenzy dangerous to herself or others. And this was particularly so since she had become thick with Mr Deamer – who was (as will appear) a thoroughly fanatical man on his job.

But at the moment Dismal Swamp was still the focal point of irritation. George from the foot of the table and Hippias from my right hand kept up an obscure sparring which naturally dominated the room. Grace put in fishing questions – no doubt suspecting that there might have been a girl-angle to this ancient misdemeanour of George's. Mervyn took it into his head to affect an inside knowledge of the affair. Bevis tried to talk kangaroo-hunting with Gerard – this by way of indicating his opinion that intimate family business should not be discussed before the servants. Lucy brought out a hazy knowledge of Australian families and fell to questioning any of the new arrivals who would listen. Joyleen would have liked to join in this, but I could see that she didn't really know the right answers and would have been stronger on the number of bathrooms so-and-so had in Bondi. Willoughby said nothing; at present you must regard him as decidedly a dark horse in what is going forward. And behind us moved Owdon, Timmy Owdon and our remaining parlour-maid, supposing or meditating I don't know what.

And that leaves Gerard, who was sitting on my left. I don't think I've mentioned that I had problems of my own to consider that night; and for a time I was quite content to leave the Simneys to their own remote affairs. But I began to get interested when I noticed how Gerard was feeling as the meal wore on. At first he had joined in this Dismal Swamp business – civilly, on the whole, but incisively enough. Then he seemed to grow puzzled, and presently said very little.

And I had an obscure feeling that it was important to gather what he was feeling puzzled about.

'Bally mean trick,' said Hippias. He glared at Owdon – apparently by way of demanding more veal. 'And it's not a trick Denzell would have played, my boy; I can tell you that.'

'Denzell?' said George blankly.

The florid features of Hippias changed from red to purple, and for a moment I wondered what could be so peculiarly maddening in this response. Then I remembered what I had in fact once been told clearly enough: that George had had a younger brother, Denzell Simney, a year younger again than Bevis, who had gone out to Australia with him and there met some more or less tragic death. To have George treating the name as if it were quite unknown to him was certainly displeasing enough.

'Yes – Denzell,' said Hippias. 'And – what's more – if Denzell were in your shoes now, and in command of a fortune, he would make reparation like a gentleman.'

Momentarily George's eyes narrowed. Then he looked impassively round at people's glasses. 'Owdon,' he said, ' – claret.'

'And let us have a rouse,' said Mervyn, 'to the departed gentility of the family. Grace is genteel, but a very Diana for chastity. I, who am all the sons of my mother's house and all the daughters too, will never be other than a little cad. Nicolette is charming, but in her veins runs only the ink of poets and the mascara of mummers. Willoughby is going to be a schoolmaster and will take his pleasure only in smacking small boys' behinds with a cane – or is it a birch? And thus, then, I conclude that on Joyleen rests the onus of restoring the old patrician dignity of our house.' And Mervyn lifted his glass gravely to Gerard's wife – who did not at all know whether she was being made fun of or not. Then a thought seemed to strike him. 'But of course there is Timmy. How often one forgets him.' And Mervyn turned to smirk at George, certain of approval for thus reviving this tiresome theme.

But George's reaction was altogether surprising.

'Mervyn,' he said evenly, 'you will finish your meal in silence.'

Mervyn blinked at him and then turned to Lucy. 'Mama, mama!' he squeaked.

'It appears that we have stopped having a schoolroom earlier than we ought. Very well. Certain of its usages we will revive.' As George made this pronouncement he looked up the table, and as his eyes swept past mine I got a vivid impression of rapid calculation. 'Get out!' he snapped.

For a moment I thought he was addressing me – and had it been so I believe that I would have risen and departed in silent seeming-obedience. They were one family, after all, and it might have been best to leave them to it. But then a scurry behind me and a softly closing door explained the situation. It was Timmy – so recently promoted to his position of prominence beside his father – who had been peremptorily ordered from the room.

It was odd. For I found it hard to see why the arrival of the Australian cousins should suddenly inspire George with a sense of the elementary proprieties in this matter. It occurred to me that I, like everyone else, had very little certain information about Timmy's origins. Was it possible that no Simney lady had been involved – nor the heavy Owdon either; was it possible that his looks came from his father, and that I had been right in my conjecture the first time I had set eyes on him? Was he George's son, after all – and the far more scandalous story we had all accepted a thoroughly characteristic perverse fiction of George's own? But then how could the story have gained credibility in the first place, and why should Owdon acknowledge the boy to be his? These were all mysteries. And I realized how sketchy was my knowledge of the precious clan into which I had precipitated myself.

But one thing was clear. The arrival of Hippias had set George some obscure problem. This might not have been evident to everybody, but circumstances had obliged me to make some study of the man, and I could sense that he felt himself in the presence of certain imponderables amid which he was cautiously feeling his way. Moreover he was rattled – a state of mind I never expected to live to see George experience. He was sitting back now, looking through his claret at the candles on the corner of the table near him – and I could see that he was reviewing his handling of Mervyn and Timmy a few moments before and by no means approving of it. But presently he looked down the table with a confident eye. 'Of course,' he said, 'my memory is bad. But all these things may come back to me. So tell me more, my dear Hippias, about this Dismal Swamp.'

'Dismal Swamp?' said Hippias blankly.

6

Well, that was queer. It was a second before I at all got the hang of it. And then I remembered how George had said 'Denzell?' in just the same blank way a few minutes before. That plainly enough had been a sort of manifesto, an announcement that George didn't intend to be disturbed by Hippias and his pesterings, and that in any trouble there might be over those distant dealings in land he felt quite secure of having the upper hand. And now Hippias appeared to be saying that he didn't after all care a damn about Dismal Swamp either. But what sense could there be in so sudden a change of front?

Gerard evidently saw none. He was looking at his father in perplexity. And immediately Hippias hedged, as if feeling that too obvious a shift of position was undesirable. 'We'll give it a rest,' he said. 'Papers to unpack, and all that.' He turned to Bevis. 'Kangaroo? They're swell enough. But if you want excitement you have to go for buffalo. You can stand in the middle of a sizeable plain, you know, and see nothing and believe you're feeling a slight earthquake. But it's a herd of those fellows over the horizon, and before you can say Jack Robinson they're coming down on you. General idea is that the Australian Bush is a dull place for a sportsman –'

'No, no,' said Bevis. He was apparently anxious to dissociate himself from so drastic an aspersion as this. 'Impression is that there's no scenery or tourists' stuff scattered about. But I've always understood a fellow could have a very fair spin with a gun. Trout, too, I've been told.'

Gerard joined in. 'There are trout in Tasmania. And they're in streams that don't belong to anyone in particular.'

'Is that so?' Bevis was civil but shocked. 'What an extraordinary state of affairs. Though for that matter I've been told that in Kenya –'

'But quite often,' interrupted Lucy, 'there *is* nobody in particular. The Shropshire Mortimers have cousins in a place called the Flinders Ranges. And they say that there is nobody in particular within hundreds of miles of them. Nobody, that is to say, except ordinary colonials.'

Gerard put down his knife and fork, and I could see that he was quite quickly learning to be less annoyed than amused by talk of this sort. 'But we are all ordinary colonials,' he said. 'Except of course those of us who are indigenous and black.'

'Black?' said Lucy. 'I thought that was Africa.'

At this Joyleen felt she must take a hand. 'There aren't *many* blacks,' she said defensively. 'Or not any longer. They were protected, and that sort of thing, so that now there are very few of them left. They are quite horrid, of course, and particularly the children.'

Gerard opened his mouth and shut it again. I felt sorry for him, for I saw that his marriage must be pretty awful. In fact we rowed in the same galley, Gerard and I. And if I'd had my wits about me I would have seen that he might be making the same observation.

'Blackfellows?' said Hippias. He applied himself vigorously to his veal. 'George and Denzell had dealings with blackfellows – of a sort.'

Grace was upon this like a flash. 'Black *women*?' she demanded.

Hippias looked at my unmarried sister-in-law, sizing her up. 'That's telling,' he leered.

And at that I saw that Hippias was the nastiest of the lot. Not even Mervyn Cockayne could touch quite this. For it was plain to me that although Hippias had intended some innuendo in this matter of George and the blackfellows it had actually nothing to do with women – or at least with immoral relations with women. Hippias was just joining in baiting Grace.

I'm not fanatical about smut. I suspect that it has a sanative place in the intimate society of young adult males. Aerated by wit, I'm prepared to stick it – even put it across – on the stage. But I don't like it at my dinner table, and in front of a parlour-maid. I can tell you I felt pretty well through with Simneys that night.

'Yes,' said George, 'it all floats back. Blackfellows, buffalo, billabongs and tepid bottled beer. A wonderful life. How eager you must be to get back. And yet how much of England Joyleen must be shown first. How her mind and spirit will expand as she actually sees so much that her education has led her to expect. Can you stop at so dull a place as Hazelwood till Wednesday – or even Thursday? Nicolette, do persuade our cousins to spare us several days.'

I uttered some decent form of words. It was unfair of George – I was thinking – to silence Mervyn and then embark on so poor an imitation of the little toad's vein. But here was only another sign that George was not so much in command of the situation as he seemed to claim. And somehow I was alarmed by this. I think I had a feeling that if, for mysterious reasons, he was going to be driven hard by his cousin Hippias he would make up for this disagreeable experience by taking it out of others nearer home.

I didn't know that George's death was going to take place just twenty-seven hours later.

And I dare say you are just longing for it – or even for a general extinction of the Simneys, as at the conclusion of an Elizabethan play. Well, don't despair. Of that blunt instrument, at least, we are within reasonable reach now. As to whether any of the others are to die I don't yet know. Somebody has declared that we shed our sicknesses in books, and perhaps that's why I'm writing. And possibly the more effective the book the more effective the cure – so I had better build up what suspense I can. Anyway, all those Simneys are alive for the moment. You might say indeed that they have the horrid vitality shown by many of the lower forms of life.

At that meal there was a certain amount of further cryptic talk. I could report it and then later on you could perhaps turn back and see its lurking relevance. But even in this sort of narrative much cryptic talk is tiresome. Certainly I was tired of it at dinner that night. And I was glad when I got the women away to the drawing-room.

Joyleen walked to the fire and said, 'Coal!' with the air of one preferring a mild indictment.

'I expect,' I said, 'that you will feel the cold, arriving in winter like this.'

'You should wear plenty of clothes,' said Grace – and seemed rather to imply that if Joyleen had her way she would appear in nothing but a string of beads and a sarong.

'And wool next the skin,' said Lucy. 'But no doubt you will know about wool. The Sussex Hallidays have cousins in Victoria – or is it Queensland? – who are said to have contrived to grow very good wool. Of course, with a special sort of sheep. I expect it would be rather like a goat.'

'Talking of goats,' said a voice at the door, 'how do you really like your father-in-law, Joyleen?'

It was – needless to say – Mervyn; he had slipped away to escape that edict of silence. But for the fact that I was coming to feel things at Hazelwood as curiously ghost-like and impermanent I think I should have taken over the schoolroom business from George and ordered him to bed.

But Joyleen didn't seem to find anything offensive or even odd in the question. 'I like him,' she said. 'He's not so slow as Gerard.'

Mervyn grinned wickedly at this cheap speech. 'No, I suppose not. In fact I should imagine him to have been quite fast in his day.'

Joyleen assumed an expression of importance and mystery. 'There are stories about him.'

'Ah,' said Grace.

'About him and Sir George and that brother of Sir George's they were talking of – the one with the funny name.'

'Denzell,' said Mervyn. 'Denzell is the funny name – Joyleen, my dear.'

I don't think Joyleen saw this – and in Bondi, no doubt, there are Joyleens in every street. 'Yes,' she said, '– Denzell. Of course it was ever so long ago and I don't really know about it. But I think they were all nearly charged with – with absorption.'

'Absorption?' I exclaimed. It seemed an improbable crime – unless indeed the reference was to some illegal attempt to drain Dismal Swamp.

'Abortion,' said Mervyn easily. 'The dear, pure girl means abortion.'

'She means abduction.' Grace was quite decided. 'It is just what one would expect of George. And of Hippias as well. As soon as he came into the dining-room I saw that he was a loose fish.'

'He is also,' said Mervyn, 'a widower, and in that sense loose too. So let Grace get out her rod and line.'

But Grace paid no attention to this. She was too absorbed

in the fresh revelation of her brother's depravities. 'Abduction!' she repeated.

Joyleen nodded. 'And on a large scale,' she added solemnly.

Grace's eye took on its most fanatical gleam. 'Is there no end,' she exclaimed with passion, 'to our family shame? Three of us nearly charged with the abduction of numerous women.'

Joyleen stared. 'Women?' she said. 'But it wasn't anything like that. It was blackbirds.'

One has, of course, heard that if a common sparrow appears in Australia whole populations go on the hunt, shot-gun in hand. And, conceivably, legal consequences to the abducting of blackbirds were merely another ornithological eccentricity of the place. This mystery would presently have been resolved – Joyleen indeed had opened her mouth to continue – when we were interrupted by a loud crash from the corridor, mingled with the horrid sound of much breaking glass.

Really sedate members of the landed gentry, I am sure, pay no attention to such domestic calamities, maintaining an air of obliviousness until the time comes to say something nasty next morning. Being only an actress, I was out of the drawing-room door in a jiffy. And the others, infected by this bourgeois behaviour, followed.

So we all saw both Owdon and Hippias. Hippias was walking away from us and in the act of turning the corner which led to George's study. But evidently he had just passed Owdon and was presumably responsible for the wretched man's condition. For Owdon was standing staring after him, a silver tray and a litter of shivered glass on the parquetry at his feet, and his arms hanging in a sort of limp tremble at his sides. You can seldom read any expression on Owdon's face – the pirates have left too little of it for that – but he retains a circulatory and respiratory system, and consequently a complexion capable of registering emotional changes. He had now gone a parchment colour, with greenish mottlings as of mildew or blight. Just such dead, it occurred to me, must Dismal Swamp render up from time to time.

Of course the damage was pretty steep – two or three decanters and quite a lot of rather pleasant old glass. But such disasters are a sort of professional risk with butlers, and I didn't see that he should be so upset as all that.

'Owdon,' I said sharply – for the fellow seemed in a perfect daze – 'all you need is a dust-pan and a broom.'

He looked at me for a second unknowingly. 'Dust-pans and brooms,' he murmured, 'baize aprons and silver polish. The key of the cellars and a book for keeping accounts.'

Joyleen giggled; I suppose she was scared by this untoward turn to things in a baronial hall. And I'm not sure I wasn't a bit scared myself, for I had never known Owdon behave in so queer a fashion before. There was something queer too in his voice which I couldn't at all define, and I was seized by that irrational and overpowering feeling of a thing's having happened before which is the product, it is said, of certain sorts of fatigue. Long ago Owdon had spoken just these words. ... Yes, I was scared, for now I positively stamped my foot at him. 'Or if you're shaken up,' I said, 'send Timmy. We can't have this mess left about.'

'Yes,' he said. He was looking at me unknowingly out of his one eye. Then recognition dawned in it. 'Yes, your ladyship,' he murmured. And he continued to look at me.

The look was stranger than his voice had been. I had a panicky feeling that he was seeing something that he hadn't seen before; or that I had suddenly appeared to him in a fresh light. 'Don't let the past come back,' he said. 'Strangle it. Anything is better than the return of the past.'

Well, it is difficult to express how confounding this was. Its most obvious aspect was that of crude melodrama – for what could be more conventionally conceived than this of the mysterious manservant acquired in the master's shady days and now thrown sensationally off his balance by the appearance of some link with the bad old times? The stricken butler and the shattered glass: ought it not to have been possible to predict the snowstorm and the blunt instrument straight away?

But there was more than this simple melodrama. There was something odd in the man's choice of words – and something very odd in the manner of their address to me. They ought to have been, so to speak, turned inward; pure soliloquy; *O what a rogue and peasant slave am I*. Instead of which they seemed addressed to me by way of serious admonition. Owdon was speaking out of his own experience – but he was speaking to *me*.

Owdon certainly has a past – in fact several pasts, including Timmy. And no doubt I have a past too. But assuredly our pasts have nothing in common and I didn't at all see why at the moment I should be dragged in. Nor, seconds later and when he had recovered himself, did Owdon himself; he stopped off squinneying at me and applied himself to picking up the larger chunks of broken decanter.

And at this Grace spoke up. It was surprising that she hadn't uttered before. I fancy she had been rather intimidated by an Owdon who had momentarily become something other than an automaton. It was true that, unless some Simney lady had possessed tastes decidedly peculiar, one must suppose him to have been this at least once before. But we had known him for years as a dummy; and for a time Grace had been disconcerted and silent. Now however, and seeing Owdon occupied in a properly menial fashion with the debris, she provided her own sort of commentary to the scene.

'Were my poor dear father alive,' said Grace, 'how he would wince at these disorderly scenes. He was a man of the purest moral principles and believed above all things in the sanctity of the home.'

'He,' said Mervyn, 'brought back no pirates from Pinnaroo, no butlers from Bumbunga.'

'Guilty consciences,' said Grace looking at Owdon. 'And hidden courses and irregular passions,' she added looking at me.

'And not even,' said Mervyn, 'the after-dinner quiet which might reconcile us to these. Willoughby throws a glass of sherry, and at once Owdon is prompted to hurl whole services of crystal. What will be his corresponding riposte should Deamer appear and defend the honour of the village maidens by shooting uncle George? Holocaust at Hazelwood. The End of the House of Simney. In one of the novels of Thomas Hardy there is an unnatural little boy – one much like myself – who hangs himself and all his relations in a big dark cupboard. Looking round the Simneys, and as a mere Cockayne, I have often thought of it. But Owdon, maybe, will forestall me.'

'Mervyn,' said Lucy, 'what you say is very clever, dear, and I am sure that your uncle George would be amused. But I do not know that it is quite nice for Joyleen, who is young and may not understand our sophisticated ways.'

'Possibly not, mama. But does she understand our mystery?'

'Our mystery, darling? I don't know what you can mean.'

But Mervyn had swung round upon Joyleen and was addressing her direct. He is an acute little beast enough, and I think he realized that something might be got out of her by sudden assault. 'Now then,' he said, '– what is it? There is more to all this than just Dismal Swamp. Or something more has cropped up – suddenly, tonight. Look at Owdon. The past is stirring, and I have an idea that it will be better for us all if it stays put. So what do you know about it?'

I looked at Mervyn in surprise, for I could scarcely remember another occasion upon which he had spoken without intolerable affectation. And then I looked at Joyleen – and it was my instant conclusion that she was just dumb. She was bewildered, of course, but I imagine that she had anticipated bewilderment in the ancient seat of the Simneys, and that even a row of bodies dangling in a cupboard might have struck her as merely part of the way in which matters conduct themselves in England. 'Know about it?' she said sulkily. 'I don't know anything at all. But I do think you were right about after-dinner quiet. We had a horrid train-journey and I would like a little quiet very much.'

Mervyn was upon this in a flash. 'Then,' he said, 'you'd better go and find your Gerard. For he is the quiet one, I think you said. But if you will just tell us first what you meant by black –'

'Mervyn, dear, that is rather rude.' Lucy shook a fondly disapproving head. 'Grace and I both want to have a quiet chat with Joyleen, and do not at all intend to worry her with mysteries. Perhaps you had better join the other men. They will be missing you – particularly uncle George.'

'They can have Timmy,' said Mervyn.

'Now, dear, don't be silly. I think you will find that they are all having a cosy chat of their own in your uncle's study. And Willoughby will be expecting you, because of course he will want to apologize.'

'I think not.' Mervyn spoke as sulkily as Joyleen had just done. 'All that Willoughby is likely to want is an occasion for further violence.'

'Nonsense, darling.' And Lucy stroked Mervyn's beautiful curly hair with a fondness which was part nauseating and part pathetic. Then she turned to Joyleen. 'You will soon,' she said, 'come to understand that we are really a very loving family. And certainly there is never any occasion for violence at Hazelwood.'

But as Lucy spoke there was a sudden angry shout from round the angle of the corridor ahead of us. And it was followed – for the second time that night – by the sound of shattered glass.

But this fracas in George's study mustn't raise false hopes. We haven't yet reached the main action of the piece. There will be no corpse available for your inspection, Gentle Reader, until you have struggled on some way ahead.

Nevertheless it is tolerably certain that without this affair in the study on the night of the Australian cousins' arrival the sensational event of the night following would not have taken place. The little business now to be related was, in fact, cardinal in the whole affair. So sharpen your perceptions and cease reading with that hurrying eye.

If George was no fool he certainly was no student either, and there seemed small reason why he should have a study any more than a smithy or a laboratory or a consulting-room. Tradition of course, decrees something of the sort. A baronet must have a library, a study and a gun-room just as certainly as his wife must have a drawing-room and a boudoir. These necessities are mysterious – a boudoir means, it appears, a room to be sulky in, and why should the over-privileged have particular need of that? – but there seems to be no harm in them. Only there was, a little – in George's case.

George's study is not in the least traditional; in fact it is one of his rather offensive jokes. A long, dusky, ill-lit room on the first floor, it is furnished with nothing more than a refectory table accommodating writing materials and scattered magazines, half a dozen hard chairs, and a few statuettes on short marble pillars. This is all the furnishing, that is to say, if one doesn't count the pictures.

Originally there were only family portraits: to be precise, the ten Simney baronets ending with George himself. I do not know that an inspection of them would have been well calculated to support any simple faith in the blessings of pedigree; from the original Sir Hippias onwards they were, I should have judged, a thoroughly dissipated lot. Still, the effect must have been respectable enough: Sir Hippias (although in fact a superior peddler who had done well out of profit-inflations under James I) was represented by Mytens as a blue-blooded person casting a casual eye over the deeds of his Trojan ancestors in a large folio of Geoffrey of Monmouth's *Historia Britonum*! the first Sir Denzell, who had been a bishop as well as a baronet, had elected to be painted by Kneller in full canonicals, surrounded by his favourite hounds; Sir Bevis, who had not only, like George, married an actress, but strangled her as well, appeared in a canvas of Wilkie's deeply absorbed in the ground-plan of an orphanage. Perhaps it was the fact that despite the disguisements of art, they nearly all suggest in mouth or eye that loose-fish quality discerned by Grace: perhaps it was this that gave George his notion.

The Simneys have quite a collection of Old Masters, brought together for the most part in the eighteenth century and, despite rising values, obstinately retained since. George had gone round these, picked out the most effective nudes, and dispersed them among his ancestors by way of female companionship. Thus over the fire-place, her lurking quality amid a heavy chiaroscuro emphasized by the elaborately carved Grinling Gibbons pillars between which she is recessed, stands a long-thighed Venus by Caravaggio, her allurements emphasized by the ghost of a lawn smock. And on each side of her stand fully – indeed elaborately – clothed Simney gentlemen, so that the total effect is not unlike that 'Déjeuner sur l'herbe' with which the painter Manet contrived to shock Paris in 1863. Opposite this, and on either side of the room's only window, are a Danae by Tintoretto and a Pasiphae by Bordone respectively. The Danae is flanked by Sir Guy Simney, depicted by Cornelius Janssen in his counting-house amid little piles of golden coin; and the Pasiphae stands next to the second Sir Bevis, a Victorian gentleman who is shown by Stanhope Forbes as leaning over a fence to examine a prize bull. These little jokes (and the ability to contrive them was probably about all that remained to George of a classical education) the reigning baronet had contrived to crown by having himself painted in a pink hunting coat which exactly toned with the flesh of a post-Matisse lady sprawled on a sofa. All this being achieved, George had added two large mirrors at each end of the room, so that from certain angles it was possible to contemplate an infinite regress of Simneys and sirens, baronets and bagnio-ladies. Such a juxtaposing of Venetian prodigality and solid English hypocrisy might be amusing on the pages of an ephemeral magazine. As a permanent set up in a gentleman's house it has never struck me – I must confess – as other than displeasing in the extreme. However this may be, it was the setting of the scene which follows. If it hadn't been for these beastly pictures – or rather for this beastly arrangement of pictures – the affair would have turned out differently. For a long time I had known that if ever I was to have a real row with George it would more probably happen in his study than anywhere else.

Lucy had been explaining to Joyleen that we were a loving family, and that at Hazelwood violence was not at all the thing – when there had been that second explosion of shattered glass following hard upon an angry shout.

I don't doubt that just this sound-sequence at just this after-dinner hour had been heard at Hazelwood often enough, and that the womenfolk of the household had stayed discreetly put until the men chose to present themselves and sober up on tea. But I have never, somehow, grown into these old-world ways, and now I pushed past Owdon – who was looking more disconcerted than just the prospect of further litter could have made him – and made for the study.

Odd factors can colour one's emotional state at such moments. I was annoyed that more Simneys seem to mean not a decent reticence and lowering of tensions but simply additional rumpus. But I was even more annoyed by something in the mere geography of the thing. All this dropping of trays in corridors and shouting and smashing of lord knew what was taking place hard by any privacy that Hazelwood afforded me. On my right as I went down this corridor were George's bedroom and bath-room, on my left were my own bedroom, bath-room and sitting-room – and this study of George's was straight ahead. Old houses are not always rationally arranged, and there was nothing out of the way in all this. Nevertheless – for now there were further shouts and angry voices – it made me feel as if I lived on the fringes of a tap-room. So did the whiskey-bottle.

Now, so far as my own part in the ensuing events was concerned that whiskey-bottle was crucial. The image of it – broken in that particular way, standing on that particular refectory table, and between the four walls of that particular room, came back to me later invested with a quite mysterious repulsiveness. But there was more to it than that. Jinn live in bottles and when a bottle is broken a jinnee may escape. From this bottle there was to come an evil spirit indeed – and sudden death was to be the consequence.

And so I would like you to *see* it – although it was, of course, a commonplace object enough, such as it would take a Chardin or a Cezanne to render significant. But there it was on the table, broken off short below the neck in an ugly, jagged line of glass such as one might cut a throat with, and standing round it were five Simneys pale and cursing. Or five Simneys, pale and cursing, in a sort of inner Circle – and beyond that ten more Simneys, immobile and watching from amid the female companionship with which George had provided them.

Something held me momentarily motionless before this scene, and as I stood in the doorway George glanced up and (I suppose) decided that there was something consciously theatrical in my attitude. Anyway, he was quite viciously annoyed. 'Come in,' he said. 'Come right down stage, my dear, take a well-deserved round of applause, and then join our domestic comedy.'

I walked in and the others followed. 'Or pot-house tragedy,' I said.

'Mama,' said Mervyn, 'are the gentlemen in their cups?'

Lucy shook her head. 'Hush, dear – I'm afraid that something upsetting must have occurred.'

'Hippias has occurred – and Gerard and Joyleen. And the upsetting has taken Owdon in the most literal way. And why, I wonder, in one's cups?' Mervyn looked round in the easiest fashion, and I almost believed that he was honestly attempting to relieve the obscure tension in the room with his badinage. 'Why not in one's glasses, or one's bottles? But now that Owdon and Hippias have done their worst there are, of course, no glasses left. And here too' – he looked at the whiskey-bottle – 'there appears to have been a clash of mighty opposites. Or has Willoughby merely been performing a parlour trick? Or has Gerard been wolfing a little broken glass by way of demonstrating the feeding-habits of the Australian ostrich?'

'Emu,' said Gerard. He was looking at the broken bottle as if he saw in it as much as I did.

'Or has uncle Bevis, perhaps –'

'Be quiet,' said George.

I looked at my husband in surprise. Assuredly he was in a vile temper – and yet this rebuke to Mervyn was half-hearted and unconvincing. Mervyn realized the fact and ran happily on. I had a moment to study the situation.

They were all angry – and it seemed to me that they were all bewildered, like men to whom it had suddenly come that they did not at all know where they stood. I decided to ask a question.

'Is this bottle,' I said, 'the result of more quiet family talk about Dismal Swamp?'

There was a moment's silence. Then Gerard answered.

'They *were* talking about that.' He glanced at me with strangely troubled eyes.

The whole group were perplexed. But Gerard, I thought, was more perplexed than the rest, so that I wondered if there had been some crisis or disclosure which he hadn't tumbled to.

'Hippias is in liquor,' said Bevis.

This was obviously true – and it was information offered as if to explain the whole thing.

'Drank too much of George's bally port,' said Hippias. 'Then felt like a lil' bit of fun. Shorry about glasses, m'dear. Shorry about bally bottle.'

Extremely clumsily, Hippias was taking his cue. There was no doubt that he had drunk too much; but then neither was there any doubt that what had been going on was more than drunken frolic – or drunken quarrel.

Grace however saw no reason to think so. 'Horrible!' she said. 'A family reunion after many years – and yet all it leads to is a debauch.' She looked round the study and her eye caught (I imagine) Tintoretto's Danae waiting for Jove's shower of gold. 'Not,' she continued, 'that more is to be expected in an apartment embellished with all the allurements of vice.'

'Or all,' said Mervyn, also glancing round, 'except the blacksmith's fair-haired daughter. And what would aunt Grace's Mr Deamer think of uncle George's Paphian shrine? Would he be reassured by the presence of the Honourable and Right Reverend Bishop Denzell?' And Mervyn affected to consult Kneller's portrait. 'I judge not. He would hold it still to be what the poet Keats calls a purple-lined palace of sweet sin. And, indeed, if any improvement could be effected it would surely be a purple wall-paper, with true love-knots heavily embossed in gold.' Mervyn turned to me. 'Nicolette, do you not agree?'

I don't know that I would have answered. But – sur-prisingly – Gerard answered for me: and with physical

55

action considerably more pronounced than Willoughby's earlier in the evening. 'You howling little cad,' he said. And at that he picked up Mervyn, strode with him to the window, flung up the sash and dropped him through. He closed the window. 'There is quite thick snow,' he explained, 'so I hope no damage will be done to the flower beds.'

'It isn't a flower bed,' I said. 'It's a rockery.'

And that got rid of Lucy as well. One may, after all, be pardoned a little maternal agitation on seeing one's only child pitched through a first-storey window. She hurried off down the corridor calling upon Owdon to follow her.

For a moment George's large laughter filled the room. But it was not the laughter with which he would normally have greeted an incident so much to his taste. And again I tried to get the hang of how these men were feeling. 'Who threw the bottle?' I asked.

What happened at Hazelwood? My question, as it happened, was really the first attempt at solving that. Or at least it exposed a preliminary mystery. For they didn't want to answer. Some queer panic or uncertainty was upon them and they were all for concealing whatever they could. But they were quite ineffective. They could, after all, simply have turned Grace (who was very much the chafing-dish again) and myself out of the room; and George ought to have been quite fit for this with no ceremony. But instead they looked at one another like third-form boys caught smoking in a barn. Bevis, although one could see that he had been in the thick of the quarrel, was endeavouring to look dignified and composed; this gave him the air of the unpleasant sort of child who, at such a discovery, edges himself towards the side of law and order.

Willoughby was a little more genuinely detached. My eye followed his straying to the Caravaggio Venus in her almost *trompe d'œil* quality over the fire-place. He was far, I knew, from seeing her as what Grace called an allurement to vice. For art is a mysterious but increasingly real other world to Willoughby, and perpetually entices him from the banal environment in which he quite willingly spends most of his time. He looked at the goddess now as one might look at some transcendental backstairs or fire-escape. Then he turned back and scowled rather conscientiously at each of us in turn.

Hippias moved with exaggerated unsteadiness across the room. 'Mush better go to bed,' he stuttered. 'Lil' dispute over cards.'

'Cards?' I said. There was no sign of cards in George's study, nor ever had been since I could remember.

'Horses,' corrected Hippias readily. 'Lil' alter – altercation about name of animal won the Derby in '06.'

'He means in '07,' said George – and as he spoke gave me a look which made me at once afraid and furious. For I could see how George's mind was working. The mystery, whatever it was, had got him in a tight spot. And (as I had suspected might happen) he was going to take it out of someone else. 'Among gentlemen such matters are always settled with a bottle. Get back to your own brand of tattle, my dear, and leave us to ours. But just see that Mervyn's all right first. And tell Owdon to bring more glasses.'

It is funny just what one won't stand. There had been times when, if George had taken a hunting-crop to me, I should have regarded it as one of the legitimate consequences of a marriage made in a bad moment. But this about the glasses was definitive.

'Owdon,' I snapped, 'has had his last orders from me. And I from you.'

I could see George hesitate, and again I knew that he had much more on his mind than I could get at. 'You are mistaken,' he said.

The significance of this – if significance it had – was obscured by Grace, who gave a sudden and indignant yelp of surprise. 'George's portrait!' she exclaimed. 'How utterly disgraceful!'

We all looked at it. Alone of all the oils in the room, this picture was for some reason glazed. And here, it seemed, was where the whiskey-bottle had found its mark. The glass was shattered, and in the lower centre of the canvas itself there was a gaping rent. Grace as she looked at this turned pale with fury; an obscure assault upon her brother plainly went very deep. Since (as I have explained) that pink hunting-coat toned George's portrait right in with the allurements to vice her attitude was really very unreasonable. But now she started on one of those tirades of hers which it would be useless to reproduce. And this annoyed Willoughby.

'Shut up,' Willoughby said. 'For goodness' sake, stow it.'

The night was full of surprises. For Willoughby to pitch a glass of sherry at Mervyn was one thing; for him to address an aunt like this was quite another. Even Hippias looked at him in befuddled surprise.

'It's a perfectly ghastly picture, anyway,' said Willoughby. 'The very worst sort of picture.' He paused and sought fleeting comfort from the Caravaggio once more. 'Do you know, every year they used to take me to Burlington House and then to luncheon at a horrible great hotel afterwards. And always I used to be sick going back to school on the train. I thought it was the luncheon, and every year I ventured to eat less and less. But I was always sick, just the same. And then I realized that it wasn't the food but the Royal Academicians. Well, this very bad picture of uncle George is just that sort. Who wouldn't heave a whiskey-bottle through it? Not that I'd throw a bottle. I'd throw a –'

'Willoughby,' said Bevis, 'you forget yourself.'

It was, I suppose, all pretty comical, and they had all very abundantly forgotten themselves. But I wasn't a bit amused. Jokes about the Royal Academy can scarcely be said to have the charm of novelty, and this one seemed altogether untimely. I could see that Willoughby was jabbering like this because he was upset; I could give him a good mark for being genuine about George's beastly portrait as well as tiresome. But certainly I couldn't be amused.

Nor could Grace. From a chafing-dish she turned to a coffee-percolator – one that suddenly bubbles and erupts. 'Willoughby,' she screamed, 'was it you who –'

'Of course it was.' Willoughby nodded savagely. 'I'm roaring drunk and I pitched the bottle through the beastly picture.'

There was an uncertain pause. Then Gerard spoke.

'No,' he said quietly. 'It was my father. Cousin George was here by the fire-place, and it is fair to say that he said something very insulting. My father, who had just returned to the room, picked up the bottle and threw it at him. It was a rash act.'

'It was a deuced ineffective one.' Bevis spoke abruptly, as on a sudden discovery. 'Try to chuck a bottle towards the fire-place and succeed in hitting that picture? It doesn't make sense.'

Well, quite a lot just didn't. And I was going to point out that Hippias, being a bit fuddled, must have got himself foxed by George's absurd mirrors when there was another exclamation of surprise. This time it was from Gerard, who had walked over to examine the damage done to the picture.

'It's hinged!' he exclaimed.

We all turned to look – and were in time to see the remains of the pink-coated George swing outwards. What was revealed was nothing so very startling. In fact, it was merely a small safe let into the wall.

But somehow the whole of the events of the evening seemed – quite irrationally – to fall into place as so much deliberate build-up for this discovery. Naturally George had a safe for his more private papers. And naturally it would be masked in just such a way as this. A wall-safe is as proper to a baronet as is a study, or a row of ancestors, or a pink coat.

Yet we all looked at it much as if here was the truth revealed at last.

8

Some nine hours later the winter sun rose for the last time on George Simney. It rose, too, upon a day full of incident. Indeed, I have something to record of the very moment in which I opened my eyes.

At first I thought that Mervyn was prowling about my room; then I realized that it was Timmy Owdon. He had set down a tray and was putting considerable subdued rage into pulling back the curtains; the light caught his curls and the fine line of his nose; it was, after all, the best of the Simneys (I came wide awake reflecting) who had been born on the wrong side of the blanket.

This didn't prevent my feeling annoyed. For one thing, Timmy was apt to remind me of that day when I had first met George and him out riding, and I could always reflect that if his beauty had not somehow set off George's vigorous physical life I might have been spared landing myself in a scrape. Then, again, the meaning of Timmy's being here was plain to me from previous experience. One or more of the housemaids had left in a hurry, and the boy had been turned on to the first necessary job. Whether newly promoted footmen are commonly given such tasks I don't know – and on the preceding night it had rather been my impression that George designed to dismiss him to the outdoors again for good. But, anyway, here he was. I sat up, reached for a wrap, and poured tea. 'Good morning, Timmy,' I said. 'Why is this?'

Timmy moved to the next window. 'If you don't like it,' he said, 'you can have Martin. Or so I would suppose. But her ladyship seems to hold it beneath her dignity to stir until you have to be got on your feet. That's why it's me.

Nothing's beneath my dignity, of course. I hope the tea's all right. I made it.'

'It's the Lapsang,' I said gratefully. 'Have a piece of bread and butter.'

Timmy took a piece. He took a quick glance at the door and then sat down on the foot of the bed. 'Oh, lord!' he said.

When we were alone together this sultry boy and I were human beings. There was much impropriety in this, I don't doubt. It had just happened.

'How is Mervyn?' I asked.

'Bruises.' Timmy's voice held satisfaction. 'But nothing broken and no sprains.' This he added dejectedly.

I pushed towards him the second of the three slivers of bread and butter which he had brought in. 'I don't think you like Mervyn very much?'

'I admire him.'

'You mustn't do that.'

'I admire him. I am ignorant enough to admire him. He has been to a public school while I have groomed horses or cleaned knives.'

I laughed. 'What's the good of a public school? It means nothing but manners and an accent.'

Timmy Owdon looked up swiftly. 'My accent is identical with his. And my manners are a great deal better.'

Both these statements, it occurred to me, were true. 'Yes,' I said gently, '– of course.'

'These are facts which tell you a good deal about me.' Timmy moved away the tray, jumped off the bed and brought me a hand mirror. 'Would this be the next part of the ritual? Anyway, you will find it heartening.'

'Heartening?'

'You bear up very well.' He smiled as he spoke, and his smile was at once wicked and friendly. 'Your ladyship is quite an example to me. But then, of course, I am young enough to feel my position keenly.' He frowned, as if catching in his own voice the echo of Mervyn's self-conscious manner of speech. 'Damn Mervyn.' He flushed darkly. 'I say – I'm frightfully sorry.'

'Sorry, Timmy?'

'For saying damn.'

I just managed not to laugh – and I should have very much hated myself otherwise. For I had stopped being annoyed. There are gentlemen and gentlemen, and Timmy Owdon belonged with a scarcer sort. 'I think,' I said, 'that you know too much and not enough.'

'Yes.' He looked at me questioningly. 'I suppose it is very unusual?'

'Very. Lots of boys are born in that way, Timmy. But either their birth is concealed from them or they are given the breeding of their legitimate brothers – though perhaps at a distance.'

'I see.' He hesitated. 'Of course I hate him a little – Sir George. But not tremendously – because of that. If – if anything ever happened, I would like you to know it was not because of that.'

I let the mirror drop on the bed. 'Timmy,' I said, 'what do you mean?'

He looked at me directly – and suddenly with flashing eyes. 'They say it was my mother,' he said. 'But do I really know about my father – though Owdon is my name? It may have been the other way. *He* may be my father – Sir George. Nicolette, how I wish I could be sure that he was not.'

I was startled by this – both by the boy's obliviously calling me Nicolette, and by the marked impression of breeding which he gave, and by the obscure tenor of his words. But instead of inquiring into these (as I ought perhaps to have done) I changed to a less awkward topic. 'There was a row last night,' I said.

Timmy nodded. 'That is why a fool of a girl called Mary has left. I shall miss her rather, because I used to kiss her quite a lot. Do you think that cheap?'

This time I did laugh – we were getting on well enough

for that. 'No, Timmy, I don't. Only don't ever positively seduce a virgin without thinking hard and long. It's incalculable.'

He looked at me with a faint flush and knit his brows, considering. 'Do you know,' he said anxiously, 'I can't promise?'

'Certainly you can't. You wouldn't be a Simney if you could.'

'You think I have a rotten heredity?'

I found this difficult. 'Heredity,' I said (not altogether honestly), 'is just a bit of jargon you've picked up from your books. And, anyway, you're good enough to kiss as many Marys as we can crowd into the servants' hall.'

Timmy flushed darkly and I cursed myself for a fool. The turn of that phrase had been altogether wrong. 'But why,' I asked quickly, 'did the little goose leave?'

'It wasn't Sir George. I mean, not particularly. All that breaking of stuff last night, and then everybody knowing that Mervyn had been thrown through a window. She just said it wasn't good service, and she would tell them so at the registry office in town.' Timmy paused. 'You know, things are getting a bit hot. This blacksmith's daughter in the village. The parson has been getting worked up.'

'But that's quite in the run of things here.'

Timmy looked slightly shocked. His knowledge of the world was insufficient to tell him how in such situations one must grow a shell, and he thought me hard, I suppose. But the truth was that I had more to think of than the blacksmith's daughter, and at that moment I was thinking of Timmy himself. If he were George's son the whole thing could have been kept as obscure as you please. But if Owdon were indeed his father, and his mother some unhappy lady of the family, how could the episode have been so successfully wrapped in mystery? I had found no answer to this when Timmy startled me once more.

'You see,' he said, 'it's Willoughby too.'

'Willoughby?'

'He was painting the girl – this blacksmith's daughter. She's very striking, but not what you could call pretty. Sir George butted in just to annoy.'

'Timmy, it doesn't get anywhere telling me these things. The only result is to make me feel like Grace. There seems to be just nothing on the horizon but these silly, shoddy, sexy scandals.'

'But there is. There's I don't know what blowing up. You know the expression about there being bad blood between relations? Well, when the blood that there is bad-ness between is bad itself – and Simney blood is bad –'

'Timmy, I think you'd better run along. You're being an old Jonah.'

'No I'm not.' He was very serious. 'I feel the devil in myself, for one thing. It's since I came into the house and saw that Sir George – and saw that you . . .'

He broke off, confused, and with a fearful rage in his eyes that told me a great deal. 'Timmy,' I said sharply, 'I can look after myself. I'm doing so. You would only –'

'If only I knew,' he said. 'If only I knew that he wasn't my –'

'You're being melodramatic. It's the result of long-lost cousins coming back with some mystery from Australia. And now you're going to stop it.' I must have spoken with something like vehemence, for I think I was almost frightened.

Timmy looked crestfallen and for a moment this com-forted me. Then professional instinct quickened my scru-tiny; I saw that the penitent face before me was a mask; and at that I really was frightened all through. I put out my hand to him. 'Timmy,' I said, '*stop it*. And listen. If I need help from anyone in this household, I'll come to you.'

'Is that a promise?' He flushed. 'I'm – I'm only six-teen.'

'It's a promise that I'll come to you. And now be off. Clean knives. Polish Mrs Gerard's exquisite Australian shoes.'

Timmy Owdon sprang to his feet, and his face was radiant with its wicked, eager smile. 'Your ladyship,' he said, 'should be about and caring for your guests. I will send your ladyship's ladyship as fast as a stick can drive her up the back stairs.'

And he was gone. I finished my tea and stared blankly into the empty cup. One cannot hold such a conversation as this with a house-boy – even though he be obscurely one of the family – without feeling oneself amid a dream-like and altogether impermanent scene of things.

Mervyn kept his bed that morning; Owdon, as befitted his dignity, was not in attendance at breakfast; but every-body else was there – including Timmy, who took round coffee like an automaton. I concluded that George had judged it futile, after all, to attempt to conceal him from the Australians (and why he had in the first case been prompted to do so I could not guess), and had therefore rescinded his banishment. That everyone should appear at once was slightly surprising after the events of the night before; one would have predicted that the family would slip in one by one after cautious reconnaissance and snatch a kipper to gnaw in the garden. But there they all were in a rather distrustful circle – and Lucy passed me the mar-malade.

A good deal can be put into passing the marmalade: adoration, cordiality, indifference, distaste. But what Lucy put in was hate – which is an altogether different matter. Just how she contrived it I could not now describe, but the impression was vivid enough at the time and wholly unam-biguous. It was the more surprising, too, because – so far as I was aware – it was something quite new in our rela-tions. Between sisters-in-law, I suppose, there must always be undercurrents of animosity; and these will be definite where it is a matter of a resident sister-in-law in such a queer household as ours. But why (I asked myself while doing what justice I could to marmalade so delivered) *hate*? Was it because she credited me with inspiring Gerard to pitch her precious Mervyn out of the window? Almost certainly it had to do with Mervyn in some way. For except in relation to Mervyn Lucy was surely incapable of any intensity whatever; she was a stupid, vague creature except when touched off at this one point of maternal solicitude. But here she was suddenly hating me – and (I could have sworn) studying my complexion. It was unnerving. And although the riddle had its obvious solution this just didn't occur to me. Perhaps I was too preoccupied with Gerard.

This was because Gerard was too preoccupied with me. Timmy had made me a bit edgy and I was reckoning that one would-be protector was a little more than enough. Yet here was Gerard so carefully not looking at me that he was obviously meditating both me and my position in the household all the time. Perhaps he was intelligent enough to be wondering not only how on earth I got there but why on earth I stayed. Even in the great Australian out-back wives are presumably not serfs – so why should they be so on the estate of an English baronet? Yes, perhaps Gerard was meditating that. And last night he had been, after all, rather unnecessarily helpful. Mervyn might very well have been let alone . . . Gerard, who was likeable, could (I saw) also be indiscreet. And he looked as if he might be taking Timmy's line on Lady Simney – and that on the strength of an uncommonly short acquaintance.

It is quite nauseous to be representing myself as a typical *femme fatale* – particularly if this aspect of the mystery is likely to prove to some extent a mare's nest. And I turned now for a little relief to young Willoughby, who had always been completely negative in all his approaches to me. Vanity is nauseous too, and I must record that for a long time I attributed this disregard of Willoughby's to the fact that we usually met in the presence of his father, and that before his father he thought it discreet to appear emotionally numb. But now as I looked at Willoughby I realized how

Hazelwood – and perhaps the world at large – had corrupted me; I couldn't look at a man without thinking of him as thinking about a woman. Whereas men have a good many other things to think about. Or rather the conjoined clamorousness and futility of the woman-business obliges them to think of other things for the sake of sanity. Hence the world's achievement of what is called culture. And hence the brooding and abstracted quality in Willoughby's eye. He was thinking of a girl down in the village – but thinking of her in terms of mass and tint and hue. This was the simple truth about Willoughby at present. He was a young painter struggling to get going in an ungenial environment, and he wasn't giving time to other things. I ought to have liked Willoughby for this, for I know very well what it is to be struggling to get down to a job. And yet I didn't like Willoughby very much. I liked him only a little better than Bevis – who would certainly never meditate mass and tint and hue, nor approve of his son's doing so – and who was now treating Hippias to a blameless dissertation on the cross-fertilization of wheat.

I looked at George. And it came to me uncertainly that he was indeed in some obscure way cornered, and that he was resolved to go down with flying colours. Or perhaps it would be better to say that he was resolved to go down with another feather in his cap. Joyleen was feather-headed enough, heaven knows.

George was experienced. On what was only a rudimentary problem he expended only a rudimentary technique. Last night he had given the girl one look and then ignored her; this morning he was all over her with everything a bad baronet can muster. He talked horses; it became evident that Bondi has a substantial acquaintance with the brutes; presently the affair turned from trot to canter and from canter to shameless gallop. And no sooner was this accomplished metaphorically than it was repeated in actual fact. Within half an hour of first putting fork to bacon Joyleen was standing in the hall in riding things. And within ten minutes of that again the two of them were disappearing through the park. Joyleen was mounted on my mare.

Bevis continued to play the gentleman farmer. And Hippias, who this morning was thoughtful if not subdued, made civil replies. But Hippias was not unaware of what had occurred, and I could see him look sidelong at his son with a speculative eye.

Whether Gerard was learning anything it was impossible to say. If these people had come from Australia on some great rackety mailboat (as I suppose they had) it would be a fair guess that he had seen Joyleen show a clean pair of heels like this often enough. But now it did seem to me as if he was startled; perhaps he didn't reckon on a host and elderly cousin behaving so forthrightly like a casual lounger on a liner. But certainly he wasn't absorbed in this disagreeable business to the exclusion of all else. Gerard (as I've said before) was turning me over in his mind; as far as he was concerned I was Hazelwood's principal mystery, and whatever had been on the carpet the night before took distinctly a second place. That he should thus be as much and as rapidly concerned with George's wife as George was with his was piquant enough in a way, and the fact that Gerard's interest was no doubt as blameless-seeming to himself as George's was downright carnal only refined upon the situation when viewed in a comic light. But I was far from wanting to invoke the Comic Spirit over Hazelwood that day. And I particularly didn't want to be meditated as a mystery.

My first impulse was simply to clear out for the morning. And, as a matter of fact, that was what I presently did. But, of course, running away is never much good. There is that book of Conrad's in which it is only the coward who comes to a really nasty end. And when I did run away it was to bump into something at least a good deal nastier than if I had stayed put.

First, however, I decided to have it out with Gerard. I wanted to explain to him quite simply that I was not a captive princess guarded by an ogre; that I was just not to be regarded as interesting in that way; that I distinctly liked him here and now but saw no future for him as a knight-errant ... And to create an opportunity for the delivery of this little homily I led Gerard off to look at the orangery.

When we got there I ought to have plunged straight ahead. The thing could only be said pretty baldly and I ought to have submitted to that. But for a fatal half-minute I beat about the bush – and in that short time lost ground which I had to struggle to recover. I don't mean that I at all felt like falling in love with this Australian Simney; but I did feel in him a simple human warmth which made me baulk rather at my frosty programme. Gerard was like a genuine piece of warmth amid the artificial climate – the product of steam-heating – into which I had led him. Incidentally it was the orangery, and the wilderness of greenhouses beyond, which gave him the initiative. He laughed at them.

Gerard looked at the orange trees and palms beneath their immense cupola of glass and chuckled. He looked at the long corridors of glass with their closely pruned vines and laughed outright. 'Of course,' he said, 'I know that it is quite august to have an orangery. And quite silly to be amused at it merely because in one's own country oranges and lemons grow in the back yard, and muscatels prolif-erate like a pest in suburban gardens, and housewives work frantically to turn a fraction of their peaches into jam. Our school-books, which are filled with the colonial inferiority-complex, loudly assert that England is very cold and very grey and very wet – whereas we have summer skies that sparkle with a myriad dyes. It is very absurd, and undoubt-edly your Nordic climate is both an economic and a spir-itual asset. But what about the emotions? Of course there are plenty of robustly animal ones galloping about.' And Gerard's glance went out through the steamy glass of the orangery and across the snow-covered park. 'But others must sometimes grow discouraged, I think, and harbour under ground.' He turned back and looked at me. 'More discouraged than the snowdrops, that will, after all, still thrust a single slender green spear through.'

Well, that was that. Gerard, like Timmy, thought me hard. And Gerard himself was perhaps ever so slightly soft – or at least subject to little eddies of poetical feeling which manifested themselves in an uncolonial cadence. I looked at him cautiously. He wasn't deliberately leading to anything with this talk – in this more honest than myself, who had been proposing to edge in something I designed to say.

So again I was checked for a moment. And again he got ahead of me. And with the same spontaneity.

'Do you believe in fidelity?' he asked.

'Yes.'

'There is a sense in which it is unnatural. We are none of us so faithful as we think. They say – psychologists who study such things – that it is just a matter of having thicker skins.'

I looked at Gerard in perplexity. 'Thicker skins?'

'Just that. A thicker skin of morality, or of the socially-sanctioned attitudes, covering the hopeless naturel promiscuity of the hidden man. What do you think of that?'

This was not the sort of talk I wanted; nevertheless I found myself considering his question carefully. 'Without his skin,' I said, 'a man would be disagreeable. He would also be dead. In fact, he wouldn't be a man. He would be a not-man.'

No doubt this was a wisp of donnish wisdom from my abortive Oxford days. But Gerard seemed to suppose that I had won it from a void. 'That's just it,' he said. 'But I could never have put it in that way.' Once more he looked out across the park into which George and Joyleen had vanished. 'Did you ever think of Australia?' he asked.

'Not, I'm afraid, very much. Or not until last night.'

'I mean, of possibly living there?'

This was a bit of a jolt. I looked at him squarely. 'You

mean that fidelity might make a better show in a second innings?'

'Something like that. At my prep school we never counted the first ball. It was called a trialer.' Gerard paused and rubbed a little steam from the glass in front of us. We were both looking at the empty park. 'Those people,' he said, matter-of-factly, 'are gone, after all.'

I think it must be admitted that in this encounter Gerard Simney had me licked. He came straight at you, as Simneys do. Once upon a time George – if on something a different level – had licked me with the same quality.

But it must not be concluded from this that I was remotely moved to proceed upstairs and pack a suit-case (as somebody else, you will presently discover, was at that moment doing). For I really *was* more discouraged than the snowdrops. Indeed, this is one of the few facts that are constant and unchallengeable throughout the whole fluid George Simney affair so far. After Christopher I was finished. And George himself had been no more than the proof of that.

I was taken unawares, and I was distressed. But I was also, I'm afraid, amused – and I must have looked at Gerard with a startled smile that his small experience took for heaven knows what. The next moment I was in his arms – and feeling unutterably clumsy at having provoked that honest, unmeaning embrace. I kissed him gently and pushed him away. 'My dear,' I said, 'you've got it utterly –'

Something like a scream of rage interrupted me, and we turned to see Grace goggling and frothing at us absurdly from behind a palm-tree. It was like an apparition – for a moment later she was gone.

We looked at each other. There was nothing for it but a good many awkward and explaining words. I just wasn't going to have Gerard feeling abased. Twenty minutes later we parted, very good friends.

9

I put on goloshes – in such things it is impossible to feel unduly tense about oneself – and went for a tramp in the park. Here and there the snow was dazzling beneath oblique shafts of sunlight, but to the north the sky was leaden: against it the fruit of the plane-trees, suspended on rime-covered and invisible twigs, showed like round black medals pinned at random on field-grey cloth. Hoof marks showed in which direction George and Joyleen had gone; I turned in another direction and walked until Hazelwood was sufficiently remote to be taken in as a single unit in the landscape. The Caroline front with its scroll-like gables faced me squarely, and to my left, like a casual acquaintance who has turned away and abruptly changed his expression, the later Georgian façade presented towards the village an aspect altogether more authoritative and aloof. The stable clock was striking; its strokes came to me with the peculiar quality such sounds take on over snow; I was suddenly aware of how familiar these sights and sounds ought to be to Lady Simney and how alien they were to me. If all that maturely proud and variously expensive pile had lost definition as I looked, if its vast solidity had thinned to gossamer and thence to a mere smoke fading into invisibility across the monotone sky, I should have been immensely surprised indeed, but the miracle as I watched it would have imparted no sense of loss.

There seemed much waste in this. On that terrace should have been children on ponies, the warm breath steaming up from them, their mother standing beside them, their father talking to his bailiff a little way off – and in the background Hazelwood itself, not particularly remarked by any of these, but nevertheless a fact as permanent as the soil on which they stood. Well, for a generation at least all that was out of the picture. Perhaps it didn't so greatly matter. For the world was passing Hazelwood by; and one generation, more or less, made small difference at the tail end of a tradition.

But it would have been better to go down with the flag flying ... And that, I remembered, was what, for himself at least, George seemed obscurely to be proposing. I tried to get the hang of it. The Australian Simneys had turned up unexpectedly and George was in some queer way cornered. *Treasure Island,* came into my head; I thought of the blind man coming tap-tapping out of nowhere and tipping Jim Hawkins's nautical guest the black spot. Had the Simneys tipped George the black spot? Gerard, I was pretty sure, had not. He had been quite ready to join in vigorous recriminations over the ancient business of Dismal Swamp – but Dismal Swamp had seemed an incident merely shabby, certainly not sinister enough to bring a black spot into play, and if graver matters had since appeared I was tolerably convinced that Gerard had not got the hang of them. Perhaps this was because he hadn't been attending, having preoccupied himself from the first with the romantic notion of rescuing his hostess from her shameful condition.

I made snowballs and pelted on oak – the windows of Hazelwood watching me blankly across the park the while. It was warming, it was even in some degree heartening, and Hazelwood seemed to grow smaller as I stood panting for breath. Bevis and his spurious respectability, Mervyn and his nauseous wit and doting mother (who had given me that glance of hatred): all these – and even the sexually-obsessed Grace with her recent snooping triumph – seemed to grow smaller too. Only Timmy Owdon, who must now be filling coal scuttles or polishing frosty bits and bridles, remained life size.

I was still thinking about the young Owdon when I came upon the old one.

The snowballing had given out on me and I had a notion that were I to turn round Hazelwood would show as large as life again, a great stone and brick and mortar fact not to be escaped from. And at that I had walked towards the north-east corner of the park, where only a narrow strip of meadow separates it from the high-road. I wanted to see a bus or two filled with country folk, or cars travelling fast across this particular stretch of England in the confident expectation of arriving at another. What I did see was George's butler – a black hurrying skulking figure against the snow. He was carrying two heavy suit-cases and looked much like a raven hobbling guiltily away with some cumbersome fruit of theft.

It was an abrupt encounter, for though Owdon too was evidently making towards the high-road we had been converging from either side of a spinney. He stopped in his tracks and I suppose I must have done the same. I remember framing a question – and then deciding that he was very much George's servant, after all, and that I need by no means concern myself with him. I glanced up at the sky. 'It looks,' I said, 'as if there will be more snow.'

Whatever he had expected it was not conversation; there was a nervous twitch to his mouth as he stood there which told of considerable distress of mind. But when he spoke it was impassively enough.

'It must be regarded as seasonable, your ladyship, at this time of year.'

This, thoughtfully and indeed heavily offered, was quite in the Owdon manner – and it was so remote from Timmy as to set anybody wondering at once. I have already mentioned the stupidity of Owdon; the thing is one of the basic facts of Hazelwood life; but now suddenly I was asking myself if Owdon's stupidity was not so obvious – so dazzling, so to speak – as to obscure what might otherwise be at least equally significant characteristics. That the man had some disreputable past, and that George cherished him for it, I had no doubt of whatever. But there was also, it struck me, something enigmatic about him here and now. There was something odd and indefinable in his relationship to the household, to George, to myself – and this was more than the aura which must surround any manservant who has long ago been implicated in some intimate family scandal. What was out of the way about Owdon – and whatever it might be I could by no means define it – was more than his being the father of Timmy (if he was that). And here I pulled myself up. For surely I had set myself romancing about the man simply because of the actual mystery before me: namely, that here he was hurrying furtively through the park with a couple of suit-cases when he ought to have been superintending the labours of such servants as were left to us.

A prosaic and yet startling explanation struck me. Were those suit-cases perhaps crammed with the Simney family silver, and was Owdon decisively reverting to his pirate days?

'Owdon,' I said, 'are you making off with the spoons?'

I think you will agree that it was queer – so queer as to deserve a little paragraph to itself. Timmy would have called it cheap, and moreover Owdon could have walked off with every stick in Hazelwood and I wouldn't have given a damn. So how I came to utter such words I don't at all know. Perhaps I was remembering the broken glasses and the man's unaccountable perturbation on the night before, and hoping to startle or sting him into some explanation of himself. Or perhaps I was just feeling oafish. Certainly I was preoccupied. The scene in that bare, horrid room of George's, the angry men, the smashed portrait with the safe behind it, the broken whiskey-bottle on the table and George stretching out his hand to it: I had got to turning these images round and round in my head as if they were going to reveal something ... Anyway, and however that may be, here I was insulting a servant.

And Owdon set down the suit-cases in the snow. 'It would be reasonable enough,' he said.

If my question had been odd this reply was surely a good deal odder. Moreover it was, in some subterranean way, a new Owdon who delivered himself of it. The man was looking at me consideringly, and for a moment I felt that I had become something more than the person to whom he was accustomed to announce that dinner was served. I was sure that he was a very bad man, with a history of villainy by no means confined to getting an illegitimate son on the upper classes. Yet I was aware that at this moment some decent human feeling towards me was animating him – and that it was so only some seconds after I had been extremely rude. And – what is more – I felt an altogether unexpected current within myself. We stood there, the two of us, in the snow – Owdon between his suit-cases like some creature led into a stall. And, if momentarily only, some sympathy, some obscure intimation of fellow-feeling, declared itself. Then my mind went back to what he had said. Why should it be reasonable enough that Owdon should make off with the spoons? Did George owe him money? Had he, too, when in Australia been cheated in the matter of a Dismal Swamp?

During these few seconds I was on the verge of having it out with Owdon. But I hesitated – it was just the sort of failure I had known an hour before with Gerard – and what followed was a lot of lies. Owdon explained that the suit-cases belonged to our departed housemaid and that he was benevolently taking them to the bus. Perhaps this was the best story he could think up. Or perhaps he had forgotten that when a new maid came to Hazelwood I had the housekeeper bring her to me and myself settled her into her room. The girl whom Timmy had kissed quite a lot was one of those whom I had received in this way. I remembered her luggage perfectly well. And those suit-cases were nothing like it.

At that I left Owdon and went on my way. He was, I concluded, preparing to make an unobtrusive bolt, and to this end was caching some of his possessions near the high-road. He had been at Hazelwood ten times as long as I had – and now within twenty-four hours of the arrival of the Australians he was getting ready to cut and run. Such behaviour on the part of an old retainer surely suggested a first-rate mystery, and it may seem surprising that as I tramped on I didn't give my mind to it. But somehow I couldn't bring Owdon anywhere near the centre of things; to the Hazelwood problem as I saw it he was peripheral only. And I think it was because of this – because, I mean, I didn't start speculating on why Owdon should be preparing his get-away – that ten minutes later the incident sprang up in my mind again in quite a different focus.

What if it wasn't his own unobtrusive departure that Owdon was preparing? What if it was Timmy's?

The notion alarmed me. It alarmed me because it brought up the knight-errant theme again. Gerard Simney had come with ludicrous speed to the notion that it might be altogether virtuous and laudable to abscond with me to the antipodes. That was tiresome enough. But young Timmy was a fowl of a different feather; it was impossible that he could have grown up without feelings of injustice and dispossession; and the suppressed rage bred of this he had somehow hitched on to the spectacle of George and myself. Of this I had been granted a sudden revealing glimpse not many hours before. Was it possible that Owdon knew more of the boy – and feared more?

The drift of my mind here must seem melodramatic enough. But remember, please, that Simneys as a race are impossibly rash – and that Timmy, whether on the distaff side or not, is a Simney every inch. Quite simply, then, I was confronting this: that Owdon feared the lad's doing George some horrible violence – and was proposing to get him out of the way either before or after such an event.

But this was not the only possibility. The matter might be altogether different. Some threat was in the air. The Australians had brought it with them. Owdon had felt it at some word spoken by Hippias. The depleted Hazelwood crystal witnessed to this. Nay, Owdon had felt it earlier; the very arrival of those people on the doorstep had discomposed him. And what if, in some obscure way, the threat were to his boy? Why had George attempted to hustle from the room the lad whom he had been so indecently ready to exhibit in the character of a footman? Were those suitcases designed to accompany Timmy to some less unhealthy spot?

I was revolving all this not without anxiety – for Timmy somehow did concern me – when the next of that morning's regular succession of incidents occurred ... This is a thoroughly artless recital, I would have you observe. I simply tramp from point to point about George Simney's beastly great park – and something happens to me every time.

This time it was a bit of eavesdropping.

It isn't easy to eavesdrop in the middle of a park covered in snow. And, of course, if you are a nice person it isn't easy to do at all. Persons who have to admit to the fact commonly are at some pains to represent how the thing came upon them unawares, and how before they knew what they were about they were landed in a situation from which there was no immediate extricating themselves without hopeless embarrassment. But it wasn't like that with me on this occasion. And when I say that in the quite near future I was to be constrained to relate the whole incident to the police I think you will agree that I more or less expiated my conduct now.

I indianed. This is something which very nice children do in books which were read to me in my early teens. The nice children indianed not, of course, for the purpose of vulgar eavesdropping but in order to lurk unseen upon the flanks of other nice children co-operating in imaginative games. I used to practise indianing, although there were no co-operative children. I could do it quite well in heather. And now – what was uncomfortable – I did it in snow. And my object was to overhear a conversation between Bevis and Hippias.

There they were in the shelter of our boundary wall, swathed in ulsters and perched on shooting-sticks, looking like country gentlemen in an advertisement designed to attract city clerks, and so very earnestly discoursing that the steam rose continuously from their mouths as from a pair of small, florid dragons. I guessed that they had tramped out for the sake of privacy – and this privacy I at once proceeded to violate. For their talk, I supposed, might illuminate whatever mystery the southern hemisphere had newly delivered on us; and it had come to me that if the facts were to be known I had better know them. The revelations and half-revelations of the past twelve hours or so had really come to shake me at last; I felt that there were factors of which I couldn't estimate the gravity; and that in fuller knowledge here might be at least some shadow of power ... So I got right down on my belly and indianed to a ditch, and along that I got on hands and knees to a point almost directly behind them. I think I have said that everything was coming to feel tail-end and impermanent with me – which is no doubt why I confronted with very tolerable equanimity the substantial possibility of being discovered in this untoward situation. If they liked to turn round and see Lady Simney squinnying at them from a ditch they were welcome. And meanwhile I strained my ears.

'A terrible thing,' Bevis was saying. 'I do beg you to see, my dear fellow, that it is a terrible thing. Shocking to think of such a stain on the family name.'

'Fiddle-de-dee,' said Hippias. 'And I don't remember that a fellow cared to talk like a parson in my day. Every Simney is pretty well booked from birth as a stain upon the family name – even if he happens to go by the name of Owdon.'

I think I crouched a bit lower in my ditch at this – for it seemed to confirm my uneasy suspicion that Timmy was somehow near the centre of the picture. And as I did so Hippias's laughter went bellowing over my shoulders. It was necessary to conclude that the little matter of a bar sinister in the family amused him greatly. There was a pause.

'Owdon,' repeated Hippias relishingly. 'It's a dam' good

name. In fact, about as plebeian as you could find.'

'In that regard,' said Bevis, 'it may be said that Joyleen runs it pretty close.'

This gratuitous stroke at his daughter-in-law by no means offended Hippias. He merely bellowed with laughter again. 'Girl's father was certainly the first to wear boots,' he said. 'But pots of money, my dear boy. Just what you will be hunting for in a few years for your own brat. Particularly –'

Bevis's voice interrupted angrily. 'Particularly what, damn you?'

For a moment Hippias hesitated. 'Particularly if his idea of earning a living consists of going after the village wenches with a paintbrush.' Again the horrid bellow blew over me. 'A paintbrush, heaven save the mark! When I was a lad –'

'When you were a lad,' said Bevis, 'there were some nasty young fellows about.'

All this was at least spirited, and I had a momentary hope that the two small, florid dragons would actually go for each other's throats. But Hippias merely tilted himself a little further back on his shooting-stick and raised an admonitory and chronically unsteady finger. 'Stick to the bally point, Bevis, my boy,' he said. 'And just try to consider what the result is going to be. Tick over the family one by one and make sure you know just how it will affect each of us.'

'A most intolerable scandal!' Bevis was evidently both alarmed and furious. 'And in its origins, confound you all, entirely colonial. I heartily wish your beastly continent off the map. It has only been there since the time of Captain Cook and could very easily be spared.'

This stupid rudeness, it occurred to me, was just the sort of thing into which the spuriously decorous Bevis might be expected to decline. But it didn't worry Hippias. 'No doubt it's a new country,' he said. 'Place where blood goes blue astonishingly quick. Fellow is no end of a swell if he can produce a great-grandfather in the honourable estate of an apothecary or attorney in Huddersfield or Hull.' And Hippias guffawed with what appeared to be quite genuine merriment at this witticism. 'Not that this is at all to the point – not to the point at all.'

'I was simply saying,' said Bevis, 'that in Australia things of that sort have their place, no doubt. But you really can't bring them over here.'

'I didn't.' Hippias was emphatic. 'All I brought was the little matter of Dismal Swamp. Do me the justice to see that, my dear fellow-me-lad. But when you ask me to hold my tongue simply to advance your own beastly interests – well, it comes to a matter of a consideration, doesn't it?'

From where I crouched I could hear Bevis suddenly breathing hard. 'You little backwoods blackguard,' he said. 'Are you asking me to write a cheque?'

Hippias gave his equable chuckle. 'The things are always dashed useful, I'm bound to admit. But talking of black-guards, my dear Bevis, just where do you stand? Are you really after avoiding scandal? Or are you after wholesale theft? It's in the blood, you know. Remember your brother and Dismal Swamp.'

There was a longer pause. 'Look here,' said Bevis, 'would you take twenty thousand?'

'Certainly not.'

'Is your boy in on this – or his trollop of a wife?'

Hippias chuckled, unoffended. 'Gerard hasn't tumbled to it so far as I know. And Joyleen would never tumble to anything.'

'Very well. You won't have to share out. I call twenty thousand a very reasonable offer.' Bevis hesitated. 'We don't positively know of any marriage, after all. Besides, you must remember that I have to consider Lady Simney – Nicolette.'

I think I almost exclaimed at this. For that Bevis had to consider me in some way when debating paying the unlovely Hippias a tidy sum in what appeared to be blackmail was a notion utterly obscure to me. It ought not to have been so, as I can now clearly see. But squatting there in the snow I could not at all understand the manner in which I was being dragged into the deal. No more had I been able to understand a certain appraising scrutiny to which Lucy had subjected me the night before.

There is matter for the psychologist in this, and it is plain that there were certain areas in my life which I was just not prepared to contemplate ... But now – and even as I was peering out at Bevis in blank astonishment – this curious interview at which I had been assisting picked itself up and receded from my ken. For no particular reason that I could discern the two disputants unstuck their shooting-sticks and marched off, still arguing hotly.

And it could not be said that I had gained much positive light. I was left, indeed, with a confused mind ... crouched like a rabbit in a ditch in my husband Sir George Simney's park.

10

Walk on. Tramp over the snow chewing on what has befallen (and very likely you will make more of it than I did) until the next exhibit presents itself.

The next exhibit is a dumb-show – rather like the queer old turn the players put on before the play-within-the-play in *Hamlet*. And here, as there, it betokens at least the first part of the catastrophe approaching. Soon Polonius will be behind his arras and the sword thrust home. The police will come with flash-light cameras and lug the guts into the neighbour room. And that will be the end of a bad baronet.

Grace was one figure in the dumb-show and the Reverend Adrian Deamer was the other. Mr Deamer is one of those clergymen who are always diving into their church for minor liturgical purposes. He would have little in common, I imagine, with that Bishop Denzell Simney who was painted by Kneller. It is true that St Francis preached to the fishes and the birds, but Mr Deamer would altogether disapprove of a bishop who conned a prayer-book amid wreaths of foxhounds. Mr Deamer doesn't approve of any Simneys – except Grace.

And at the moment perhaps he didn't much approve of her. For she had intercepted him when emerging from some interim devotions and probably proposing to himself a rewarding cup of Oxo in his study. A chilly wind had sprung up; it fluttered the surplice which Mr Deamer clutched in one hand and the unrolled umbrella which depended from the other; it disarranged his thinning hair and reddened his inquiring nose. Grace, in her character as an intelligence officer straight from Sodom and Gomorrah, stood strategically placed in the narrow defile of a lich-gate, and there raised to heaven the supplicating voice. Or to heaven and Mr Deamer – the latter, at least, being obliged to listen, since the lady regularly worked him embroidered slippers. Not that he was in any way reluctant, really, for he is a man who has come to feed on that with which he wrestles, and Hazelwood is inevitably both his principal gymnastic appliance and his principal trough. Presently the two of them had their noses well into it together.

I think I ought to say that, despite this tone into which I have fallen, I don't object to clergymen and churches and whatever superior verities these stand for. If I were myself by way of embroidering slippers for a revered vicar I should be pleased. But I had never managed to like Mr Deamer, perhaps because he on his side had distrusted me from the first. There had been a plan between Grace and him, I believe, to secure George's salvation by marrying him to another slipper-embroiderer of superior station in the county. It was a laudable plan if not a very likely one, and if it had matured everything (so far as I am concerned) would have been a great deal better. So I ought to have felt a kind of gratitude for the attempt. And for the man himself and his rather exclusive fanaticism about one sort of sin I ought to have allowed. And I ought not to have minded his having a low view of actresses. In fact I ought to have been able to be Lady Simney to the vicar even if Lady Simney was patently a scarlet woman to him. But somehow I hadn't managed it. And now here, as I came out of the park and approached the village, were those two communing over the Hazelwood situation in general and the recent affair of my supposed guilty embrace in the orangery in particular. It was a dumb-show – if only because I kept well on the far side of the road. But it was good of its kind. If the villagers felt like joining in and playing charades they would have had no reason to complain on the score of lack of expressiveness and intelligibility.

There was a field-path on the right, and discretion would have taken me up it. But something in me revolted against dodging and I walked straight on. I even moved out a bit on the crown of the road. For, of course, the natural thing to do was to tramp briskly past and speak a civil word while doing so. Cordiality would have been false. But to avoid these two would have been to play their own silly game.

Grace, who had been achieving gestures of repulsion, was now flapping her arms in resignation and despair. Mr Deamer had contrived to dispose of the umbrella and surplice and was thus able to clasp his hands before his chest – which was a way of suggesting that the matters on hand were supportable to him only by virtue of his professional character.

I was less than ten yards away. 'Good morning, Mr Deamer,' I said.

Grace turned round and stared at me with a sort of fascinated dread that I didn't much mind. But I minded Mr Deamer, who compressed his lips and looked straight through me.

One can always be disconcerted by something new, and I don't think I had ever been cut like that before. The effect on me was out of all proportion to its occasion. For, after all, I knew exactly how those two worthies felt – and why should just this upset me? But the fact is that I wanted to cry and that I had to be careful not to stumble until I was past them and with a clear road in front of me. The man had betrayed his calling – a shepherd being the last person who should look straight through a lost sheep. But that was his business, not mine. Why should I bother? Perhaps a very different sort of clergyman had sustained me in some forgotten passage of my childhood; perhaps it was something like that. Anyway, I was most irrationally humiliated and hurt. And I no longer disliked Mr Deamer. I hated him.

Mind you, I don't go in for hating. I don't think I hated George, though I greatly loathed him. And so I walked on, a good deal shattered both by the thing itself and by an emotional response so unexpected and extravagant. But don't think that all this is thrown in merely by way of canvassing sympathy for a sensitive plant. Don't condemn my morning's wanderings as so much beating about the bush; don't, like mad Hamlet, yell at me to leave my damnable faces, murderer, and begin. All these things have their place.

But I had no idea of what toils this walk was weaving.

And now the morning's last episode. If I had been indulging myself in too much fuss over the preceding one here was something which might have been sent to point me a fool.

I have forgotten to say that Gerard was abroad in the park at this time; once or twice I had glimpsed him walking moodily about some quarter of a mile away. It was to avoid the chance of meeting him that I took the homeward route I did. When I returned from the high-road I took a path which skirted the fringes of the path and led past Sir Basil's Folly.

Sir Basil Simney hangs in George's study with the rest of them – Zoffany is the artist – but I haven't, I think, mentioned him. He is unmentionable, even as Simneys go, and his Folly — which is a retired little classical temple erected to facilitate the pursuits of certain excessively recondite pleasures, is about the most innocent thing recorded of him. Outside this sinister little place two horses were tethered.

Well, as Gerard had remarked, those people were gone, after all. And if George amid the obscure difficulties gathering round him chose to find a little light relief in the high-speed seduction of Joyleen Simney it was just no business of mine, any more than was Mr Deamer's failure in pastoral care. Nor was it of any *use* to me. A couple of private detectives snooping round this chilly eighteenth-century love nest with cameras would have added very little to what my solicitors already had neatly tied up in pink tape. All that I had to do was to turn away from the Folly, walk back to Hazelwood, change my shoes and eat an undisturbed luncheon. I ought to have done this even when I became aware that there *was* somebody snooping round. But suddenly I was terribly frightened. And with a beating heart I advanced straight towards the little building before me.

To explain this would require a command of atmosphere that I don't remotely possess. George had told me in some detail about his ancestor Sir Basil and I knew that those elegant Ionic pillars supporting their dome of snow, that those surrounding oaks rising dark above a stainless carpeting, were heavy with old, unexpiated sin. Melodramatics or hysteria is the word for this talk, I suppose — and yet I did truly feel the place to be fit only for some horrible sacrifice, for the appearance, perhaps, of a hooded figure gliding through the druidic trees with a ritual and cleansing knife poised in air. Plainly I hadn't recovered from the nastiness of my encounter with Mr Deamer and Grace. Nevertheless there was a rational basis too for my alarm. For through these same trees a figure *had* glided. Somebody was lurking behind the Folly now.

I tried to think of harmless explanations. Upon persons retired as George and Joyleen were, snooping may be practised by any casual Peeping-Tom. Possibly it was no more than that. Or, again, Mr Deamer might be on his familiar beat as a one-man anti-vice squad – and this called for no more than a resolute turning of the mind to some less silly and squalid theme. Or it might be Grace – and here the same consideration applied, only rather more compellingly. But might it not be Owdon – a man become so enigmatic and mysterious that one could not calculate upon consequences in regard to him? I tried to persuade myself that the possibility of its being Owdon who was spying on his master represented the worst I could conceive in the matter. But this self-deception was no good – and already I was hurrying forward with that pounding heart. It might be Gerard. It might be Timmy.

Gerard had been in the park. Gerard was the wronged husband. Here were both a practical and a conventional reason for thinking of him. I forgot his matter-of-fact announcement that those people were gone, after all. But this was only because I *wanted* to bring him into the picture. If it was Gerard, it was bad. But if it was Timmy, it was a great deal worse.

For in some way I had taken Timmy Owdon to my heart. By some queer twist of the mind I saw him as very young – much younger than his sixteen years. And I think I saw him as one of that non-existent group of dream-Simneys on the terrace with their ponies. It was, no doubt, something very silly like that. But I just wasn't going to have Timmy destroyed in the working out of all this beastly and gathering wickedness and mystery. Or not while I was still about. Perhaps the Simneys – even appealing ones like Timmy – must have their disasters and there was no saving them. But *I* was going to be out of it *first*.

There was nothing very beautiful about this. Still, that's how I felt. Violence was part of the Simneys' story, and more or less imminent family violence I had intuitively come to expect. Perhaps it was the jagged line of that broken whiskey-bottle and the rent canvas of George's pink-coated portrait cheek by jowl with his nasty pink-fleshed lady. Cer-

tainly if I shut my eyes I could see, with almost halluci-
natory vividness, each of these pinks splashed with a ghastly
scarlet.

So it looked as if, rather suddenly, I was going a little
mad. From feeling that all this family quarrelling and
mystery-mongering left me cold I had swung round to panic
about it. I wanted if possible to get Timmy out, and was
quite resolved to get myself out, before the intolerableness
of Hazelwood was increased by some nasty newspaper
tragedy. Moreover I was quite prepared to take risks –
which was why I was hurrying towards Sir Basil's Folly
now. There before me were the horses, and there must be
George and the little wanton who had last night arrived
on us. And there, too, was someone skulking behind the
building.

Both in simple location here in its secluded corner of the
park and in atmosphere and traditional association the
place could scarcely have been better suited to some rash
act of jealousy or rage. Or – for that matter – to some
calculated crime, and if I had ever sat down to plan the
liquidating of George Simney it was here that I would have
set the scene.

But all this is idle talk endeavouring to explain away what
was doubtless a flustered and altogether injudicious reaction
to the sight of those horses – one of them my own – and
to the sense of that lurking figure behind. I was going to
call a halt to violence. And forward I ran.

Recognizing me, the horse whinnied; then, as if disturbed
by my pace, it neighed and reared. I realized how still everything was. The little temple – erected to I don't know what
murky god or goddess – was silent and shrouded; it was no
place upon which to break. Nor could I, after all, bring myself to run up its short flight of steps and enter. I stood before
them, panting, and took breath to give a shout. Short of the
blindest passion, no utterly sinister purpose was likely to
accomplish itself after that.

But it was the horses who sounded an alarm. They took

fright and sent up a flurry of snow and gravel – and at that there was an exclamation from within and George came striding out with Joyleen, flushed and doubtful, behind him. He took one look at me and strode down the steps, calling to her to follow. And follow she did, like a bitch at heel.

The lurker behind the Folly stirred and I heard a twig snap dully beneath its covering of snow. But of this George was oblivious – and the situation was such that he saw me only as a lurker myself. Clearly my apprehensions were needless now. Perhaps they had been groundless all the time. And certainly they had landed me in a position from which there seemed no possible retreat to any form of social pretence. It was best just to stand still, keep silent, and let them go.

And George, I thought, was for that. He strode unheeding to the horses, unhitched, and mounted. He paused a moment to let the girl do the same. They rode forward as if to pass me, and all I could see at first was Joyleen's face in a shapeless flabby grin. Embarrassment and sheer funk had made her lose control of the muscles round her mouth – and the result was so nasty that I turned my eyes on George instead.

George was in a flare of passion – a resounding bestial Simney rage. He reined in and leant down over me. 'I've seen your lover,' he said.

It was an unexpected remark. I looked at him blankly.

'I've seen your lover,' he repeated. And then he slapped my face.

Joyleen gave something between a hysterical giggle and a cry of protest. George turned and cut her mount hard on the croup. Seconds later they were both cantering across the park.

I stood quite still. And then, behind me, I heard the sound of somebody – the lurker who had led to this scene – coming rapidly round the Folly. But I felt no curiosity and sought no interview. Straight before me was the façade of Hazel-wood – half-a-hundred crouching windows regarding me over the park, Argus-eyed. And I marched straight forward. It was where I lived, after all.

II

George died at midnight.

Persons of what is called irregular life often have regular habits, and George was one of these. Whatever he had been doing during the day, and whatever happened at dinner or immediately thereafter, the evening ended with an unvary- ing ritual. It involved George's keeping late hours, and Owdon's perforce doing the same.

And on Tuesday night I was keeping late hours myself. When Owdon came stumbling out of the study calling murder I was in my bath. Or rather I was under it – for I think I have mentioned that George brought back from Australia the conviction that only shower-baths are proper- ly healthy and cleansing. I rather dislike shower-baths. Still, there I was, trying (you may say) to wash Hazelwood off myself at midnight – when I heard Owdon's voice raised in a ghastly yammering. Nobody could have mistaken the gravity of what such an uncontrolled hullabaloo must portend. I didn't stop to dry but grabbed what was no more than a towel and was out in that corridor in a flash. And there the man was – a bulk of a fellow in a tremble – and looking as if the grave gaped for him. I don't think my head was very clear. But I know that I was at once struck by the immensity of our butler's dismay.

Somebody had to be controlled, more or less; and I pulled myself together. The first consequence of this was the reflection that even if the whole of Hazelwood was dis- solving in chaos that was no real reason for looking like an advertisement for bath-salts. I dodged back and got rather damply into my wrap. And then I came out again. 'Come, come, Owdon,' I said. 'What's all this?'

On such occasions one says and does the most conventional things. Here I was piping up with what is supposed to be the superior calm of the educated. Owdon peered at me, moving his head in an odd way as if trying to discern me through a mist. 'He's dead,' he said.

I think that what I chiefly felt was a kind of breathlessness. But I still played the controlled gentlewoman. 'Dead, Owdon! Who is dead?'

His mouth opened – and abruptly shut again. He was rather like a fish in a tank. He passed a hand over his forehead. 'Your ladyship,' he said, 'I'm afraid this is bad news. Sir George has had an accident – in his study. He's dead. But Dr Humberstone must be called.'

'Then call him. I will go in and do what I can.'

'Very good, your ladyship.'

But Owdon didn't budge. He stood barring the way – or virtually that. And on his face I seemed to read both suspicion and fear.

'If your ladyship will allow me, I will remain with you until some other member of the family arrives. It – it is very unpleasant. You must be prepared for a shock.'

Owdon, once recovered, could take a conventional line too. And I was not sorry at the idea of some support. The news that George was dead came to me with the quality chiefly of something merely bewildering. This must have been because of the diversity of emotions which, when digested, it was bound to arouse in me – incompatible emotions one of which my conscious mind would presently have to assert as dominant. But now I was in a mere confusion. Owdon made way for me and we were about to enter the study.

'I say – did I hear a row?'

We turned and saw Willoughby coming rapidly up the corridor behind us. He was in dressing-gown and pyjamas.

'Owdon says that George has had an accident – that he is dead.'

I heard my own voice as if it were speaking rather far

away. And Owdon appeared to be under the weather again too; fleetingly I noticed that his arms were dangling in the same helpless way as when some approach of Hippias's had made him drop his tray the night before.

'Dead?' And Willoughby raised his eyebrows. 'Why, that's very bad indeed.' He looked at me seriously as I stood there with my wet wrap clinging to me. It was an appraising look but with nothing remotely indecent to it. At this unlikely moment this most unlikely of the Simneys was rather taken up with me as a possible work of art. And in this there was an element somehow so macabre that I shivered as if the cold air in that corridor was piercing me to the bone.

'No point in talking,' I said. 'Come with me, Willough- by. And you, Owdon, get the doctor at once.'

'Your ladyship, I am afraid I had better call the police too.'

'As you think best. And then rouse Mr Bevis. Willoughby, come.'

Willoughby appeared to wake up. 'Nicolette,' he said, 'won't you let me go in and see first? It may be a bit horrid. Go and sit down in your room.'

I looked at him queerly – perhaps because he spoke with unexpected authority. And suddenly I realized that Hazelwood now held a Sir Bevis Simney, and that here before me stood the next in succession to a baronetcy. Well, all that was no business of mine. 'We'll go in together,' I said.

Owdon had gone away to telephone, but his voice could be heard raised in question or explanation somewhere behind us. A moment later there was a patter of footsteps and Mervyn Cockayne came running down the corridor. He too was in pyjamas – an old pair of schoolboy's pyja- mas still – and these and his slippers were both splashed with melting snow. 'I nearly caught him,' he said quietly. 'But is what Owdon says true?'

Willoughby halted. 'Caught him?'

'The burglar or whoever he was – out on the west terrace.'

'Rubbish. You couldn't come within a mile of catching a henwife. And now you'd better cut off to bed.'

I could see Mervyn flush unexpectedly – and in that moment he was extraordinarily like Timmy. He turned to me. 'I think,' he said, 'that we had better go in?'

Willoughby was at that moment disagreeable to me, and Mervyn I had certainly never had cause to care for. Moreover they were scarcely more than boys, and at what was in front of me I would have preferred the company of a grown man. But it was no good standing there and risking the start of an indecent quarrel. 'Yes,' I said. 'Come along.'

George's study was a bare, bleak place in which the comparatively crowded pictures set off the almost empty room. The long refectory table was the only substantial piece of furniture. And George's body was sprawled on it, face downwards. There was a chair behind him, and it was as if he had been sitting there at the end of the table, reading. And that, indeed, was his habit. And the impression one received was obscurely this: that some preternaturally powerful force from behind had picked him up and flung him across the table. Only his toes touched the floor.

George's end was ugly. Even if the back of his skull was not as I now saw it to be, there would have been something peculiarly horrible about that sprawl across the table – the posture of a man hopelessly drunk, or of a schoolboy about to be caned. His left hand was violently splayed out, as if desperately spanning the octave of a gigantic piano; his right hand had closed upon a tumbler with such force that it was no more than shivered glass within his fist. There was nothing on the long table but writing things and a litter of magazines – stupid magazines full of horses and dogs and stupid, arrogant faces, for George's brains he had kept for the prosecution of his own peculiar affairs. Now, his brains were rather widely scattered about the room.

I turned towards the window behind him – this because

I felt sick and there was coming from it a blessed breath of cold night air. The boys – they were no more than that, after all, and so far the world's violence had passed them by – turned towards it too. And I could see them stiffen as its significance struck them.

The room's single window stood in a shallow embrasure across which thick curtains were now drawn, and these were stirring in a way that showed the window behind them to be wide open. This was, of course, unusual on a winter night, and the moving curtains held their own powerful suggestion at once.

But there was more than that. Here was the room's only possible lurking-place. And it is only in books that, when murder has been committed, it is at once taken for granted that the murderer will have fled from the scene of his crime. I looked at the curtains and felt no assurance that George's assailant was not still behind them; I looked at Willoughby and Mervyn and guessed that the same thought was in their minds.

In that moment it required positive courage to move. And it was the youngest of us who moved first. Mervyn strode towards the window – the very window from which he had been so ignominiously dropped by Gerard the night before. I could see his spirits rise as the discovery of his own sufficient courage came to him. Of course if he had really tackled somebody outside, and that somebody had fled, there could scarcely be any actual danger now. But I doubted if he remembered this – for those slightly swaying curtains were simply sinister in themselves. During this first brief period of tension, in fact, they represented a sort of magical or *tabu* locality against approaching which the blood rebelled. Murdered baronets sprawled across tables at midnight are sophisticated enough. But, confronted with them, the mind works in uncommonly primitive ways. I didn't want my own mind to do this, and I was fighting to be calm. But here was the little toad Mervyn striding across the room. His voice rose – shrill, affected, but confident –

94

in the first words uttered since we had entered the study. 'Nicolette,' he said, 'I will just have a look round while you get poor Willoughby a glass of brandy.' And he disappeared behind the curtains.

I remembered that, if not brandy, there ought at least to have been whiskey, sugar and hot water on the table, since it was one of Owdon's routine duties at this hour to provide these for the making of George's final and solitary toddy. And then I saw that these were lying spilt and smashed on the floor, having apparently been pushed over, tray and all, when George's body pitched across the table. And I remember – so strange a contraption is the human mind – feeling a kind of automatic annoyance that here was more cut glass gone. If involuntary, this was none the less indecent. And then I became aware of something not less indecent. Willoughby and Mervyn were quarrelling fiercely behind the window curtains.

I was tiptoeing about the room now – rather, I suppose, as if George were a light sleeper whom it would be inconsiderate to waken. The Simneys – the other dead Simneys – and those ladies whom George had associated with them looked down at me impassively; the lads quarrelled and were seemingly jostling each other; I could hear Owdon's footsteps returning heavily up the corridor. There was something peculiarly horrible about this moment; a tall flame suddenly leapt up in the great fire-place, and amid the resulting flickering shadows everything seemed to be moving, so that I had a wild feeling of that splayed-out hand of George's as something in the act of making a last desperate clutch – perhaps at the leaping flame, perhaps at my throat. ... And then Willoughby and Mervyn appeared again, decorously enough. I believe that there, and in the very presence of the dead man, they had fallen out over some coveted possession that might now come to one or the other of them: a shot-gun, perhaps, or some little secret collection of smutty books. And now this made them (sincerely enough, I think) all the more gentlemanlike and solicitous for the unhappy widow. And the unhappy widow was calculating in just how many days she would at last be able to leave Hazelwood for good. ... There is nothing pretty in this chronicle of Sir George Simney's end. It is all ugly from start to finish. But then if one marries out of some bitter negation of decency – well, what has one to expect?

At least not perhaps murder. But what, other than murder, could this be? I believe that George Simney must be called satanic – I have ample reason to believe it. Had he resolved to commit suicide it was only too likely that his last hours would have been spent in contriving to bequeath posterity the appearance of a murder-mystery. But no man could contrive to stave his own head in like that.

Or could he? By some extreme of ingenuity could he manage just that? Was the expression of inordinate surprise which was to be revealed when the body was turned over occasioned by his pleased knowledge that he had brought off some peculiarly difficult technical feat?

Gentle Readers – you who are skilled in conning chronicles of violence – these questions are yours!

Part Two: Harold

I

... Speculations, he says, are useless until you have all the facts. But I've noticed often enough that it isn't like that with him, really. He begins speculating straight away, if you ask me, and his speculations suggest what facts to hunt for next. You know I always do a bit of serious reading at bed-time, as auntie Flo advised? Well, the other night I was reading a book about Darwin, and it said how Darwin's great strength was in his extraordinary fertility in hypotheses. This just means that he was always guessing. Give him a few facts and he would start guessing at once. He couldn't peer into a cage at the Zoo without forming a hypothesis, and then he would go hurrying round the other cages trying it out. Most likely there would be nothing in it, and he would discover this before he had got from the lemurs to the spider-monkeys. But by then he would have another hypothesis – or guess, that is – and quite soon one of these would look sufficiently promising to be called a theory ... Well, you know, it's very much that way with *him*.

But, of course, he says little, and you just can't tell what the hypothesis of the moment is – or even the theory when one develops into that. Still, I really believe that he is guessing all the time, and that this is what makes him so good a Detective Inspector – far the best at the Yard, as I've often said. It's a bit of luck, isn't it, to work with a man like that? Tell auntie Flo about Darwin. Anything of that sort always interests her.

If you ask me, he's wasted no time in beginning a few

speculations about this Lady Simney – Nicolette, as she seems to be called by the men folk here. I must say, my dear Dad, that I would like to have seen her when she came out of that bath-room in a towel – a regular Venus, she must have been. But then she's an actress and famous on the London stage, and no doubt the dead man married her for what the queer kid Mervyn calls her charms. What *she* married *him* for nobody knows; he seems to have been quite as nasty as most of the people who get murdered. Don't tell auntie Flo that about wanting to see Lady Simney like I said. I told *him* and he was down on me like a ton of bricks. Only 'tecs in American shockers, he said, can afford to have those sort of feelings when on duty. Keep them for the cinema, he said, or for Jane; it's safer. Well, that's just like him.

And it must have been just a guess (or a hypothesis) that those clothes were not Sir George's. For if you find a suit-case in a married lady's room with a complete outfit of men's garments you would naturally take them to be her husband's, wouldn't you? But no sooner had I opened the thing than his eyes narrowed on them the way they do. 'Harold,' he said, 'take them across the passage and measure them against some of Sir George's. And I did, and they were nowhere near the same. Then he made me snoop all over the house (and a huge great place it is – I think the most aristocratic I've been in yet) and measure the things against everybody's – all the men, I mean, who live here. And they were nowhere near a match anywhere. It was like going round with Cinderella's slipper in a pantomime with four times as many ugly sisters as usual. 'So what do you think of that?' he asked. And I said it looked suspicious. 'Suspicious?' he said; 'well, it may be a straw in the wind – or a feather.' 'A feather?' I asked. 'Just that,' he said; 'Cuvier's feather.' 'Cuvier?' I asked. 'Ah,' he said, 'I see you haven't got to the chapter on Cuvier.' I think this was some sort of joke – *his* sort of joke – on my reading a book about Darwin. I'll find out one day soon. That's one thing about him. He always explains his little mystifications later on.

But now I had better go back. I'm afraid my first notes were a bit disjointed. The truth is, I haven't been brought out before on so big an affair, and I was a bit worked up. Besides, there was Lady Simney; it did seem a shame that such a woman should be mixed up in a dirty affair like this – blacksmith's daughters, and that sort of thing. I felt I would like to take her right away – to New Zealand, or somewhere like that. When I first saw her I said to myself: 'There's a woman who has had enough' – and for a time I couldn't get anything else into my head. But I wouldn't like to tell *him* that – or auntie Flo.

We got here just before luncheon, which means about twelve hours after the commission of the crime: an attack *a tergo* with a blunt instrument upon a well-nourished middle-aged man (upper class). That's how it goes in my notebook. It's difficult to get rid sometimes of the awful bosh they taught us in the lectures. And practical work is miles better, I must say. Lady Simney –

But that's wandering. We got here at lunch-time, and I could tell by the pace at which he let me push the Bentley along (the yellow one, you know, that poor Inspector Appleby had before his marriage) that he felt there was something out of the common in front of us. We were met by local men and shown in on somebody called Sir Bevis – who talked as if he was a chief constable or even a lord lieutenant. *He* let him talk until he had talked himself thoroughly uneasy, and then we could see that this Sir Bevis was hiding something. But then they all are, and we can't even be sure that it is the same thing. It looks as if the investigation might be quite a long affair. However, I rather look forward to settling in. This C.I.D. business, you know, has turned out almost as *peripatetic* (just ask auntie that one) as being on the beat. So here's a change, anyway.

They all have something to hide – and they all have something to gain. This Sir Bevis has got a title and a fair-sized estate. His son, Mr Willoughby Simney, has got one step nearer to the same. Lady Simney has got rid of an awful beast of a husband. Young Mr Mervyn Cockayne is believed to have come into a considerable legacy, and this may also benefit his mother. As for the relations from Australia, it appears that the deceased and Mr Hippias had quarrelled, that Mrs Gerard – the girl called Joyleen – had let the dead man seduce her and may have been terrified of being given away, and that therefore her husband (if he knew) had a very sufficient motive himself. Finally, of course, there are the servants – as *he* says there always are. Well, when I say that the butler, Owdon, once had an illegitimate son by one of the ladies of the family, and that the son is here on the spot as a sort of footman, you will see that the menservants, at least, can't quite be counted out. In fact, the only person who seems to have no interest from a police point of view is Miss Grace Simney, the unmarried sister of the dead man. But he says he's not so sure. It isn't often he says so much. He says that it's very classical – and looking out of the window at the yellow Bentley he murmured something about What would Appleby have done? From what I've heard of him I'd say the answer is Talked Greek and swopped tags out of Shakespeare. Whereas I bet *he* will get straight on with the job. We've got to find out what happened at Hazelwood. And the thing may have been done by any of them, I should say – I mean just reckoning by the sort of people they appear to be. I can't be sure that Nicolette even – Lady Simney, that is – is *nice*. I'm sure she's *been* nice. But there's something rather hard about her, and perhaps a woman can go a bit bad when she's had enough and she's through ... And now to throw in the clutch.

'Sir Bevis,' he said after he'd bided his time, 'I understand that on Monday night there was a family quarrel in this room?'

The new baronet didn't like it. 'I don't think it should be called that,' he said. 'No doubt there was a little heat.'

'And the heat resulted in the throwing of a bottle and the smashing of that picture?' He pointed to the portrait of the late Sir George in his hunting-coat. 'In fact there was attempted violence?'

Sir Bevis frowned. 'Mr Hippias undoubtedly – ah – tossed the bottle. Sportfully, no doubt. Colonial manners are a little bluff.'

'Sir Bevis, are you disposed to a little bluff yourself?'

That got him. He went as red as a turkey-cock and made much the same gobbling sort of noise. 'Perfectly scandalous!' he said. 'And I may mention that a particular friend of mine at the Home Office –'

'Quite so, sir. That is what everybody says – when caught speeding, for instance, or anything of that sort. But in thirty years' experience of police work I've never known it to cut any ice yet. So we'll spare your influential connexions, if you don't mind. But my question should have been more precise. Have you not, so far, concealed information which it is your duty to divulge?'

Well, that's the straight way to talk to a baronet. And perhaps in a year or two I shall have picked it up. And this one wilted a little. 'I don't know what you mean,' he said.

'Thank you. That, in my opinion, is one of the most significant replies a police-officer can receive. It invariably indicates deception.' And he turned to me. 'Harold,' he said, 'write it down. The words were *I don't know what you mean.*'

In America they're said to use wearing-down tactics – which must take a lot of time considering the hurry folk are in there. *He* uses sudden little unnerving bits like this. And – sure enough – our grand Sir Bevis begins to babble, and has a lot to say about some unpleasantness over a place called Dismal Swamp.

He listened to this for a while. And when he spoke again it was with a sort of relaxed tension as if the air had been cleared a good bit. Well, I've got to know a number of his tricks in the last few months, and I knew this one.

'Ah,' he said. 'Very interesting, no doubt. But nobody would think to kill your poor brother over an old affair like that, would they?'

'Of course not. Which shows that the turning up of these Australian relatives is purely coincidental. The truth is that there are a lot of dangerous characters about, and that the police are very far from having the situation in hand. The local police, that is to say.'

The afterthought was a handsome one. But I don't know that we showed gratification.

'Only last week old Lady Longer lost a lot of poultry. And the constabulary were helpless, it appears – absolutely helpless. I have promised her to take the matter up with the Chief Constable.'

The Inspector gave me the sort of quick grave look that would be a wink in another man. 'Very kind of you, sir, I'm sure. And perhaps you might take up your brother's death at the same time.'

This was a nasty one, and I'm bound to say that Sir Bevis reacted with some spirit. 'In my opinion,' he said, 'you ought to be out and about combing the neighbouring pubs for dangerous ruffians. It might be more rewarding than aspersing my family and contriving impertinent witticisms. For the situation is abundantly clear.'

The Inspector looked relieved. 'Harold,' he said, '– your notebook. Here is to be light.'

Sir Bevis went his turkey-red. 'Abundantly clear!' he repeated in a sudden bellow. 'There has been a widespread cock-and-bull tale of my brother's keeping considerable wealth in this study. To the window of this study – which a trellis makes perfectly accessible from ground level – it has been found that a man's footsteps led through the snow. While sitting with his back to that same window my brother was struck on the head from behind and killed. Outside that window again – and seemingly only seconds later – an unknown lurker was tackled by my beastly – that is to say by my courageous nephew, Mr Cockayne. Unfortunately the intruder got away, and his footsteps could not be traced very far ... May I ask if you support me in these statements?'

'Yes, Sir Bevis – I do. But just what these statements in turn support is another matter. I cannot see that attempted robbery such as you suggest would be very likely to transform itself into sudden and savage attack from behind.'

'The mirrors!' Sir Bevis came out with this a bit too quick. 'My brother looked up and caught sight of the thief's reflection. That accounts both for the look of surprise on my poor brother's features and for the instantaneous attack made upon him.'

'Not quite,' I said. 'Not quite for either.'

The Inspector looked at me gravely. He likes me to speak up at times. But he expects me to have good occasion for doing so. And I must say, my dear Dad, that I felt more than a little nervous at this moment

'It doesn't quite account for the surprised look,' I said boldly. 'Because, you know, it was a *very* surprised look. And – again – why should the intruder, even if spotted in the mirror, be prompted to strike to kill? Would it not be because he was known to the late Sir George, and could not save himself from discovery by mere retreat? And as for the dead man's astounded look – must we not suppose that he saw in the mirror somebody both known to him *and totally unexpected*? If so, a pot-house ruffian just doesn't fit, and a good deal of investigation at Hazelwood itself may be justified after all.'

'Do I understand,' said Sir Bevis, 'that you are proposing to hold suspect members of my household?'

This was spoken as grandly as you please – but you may be sure it didn't cut any ice with the chief. 'Of course we do,' he snapped. 'There were new arrivals, disputes over Dismal Swamp and we don't know what else, and then a regular rough-and-tumble with trays falling, glasses smashed, bottles flying and people being pitched out of windows. In fact, quite a pot-house in the home. And then

Sir George gets murdered at a moment when not a single one of you, with the possible exception of his wife, can give a convincing account of himself. A police-officer who went off looking for tramps before carefully sifting every circumstance here at Hazelwood would be gravely failing in that course of duty to which the available evidence pointed him. And now, Sir Bevis, and for the moment, I have only one question more.'

I must say that even for him this was pretty strong stuff. But then he never gets anybody riled unless he means to. And so I waited with a good deal of curiosity for this one last question.

When it came it was odd enough. 'Do you think,' he asked, 'that this murder was prompted by the fact that dead men tell no tales – or leave no males?'

The new baronet had already been made very angry. But he was much angrier now. His words came with difficulty. 'I think,' he said, '– I think you are . . . a foul devil.'

'Thank you, Sir Bevis. And I must apologize for having detained you so long.'

2

We were left alone in the study. Inspector Cadover looked at his watch. 'I hope they'll send us in some tea,' he said. 'Crumpets, perhaps – or even muffins in a big silver dish.'

He had become cheerful, as sometimes happened when he had found reason to think a little less ill of somebody than he had feared. 'You don't think,' I said, 'that this man killed his brother before Lady Simney could get going on a family?'

'You saw what happened, Harold; answer for yourself. I led up to the idea as nastily as I could and you may think that his reaction was a little too forthright for a guilty man's. Besides, does Lady Simney look like starting a family? I don't think she does.'

'I'm afraid,' I said, 'that I wouldn't be very skilful in telling. We never had lectures on that.'

He smiled grudgingly. 'I don't mean that. Of course, if there was actually a baby coming it might have been too late for this action' – and the chief swung an imaginary blunt instrument in air – 'to nobble the estates and the baronetcy. I only mean that I scarcely think her of a mind to perpetuate Simneys.' He shook his head very seriously. 'I'm afraid it cannot have been a happy marriage.'

Every now and then (and particularly in his understatements) you can see that it all weighs on him a bit; that the endless semi-tragic messes amid which he moves prompt him to a great deal of concealed moral concern. It makes me feel that I must become wiser as well as nippier if I am to go on at it myself. But I was content to be nippy now.

'I had a word with the boy Timmy,' I reported. 'He says that they most of them hated Nicolette, and that Mrs Cockayne – the dead man's sister Lucy, that is – used to be studying her complexion just as if she were wondering whether there was a baby starting. She hated the idea of anything that might cut down Mervyn's legacy.'

The Inspector was lighting a pipe. 'That's a queer sort of thing for this Timmy to notice and get the hang of. He must have a watchful eye and be rather exceptionally perceptive for his age.' He blew out his match. 'Might the lad perhaps be devoted to Lady Simney? As you've observed Harold, she's an uncommonly beautiful woman.'

'No doubt. But about this Sir Bevis, sir. You wouldn't go so far as to say that he came out of the interview well?'

'Dear me, no. He finished strongly, that's all. Foul devil was a great deal better than conjuring up his friends at the Home Office. But he is certainly concerned to conceal something.' The Inspector sighed. 'You might have a little rubber stamp, Harold, to save yourself copying that phrase into your notebooks ... He's concerned to conceal something, and he's apprehensive. But then, perhaps the majority of human beings have something furtive on hand as often as not. And then some accidental spotlight comes creeping towards them and they are terrified. I think we'd better have the butler.'

I nodded and moved to the bell. 'He's certainly apprehensive too.'

'He's the key to the affair. If he's telling the truth so far as he knows it, our understanding of the physical framework of the crime is very substantial. If he's lying, we're nowhere. But hold your hand a moment. Before we have him in we'll do a little stock-taking. And to begin with, my boy, just turn on the lights and slip behind those curtains.'

I did as I was told. A man could certainly have concealed himself in the window-embrasure; indeed two or three men could have done so, for the space was unencumbered except by a bronze head of a boy set on a marble pedestal. It looked rather good to me – and often my guesses are right about such things – and I was inspecting it more carefully when the Inspector's voice came through the curtains. 'Now then,' he said, 'quick march.'

I pushed the curtain aside and entered the room. With all those folk round the walls it was rather like coming on the stage of a theatre – and even as I felt this I realized that somebody was really and truly looking at me. In fact what Sir Bevis had said about the mirrors was feasible enough. For the Inspector was sitting at the long table with his back to me, just as the dead man must have been doing. In front of him at the other end of the room was the fireplace, and at some remove from it on the same wall was a sizeable mirror. In this mirror our eyes met.

He sprang to his feet, still eyeing me. I saw my part and strode into the room, an arm raised above my head. For a second he watched me still, and then turned round. 'Well?' he asked.

'There's not a doubt of it, sir. Only you forgot to look uncommonly surprised.'

'So I did. But then, my dear Harold, you were not only a familiar face but an expected one as well.'

I looked at him rather uneasily. When he says 'My dear Harold' just like that it is a sign that something has gone wrong.

'You think,' he said, 'that we may have got the hang of it?'

'Yes, sir.' I could see that somehow I had fallen down on this, but of course I knew it was best not to fox. I've stuck with him longer than any other detective sergeant in the Force largely through not pretending at these moments.

'Then you're wrong, lad. But sit down and spread your notebooks before you. And speak up when I go wrong in my turn.'

Sitting again where Sir George Simney had sat, Inspector Cadover let his eye travel slowly round the study. 'It's an uncommonly bare room,' he said. 'It has one window, which is behind me, and one door, which is there' – and he pointed mid-way down the left-hand wall. 'Now, listen.

'Two things are very important, in my view. The first is this. Late at night, this study is very much like the courtyard of Buckingham Palace.'

My eye too went round the study – and took in all those paintings of ladies in their birthday suits. 'I don't see it,' I said.

'But it's obvious enough. In that courtyard certain events conduct themselves with astronomical regularity. You've watched the changing of the Guard?'

'Yes, sir. In fact, my brother is a Guardsman.'

'That's very good – very good indeed.'

I knew from this that he was thinking hard. He never likes to be caught thinking, and so he often falls on such occasions into unmeaning remarks. And indeed this whole palaver about Buckingham Palace was no more than that.

'There's a routine,' he pursued. 'This and that happen at a stated time. And so with this dead man in this room round about midnight. There was a sort of ritual and it didn't often vary. Even with guests in the house and untoward things happening, the final routine of the day remained. Here were dispositions that could be calculated.'

'A crime of calculation,' I said. 'Not tramps from pothouses.'

'I don't say that. So exclusive an inference is quite unjustified, really. I merely note that here are circumstances admitting of calculation. The fact is suggestive – no more than that. And now my second point. Unless the butler is lying – and we'll have him in presently – the murderer entered by the window.'

'Of course he did!' I exclaimed. 'The marks of his climb are there on the trellis; even the local men found them. And the footprints were there in the snow. And he left as he came, and young Mr Cockayne had a fight with him.'

'Well, all that is evidence, of course. And what is the conclusion?'

'That it was an outside crime, after all.'

'Listen, Harold. It looks as if somebody came up the trellis. But it is only if the butler, Owdon, is telling the truth that we can be sure of that. His story seems to be that he was virtually on sentry-duty out there in the corridor. And nobody, he says, could have come into this room by the door. Now, where does that take us? Remember that this sentry-duty of Owdon's was also part of the routine.'

'You mean Buckingham Palace again?' I said this rather anxiously, for I felt that it was about time to understand what he was talking about. And then I did see. 'You mean, sir,' I went on, 'that the certainty of the murderer's having come up the trellis is rather an obtrusive certainty. Owdon's being out there in the corridor establishes it. And yet it is only somebody inside the house – another servant or a

108

member of the family – who would be very likely to know about the routine and count on it.'

'Just that. And I can't see that there was much to prevent anyone here from simply slipping outside and making the climb to the window. Sir George was known to be alone at that hour, but nobody could go to him unobserved through the house because of the habitual location of Owdon at the time. Very well. Circumvent this in going by the window, and at the same time so convey the strong impression of a burglar or the like. Any of them might have planned it. They all seem to have been alone and unaccounted for at that late hour. Lady Simney, for example.'

I stared at him in surprise – and perhaps with an obscure feeling of indignation too. 'Lady Simney was in her bath,' I said. 'It's scarcely reasonable to expect that she should have had an observer attached to her to provide an *alibi.*'

He frowned. 'She may actually prove to have one, anyway. And she needs it. But she and this fellow Owdon are the only people who were pretty well hard up against the thing here when it happened. Their stories interlock and may be a put-up job.'

'Well, as you've said, sir, if the butler is lying, or deceiving himself, we are pretty well nowhere, and Lady Simney is not necessarily more involved than anyone else.'

'Perfectly true, my lad ... Is there going to be more snow in the next twenty minutes?'

I looked at him in surprise. 'Almost certainly not.'

'Then we may defer the one vital inquiry about your beautiful Nicolette until we have got Owdon's story a little more precisely than we have it in the notes of the local men. Ring the bell.'

I didn't much like him speaking of Lady Simney in this way. But policemen, I suppose, are bound to get a bit coarse in the grain. I rang for Owdon.

3

He was no beauty – and today probably less of one than commonly. That the late Sir George Simney's butler had got any sleep since his master's death I didn't believe. His hand trembled. He had cut what remained of his face while shaving.

'I think, Mr Owdon, that the late Sir George had fairly regular habits late at night?'

'That is so.'

The man's distress didn't get into his voice. But something else did – which I sensed as important but couldn't at all place. That's what's so fascinating about this detective investigation I've managed to win my way to. At a bound, as it were, you feel yourself almost at the heart of the maze, so that a single further turn would take you there. And then in next to no time you have followed the wrong track and are back near the perimeter.

'Perhaps, Mr Owdon, you would be good enough to run over that routine again?' The chief consulted a notebook. 'Round about eleven-thirty would appear to be a convenient start.'

'Very good, sir. It is about that hour that I commonly come to this part of the house. I always did some little valeting for Sir George, and I would go to his bedroom and see to one or two things there. Then I would come out to the corridor. You will have noticed that it is a straight corridor running directly away from the door of this room, and that it has Sir George's apartments on the one side and Lady Simney's on the other. You may also have noticed that outside Sir George's bedroom there is quite an elaborate arrangement of wardrobes and cupboards. I get through a number of jobs there, and when I come out of Sir George's bedroom I am commonly engaged there for some five or ten minutes. Just before a quarter to twelve I am in the habit of boiling an electric kettle and taking it along to the study for the making of Sir George's final toddy. I set it down on the table, stir the fire, tidy round, and close the window. At this hour, you will understand, the study is empty.'

Inspector Cadover looked about him. 'You close the window?'

'Yes, sir. The curtains are, of course, drawn to, but I step behind them and close the window from the bottom. It is a sash window and the upper part remains open.'

'I see. And it would therefore be perfectly possible to push the lower part up again from the outside and enter?'

Owdon hesitated. 'Really, I have no idea.'

The Inspector frowned. 'Chilly nights,' he said. 'But no doubt your master was an open-air man and wouldn't want the place shut up altogether.'

I felt a tingling in my spine. For this purposeless speech meant something. It was an example of that sort of camouflage I have mentioned. The chief's mind was leaping at something, and he was concerned not to give away the fact. I had a very queer feeling that my own mind had leapt at it too not very long before – and just failed to effect a lodgement.

But now the Inspector was speaking briskly again. 'You tidy round and close the window. And then?'

'I leave the study and return to my pantry – for it is really that – in the corridor. I have some ten or fifteen minutes to fill in, and I employ them on accounts, the cellar-book, and matters of that sort.'

'I see. But by this time it must be getting pretty late. Why have you time to fill in?'

'It is about eleven-fifty. Very punctually at this hour Sir George comes – I ought to say was in the habit of coming – up to the study. He would enter, close the door behind him, and spend some ten minutes glancing at magazines and drinking his toddy. Then he would come out, turning off the lights behind him, and enter his bedroom. I would follow him a few minutes later – perhaps just on midnight – and collect his dress-clothes. These I would put in order in one of the wardrobes before finally retiring to bed myself.'

I think I looked at Owdon with a mixture of compassion and respect. That sort of upper-servant business, and shuffling round with other men's drinks and pants while having to keep one's own dignified end up, seems pretty awful to me. And I suspect the world is about through with it. But if Owdon thought it pretty well sub-human he concealed the fact effortlessly enough. He was as respectful as one's silliest self could wish. At the same time he might have been a cabinet-minister giving an account of the organization of his Ministry to the P.M.

And it occurred to me that there was more to Owdon than there was supposed to be. But then hadn't he once struck one of the Simney ladies that way? Plainly, he was a man to keep an eye on.

The Inspector was doing that. And it was a narrowing eye. 'All this is very good,' he said. 'It is very clear – this exposition of your routine. And I am particularly impressed by your stepping behind the curtains.'

'Is that so, sir?' If Owdon was perturbed he didn't – save for that now chronic slight trembling of the hand – at all show it.

'Of course it was simply to close the window in your regular fashion. . . .' The Inspector paused. 'I suppose you didn't happen to glance out of the window?'

'No, sir. I simply pushed down the sash.'

'You didn't happen to make some sign or signal to somebody waiting outside?'

He can be pretty effective in these transitions to the really nasty questions. But Owdon declined to be shaken. 'I did not,' he said.

I must say I believed him – just as I was going to believe him presently on other vital matters. There was something in his voice that convinced me. At the same time I was puzzled, and I looked at the Inspector. He was making jottings in a notebook – never a very significant process with him, I'm bound to say. And then he looked up and went evenly on. 'Very well. And now we'd better come to last night, and to your discovery of the murder. For the moment, you may as well again begin at eleven-thirty.'

'Very well.' The words were almost snapped out – but decisively rather than defiantly. I realized that Owdon was a man who had received a tremendous shock and still showed it – but that the signs of this shock would be misleading if they inclined one to suppose that he was not fully in possession of himself now. 'Very well, officer.' And Owdon looked quickly about the room. 'I came in here as usual about eleven forty-five, and everything was much as it is now. But just before that, I remember, there was one incident. Her ladyship sent me for *The Times*.'

'You would call that an incident?'

There was no more in this, I suppose, than the more or less routine police trick of giving a witness the impression that his statements are being closely scrutinized. But Owdon appeared struck by the question. 'Well, yes,' he said. 'There was something a little arresting in the way it happened. I had been working in the corridor there since about half past eleven, and Lady Simney was already in her boudoir. It must have been about ten minutes later that she opened her door and asked me to fetch her *The Times* of the day before. She had already dismissed her maid, Martin, for the night, and, of course, I was very ready to do her bidding.'

'I see. And what was arresting about this?'

Owdon hesitated. 'Perhaps I used too strong a word. But in the first place there was the fact that she was already undressed and in what is called, I suppose, a bath-robe. Commonly her ladyship did not appear like that. I have the impression that she resented the comparative lack of privacy resulting from the study's being set at the end of a corridor upon which her own apartments gave. It is un-usual.'

'Ah. You have been in service in other great houses?'

This time Owdon did jump. But at once he controlled himself. 'You would wish me,' he asked, 'to turn aside to some account of my own history?'

The Inspector frowned. 'Go ahead,' he said abruptly. 'About *The Times.*'

'I think it must be said that her ladyship burst from her room. And she was holding that day's *Times* – yesterday's, that is to say – as she appeared. I saw that something she had just read made her uncommonly anxious to consult the issue of the day before. There was nothing more arresting about the incident than that.'

'It has its interest.' The Inspector looked up sharply. 'Has it occurred to you that Lady Simney may simply have been contriving to get you out of the way?'

'That wasn't the way of it at all. She very much wanted that *Times.*'

'But I think I am right in believing that she is by pro-fession an actress? If she wanted to get rid of you she could think up and execute this little business of the newspaper without effort?'

Owdon hesitated for a moment at this ingenuity. 'No,' he said. 'It sounds likely enough, but I don't think so. I found the paper in the breakfast-room, and I remember that the clock at the end of the corridor here was chiming eleven forty-five as I passed it. Her ladyship had gone into her bath-room – I could hear the water running – and so I left the paper on a table in the boudoir. As I came out I found that my electric kettle was boiling, and I therefore proceeded straight to the study. The room was, of course, empty. I stirred the fire, closed the window from the bottom, and withdrew. In the corridor I met Sir George; he said nothing, but entered the study and closed the door behind him as usual. You must realize that during the next few minutes that door was steadily within my observation. I was not, of course, watching it idly, and I began, indeed, the inspection of some bills which had come in that morning. Nevertheless it was impossible that anyone should pass me unnoticed, or even slip out of one of the other rooms on the corridor and enter the study. Lady Simney, for example, could not have done so.'

Inspector Cadover stirred in his chair. 'And you are positive that this room had, in fact, been empty when you visited it?'

'I am quite positive. It is, as you see, sparely furnished – and to its one possible hiding-place behind the curtains I had, of course, to penetrate in closing the window.'

'Very well., Sir George is closeted here alone; the curtains are drawn across the window-recess with the window still open at the top; and you yourself are only a few yards off down the corridor. What then?'

'Whatever happened, sir, must have happened within a couple of minutes of Sir George's entering. I heard –' And Owdon hesitated.

'Yes, Mr Owdon?'

'I heard a scream of rage and terror.'

'Dear me! And was this from Sir George?'

Owdon shook his head. 'It was a man's voice, sir – but definitely not Sir George's.'

At this I was prompted to chip in. 'Come, come,' I said. 'Sir George cannot have been in the habit of uttering screams of rage and terror in your hearing. So how can you rule him out so certainly?'

'It was not Sir George.'

This was no sort of answer – but again it was convincing. That he had seen his employer go into an empty room, and that within a couple of minutes he had heard a strange man scream with terror and rage: these, I was tolerably sure, were true reports on Owdon's part.

The Inspector had twisted round to look at the curtains behind him. 'Well, Mr Owdon,' he said without turning back, '– what then?'

'The scream was followed immediately by a crash, and a sound as of a heavy body being flung forward. I hesitated for a moment and then ran up the corridor.'

'Mr Owdon, please attend to this. It has been my duty to listen to a good many narratives such as yours, in which an unsuspecting man is suddenly embraced within some context of violence. And over and over again I have heard the words, *"I hesitated for a moment"*. Sometimes that moment proves to have been no more than a second or two; sometimes it has been a minute or more. And now, as commonly, the exact truth is very important. Let us have it, please.'

I could see Owdon suddenly lick his lips. 'I was frightened,' he said.

The Inspector looked at him curiously – struck, I think, by some importance that the man seemed to attach to his confession. 'Likely enough,' he snapped. 'But with just what result?'

'I believe I ran up the corridor almost at once. Only when just outside the room was I seized with a horrible dread.' Again Owdon licked his lips. 'My feet would not move. It was as if they were tied together. Nothing of the sort has ever happened to me before.'

'Quite so. It is nothing out of the way, I assure you. And it lasted?'

'No more than half a minute, I should say. It passed, and I felt intensely ashamed. I flung open the door and ran into the room. Sir George's body was lying across the table, and behind him the curtains had been disarranged. I bent over him and – and saw the back of his head. It was impossible to doubt that he must be dead – nevertheless I knew that medical aid ought to be summoned at once. I turned and hurried from the room. As I reached the corridor Lady Simney appeared from her bath-room, much alarmed. She had heard some involuntary cry of my own.'

'Quite so. We are all liable to bellow at times, Mr Owdon. And I judge that we have reached a point at which your testimony may end for the moment. I think it fair to say that it will be scrutinized, and that we may require some inquiry into your personal affairs. ... I take it that in the interval between Lady Simney's asking for *The Times* and her subsequent reappearance from the bath-room there was no one who caught a glimpse of you and could in part substantiate your story?'

'There was Sir George; he passed me in the corridor.'

'But it is Sir George, unfortunately, who has been killed.'

And suddenly Owdon looked at us stupidly – as if the fact were one which he had only confusedly realized before. 'Yes,' he said. 'It was Sir George.' His knees crumpled beneath him and he slithered to the floor.

4

Had Owdon expected to find *somebody else* dead in the study? Why otherwise should he display this sort of delayed shock over the dead man's identity? Was he lying, after all, when he said that his employer had entered an empty room? Or had he known of some tryst that Sir George was to keep there, and would it have been more in accord with expectation if it had been the visitor who was killed? Again – and to take the matter another way – had the butler really given some sort of signal through the window, as the chief had hinted? Standing out there in the corridor like a sentry, had he really lured his master into a trap? We knew obscurely that those two men had shared rough and mysterious days long ago. Might Owdon have been living here at Hazelwood simply on the strength of black-mail? Might some element of the sort be connected, too, with what was known of the parentage of the boy Timmy? And had the arrival of the Australians in some way turned the tables on Owdon, who had hastily arranged with some confederate that Sir George should be silenced? Was it simply some stroke of remorse that made his mind veer away from the simple fact that in the resulting encounter it was indeed the man plotted against who had died?

You see, my dear Dad, that I am doing my best to follow in Darwin's footsteps. I have entered the Zoo, taken one look at the baboon – the effect of looking at Owdon, I must say, is not altogether different, poor chap – and hurried off round the cages being as fertile in hypotheses as you could wish. The difficulty, of course, is to know how to test these out rapidly and scrap them if they are no good. Perhaps the chief was already doing so. After we got Owdon on his pins again and away, he sat in a muse, staring at the dark grain of the table before him. I could hear my watch ticking in my pocket.

And what, I wonder, would auntie Flo think at this point? Her eye, if you ask me, would be decidedly on Lady Simney. A really beautiful actress, who had good reason to hate her husband. Where could you have a better point than that?

Inspector Cadover, I think, was turning his mind the same way, but for a different reason. Lady Simney looked like having quite an obtrusive *alibi*, and no C.I.D. man likes that. Perhaps this is just the influence of fiction. Certainly we spend a lot of time trying to convince ourselves that in regard to this or that person the laws of space and time just don't apply.

We went down to the terrace. If the late Sir George had wanted to provide a convenient back-staircase for murderers he couldn't well have done better than put up the trellis that here arose from ground-level to his study window. And he *had* put it up. This the chief, with his queer faculty for asking questions that bring all sorts of unexpected information, had discovered when we had first inspected the thing. Were there to have been roses? Yes, it was believed that such was the idea. Had anything, in fact, been done about them? Nothing at all. Sir George's interest in gardening was nil, and it was an activity from which his young bride had very quickly withdrawn ... We stared at the trellis once more – and then looked at each other doubt-fully. It seemed difficult to escape this conclusion: that the trellis *was* a back-staircase and nothing else. Sir George, presumably, had used it as a quiet means of playing truant. But it was a queer way for even a bad baronet to behave.

There was no doubt that somebody had climbed the thing the night before: Dr Watson himself could have read the signs unmistakably. There was no doubt that somebody had approached the terrace from the direction of the drive, and one could just distinguish that he had later retreated as he came. There was no doubt that a little way along the terrace somebody else had emerged from the house and made his way to a spot just beneath the study window – and this, of course, must have been the courageous Mervyn Cockayne. There was every sign of some sort of dust-up or flurry, in the snow, so that nothing contradicted his story of a struggle with the intruder. All this could still be read in the snow, and it pointed as plainly as could be to the crime being the work of an intruder. Except, of course, that any member of the household, granted the necessary time, could have left the house unobserved by one of several swept paths on which no tracks would be visible, could have made a detour and approached again through the snow from the drive, could – after breaking away from Cockayne – have regained the house by reversing the manoeuvre.

We went over these facts and appearances carefully enough. Nevertheless I could see that Inspector Cadover's mind was elsewhere. There was one stretch of territory which irresistibly attracted him. It was that which rounded that whole wing of the house with which we were immed-iately concerned. In other words, it started under the win-dow of Sir George's study and ended under the window of Lady Simney's bath-room. We covered this route hugging the terrace and the wall. We covered it making a wider cast. Snow, of course, had been falling at the time of the crime; and there had been some wind since. I could imagine that every track and trace would by no means remain – and indeed there were here and there appearances in the snow for which I could only account by supposing a stiff wind blowing it into drifts and ridges. But it was, and had always been virgin of footprints. There could be no doubt of that.

'Nothing could cross this,' the Inspector said disconsolately. 'And no trellis here, either.'

'Something like an eighteen-foot drop.'

He shook his head. 'We've a good long way to go yet. Almost a dozen folk who are unknown quantities still. I think we'll go back inside.'

But where he took me was Lady Simney's room. I didn't like it, for I had no reason to suppose that she mightn't turn up at any time: after all, nobody had clapped her in a police-cell yet. Of course, *he* didn't mind that. We started with the bath-room, which smelt of something pretty special in the way of soap. There was something, it seemed to me, downright indelicate in this. And I know that auntie Flo would agree with me.

Not that it was really a bath-room at all. There was nothing but an elaborate shower in it – all chromium-plated sprays and nozzles and taps, surrounded by yards and yards of oil-silk. I am sorry to say that I found this shower-bath a little haunting (if you understand me); more so than if there had been just an ordinary bath. I couldn't quite get the lady out of my head.

Inspector Cadover didn't waste much time here, and we went poking into the bedroom and the boudoir. The bedroom was very handsome and curiously neutral, so that here the lady just didn't come into my head at all. We might have been in a shop. I mean a furniture shop of a tremendously expensive sort, with a whole room faithfully got up for living in. But here nobody really lived.

The boudoir, on the other hand, was quite different; in fact it had a very definite personality stamped on it, and I felt at once that it shouldn't go by so stupid a name. Into this room Lady Simney had brought her past life with her, and although it didn't come together in any clear picture the effect was pleasant enough. There were old theatrical prints and hockey sticks and skis; there was a shelf of delicate Chinese pottery and on top of that a shelf of pretty stiff-looking books on drama; on the walls there were half a dozen magnificent photographs of Papuan children caught in the several stages of some intricate game. It was an excellent room for living in. It was also an excellent room for spying and snooping round – and this was our business now. The Inspector prowled about looking sombre – it was just as if he had already spotted something that depressed him – and I did the work. It's commonly like that. He says that my generation has been taught the technique, and that he isn't going to compete with it. But sometimes I suspect that he has preserved from a well-brought up childhood a distaste for poking about in other people's drawers.

There were several large cupboards and it was in one of them that I came upon the suit-case – a battered old suit-case with the labels of a dozen steamship companies – Matson and Orient and P. & O. – and of a score of out-of-the-way hotels. Perhaps, I thought, Nicolette in her salad days had done a colonial tour, taking Ophelia to the citizens of Bulawayo or Pago-Pago. And then I opened the thing and there were all those men's clothes. I'd hardly had time to reflect that Lady Simney's theatrical career was not likely to have included male impersonations when the Inspector strode forward and ordered the Cinderella's slipper business which I've mentioned already. So off I went across the corridor, more than half suspecting that it was an occupation he had thought up merely to get rid of me. Well, you know the result; those clothes would fit no one at Hazelwood. They were for a man taller and slimmer than any in the house. The Inspector was almost out of temper at this, and I could see that it upset something which was moving obscurely in his mind. Whatever the idea was, he didn't want me to spot it there and then – which was why he made his joke about Cuvier's feather. There's quite a grand library at Hazelwood, though I doubt whether Sir George much used it. Perhaps I'll slip in presently and look this Cuvier up. I might manage to surprise the chief, that way. And, of course, it's something to surprise *him* ... But that's just what was successfully achieved within the next five minutes.

For the door opened – the boudoir door – and in came a handsome youth in ill-fitting dark clothes and a yellow-and-black striped waistcoat. 'How do you do?' he said gravely.

The chief isn't often at a loss, but he blinked at this. 'What do you mean, *How do you do*?' he said. 'Aren't you the footman?'

At this the youth shook his head. 'No, I don't think I am. But I suppose that you are the policeman – the important one who has just arrived?' As he asked this question the youth had turned deliberately to me. Then he nodded curtly towards the Inspector. 'And that this is the man who photographs the body, and that sort of thing? But won't you both sit down?'

Now with this youth – Timmy Owdon – I had already had a word, as I've mentioned. He knew very well who was who. In what he had just said he was simply sailing in, head on, and showing that he was a Simney too. And I'm bound to say that he succeeded. We both sat down.

He crossed to a door communicating with the bedroom. 'Nicolette?' he called. And when there was no answer he turned to us again severely. 'Did Lady Simney,' he asked, 'invite you into this room?'

The Inspector looked at him with a severity answering his own. 'Young man, am I right in thinking that you are Owdon the butler's son?'

'I am Mr Owdon's son.'

'Master Owdon the butler's son.' A new voice spoke from

the doorway and we turned to see a slightly older youth, the split image of Timmy, advance into the room. 'Where other than to Hazelwood,' the newcomer asked in a high-pitched voice, 'would one turn in inventing a new form of Happy Families?' And he turned away from Timmy and bowed to us. 'Mr and Master Copper, I presume,' he said. He waved his hand round the boudoir. 'Picking up tips, no doubt, to assist Mrs and Miss Copper in interior decorating.' He pulled out a watch. 'Timmy, my good fellow,' he continued, 'something tells me that your services are required for marshalling the cake-stands.'

Timmy shook his head. 'No, Mervyn,' he said. 'My last cake-stand has been marshalled – at Hazelwood or anywhere else.'

Mervyn Cockayne – for, of course, it was he – opened his eyes in surprise. 'And may I ask, my dear kinsman, what activity you propose instead?'

'Responsions. I think I can manage it in a year.'

'God bless my soul! You want to go to *Oxford*?'

Timmy nodded. 'I think that is what uncle Bevis will propose.'

'*Uncle* Bevis!' And young Mr Cockayne put a hand in an affected way to his beautiful forehead. 'You think you will get somewhere with him by taking this sort of line?'

'I certainly shan't get anywhere with him by being content to go on marshalling the cake-stand.'

Mervyn sat down. He had the ability to recognize a true word when it was spoken. 'You interest me,' he said. 'And you interest these gentlemen too.' His expression became ugly. 'You regard your prospects as happily transformed by the death of my uncle George?'

'Everybody's prospects are transformed – including Nicolette's, I am glad to think.' As he said this Timmy looked directly first at one and then another of us. 'Haven't you thought that out, Mervyn? It means that if we are all to be suspected we do at least so far as motive goes start all square.' He turned gravely to the Inspector, no longer pretending to suppose that he was the man who had come to do the photographing. 'Sir George was mostly bad,' he said. 'And he loved holding people in a kind of thrall. For instance, me. You see' – his voice faltered for a moment on this – 'my mother was a Simney, and for sixteen years he exploited the fact for his own amusement.'

I looked at Timmy with some sympathy. He felt himself to be a gentleman and he had taught himself to talk like one. Or rather he had been prompted never to talk otherwise. The difference is important; it meant that there was nothing synthetic or bogus about him in this. His model, it occurred to me, must have been largely the intolerable Mervyn, and this increased the oddly twin-like effect they gave. And perhaps the main difference between them reduced itself to this: that no mother, or a mother who is only a speculation and a dream, is a good deal better than a thoroughly foolish one. This wasn't a point I could make to myself at the moment, for I hadn't yet met Mrs Cockayne – the dead man's sister Lucy, that is to say. All I could feel was that Timmy Owdon wasn't so bad; that he showed up his cousin (or whatever he is to be called) Mervyn rather badly; and that there was inevitably a lurking antagonism between these two – but just conceivably other lurking feelings as well.

'Look here,' said Mervyn, 'it's not very decent to treat the Coppers *père et fils* to that sort of thumb-nail sketch of uncle George. It's true that he was constantly having immoral relations with women. But at least it's less out of the way for a man to seduce his wife's parlour-maids than for a woman to seduce her kinsman's butler.'

Timmy Owdon took two strides forward. Mervyn Cockayne (oddly enough, I thought) did the same. Both flushed, they looked into each other's eyes. Neither the chief nor I interfered – and I really believe that this was because the scene was so oddly beautiful. I remember thinking fleetingly that they ought both to have been stripped – in which case they would have been just like some of those reliefs cut in stone which auntie Flo (rather surprisingly) once took me to see in the British Museum.

'You know,' said Mervyn, 'two nights ago I let myself be pitched out of a window. But last night' – and he took another step forward – 'I found out that I could do this sort of thing. Not expertly yet, of course. Still, I think I'm coming on.' And suddenly he leant forward with a sort of wicked and radiant smile and slapped Timmy's face. The gesture had an odd effect of clapping on a mask – for there instantly on Timmy's face was the identical joyous and Satanic expression. A second later they were punching each other about the room. They were also kicking. And I think perhaps they were biting too. In these ways – it's not unpleasant to record – they just weren't gentlemen at all.

Inspector Cadover looked on for some moments a shade helplessly. It must be a good many years, I suppose, since he has tackled that sort of thing outside a pub. 'Stop it!' he called out. 'Don't you realize that your behaviour is disgraceful – here in Lady Simney's room and within a day of her husband's death?'

Well, considering that he and I had just been sneaking through Nicolette's drawers and cupboards there was more than a shade of hypocrisy in this, nor could I feel myself – although it was now a thoroughly dirty fight – that anything disgraceful was going on. I haven't the Inspector's brains, and one result is that I get feelings about things from time to time. I was just trying to formulate these particular feelings when I happened to look round, and read them in another person's eyes.

They were eyes wide-open with surprise, and they belonged to Lady Simney herself who now stood in the doorway. But there was more than surprise as she watched the two young men. At first I thought it was just the look with which women do watch men fighting – which is by no means a look of simple moral disapproval, such as Inspector Cadover could contrive. Then I saw that there was more to it again than this. A sort of dawning relief, as of the first lifting of the corner of a cloud, was on Nicolette Simney's strained face. 'Timmy!' she called out. 'Mervyn!' And then – and most unexpectedly – 'Oh, hit him, Mervyn – *hit* him!'

But it was Timmy Owdon who was inspired by that; with a big effort he broke free and jabbed his opponent under the jaw. And Mervyn Cockayne – whose nose was already bleeding on Lady Simney's pale ivory carpet – went down like a sack.

Timmy had turned in a flash, his face flushed the darkest red. 'How dare you!' he cried. 'You are my friend. How dare you back the conceited, foul-mouthed little milk-sop.' And Timmy paused to give the prostrate Mervyn a vicious kick on the behind.

And at this shockingly unsportsmanlike action Lady Simney laughed aloud – which the Inspector, I think, didn't like at all. She stepped forward and ruffled Timmy's already disordered hair; she knelt down and gave Mervyn her handkerchief. He looked at her in comical woe and she kissed him on the forehead. 'But you admire him,' she flung back at Timmy. 'And he's not a milk-sop; he's taken to rough-houses every day. Of course I backed him. You're younger, it's true. But in your time you've fought every stable-lad in the county.' She mocked him charmingly. 'I just don't know what the gentry are in for with their new recruit.'

Timmy looked sheepish. So did Mervyn, who was now scrambling to his feet. The two lads eyed each other and I could see that they had made some largely satisfactory discovery. 'Gentry?' said Mervyn, his voice at its highest pitch. 'The little thug is poor uncle George's house-boy. And he says he won't get us any tea.' The high voice rose to a wail. 'No tea – and it's after half past four!'

I heard the Inspector breathing rather heavily beside me – a habit he has when overhauling a situation which has got a bit ahead of him. 'Lady Simney –' he began.

But Nicolette was dusting Timmy down. She tugged at his ridiculous waistcoat and it came in two in her hand. They were all three quite still for a second and I guessed that they read it as a symbol – as a sort of sartorial token of the disruption of an old order at Hazelwood. For that was the fact. Sir George Simney was dead – and the place was becoming more wholesome hourly. Somebody was surely going to be morally infinitely the worse for what had happened. But a number of people were going to have at least the appearance of being a good deal better.

'Mervyn,' Lady Simney said – and she glanced from the one lad to the other – 'surely your flannels would fit?'

Timmy's late antagonist hesitated, and I supposed that he was fleetingly wondering about the attitude to all this of his uncle Bevis. 'Why, yes,' he answered. 'Let's go and see.'

They went out like brothers. 'Whereas,' said the Inspector as the door closed on them, 'these would *not* fit.' And he pointed to the suit-case we had discovered. 'They fit nobody in this house.'

5

There are times when I hate him, and this was one of them. Hounding people about is a disgusting trade. I wish it wasn't so fascinating.

Lady Simney paled when she saw the suit-case and I could see that this particular triumph of our nosey-parkering was a real shock to her. She sat down. 'I didn't kill my husband,' she said. 'Nor do I know who did.'

The Inspector crossed the room and stood beside her – a little too close up, so that he was almost standing over her. 'Now,' he said, 'that's a very extraordinary remark to make. Nobody has breathed a word of such a suspicion, and you start off like that. It sets one wondering at once.'

But he got no change with this. 'There's nothing extra-ordinary about it,' she said. 'I'm simply not beating about the bush – and I expect the same of you. Poke among my private possessions if you like. But don't waste time on making your approaches cunning and foxy. Of course I'm suspected.'

'Since you're so sure of that, Lady Simney, perhaps you wouldn't mind telling us why?'

She gave a sort of quick, severe smile. She had the trick of expressions and gestures which were at once beautiful in themselves and unrelated to any clear conception of her character which you could form. And so, although she was frank and direct enough, and gave herself no airs of mystery, there was a point at which you came to feel that she was a perfect walking Mona Lisa. (But can one conceive Mona Lisa as having legs and going for a stroll round that land-scape? I'm talking about a picture. Show this bit to auntie Flo.)

'Yes, I can,' she said. 'I can tell you in a dozen words. My marriage was bad. It began in disillusion – which means sin – and ended downright squalid. My husband's infidelities were tiresome. But his fidelity was intolerable.'

Well, it sounded straight talk. And again the Inspector was breathing heavily. This was the sort of thing he was accustomed to bully out of the commonalty, or to worm out of their superiors by an elaborate bedside manner. You mustn't have any pretty fancies about this job of ours.

'Moreover, yesterday was a sort of crisis. A number of things happened. The young Australian who has arrived here started making love to me in a hot-house. One of my sisters-in-law disapproved. Then George did rather more than start on the same lines with this young man's wife – and incidentally in what must have been pretty well an ice-house. I came upon them, more or less. He shouted something about having seen my lover – he must some-how have got wind of the hot-house business – and then

128

he struck me. And, of course, before that, life has been hopelessly disordered: quarrels and smashings and fights.'

'It does appear, Lady Simney, that folk here about are a bit free with their hands.' He fished out a notebook and affected to consult it. 'For example, I understand that only a few minutes after the discovery of Sir George's death there was some sort of quarrel between the young man who has just left us – Mr Cockayne, is it not? – and Mr Willoughby Simney?'

'I believe there was. They went to have a look at the window through which the attacker had fled, and they seemed to fall into some sort of dispute about I couldn't hear what. But then, they have never been on very good terms, and they were considerably overwrought.'

'That, as far as I understand the matter, would apply to several members of the household. And now, will you please explain this suit-case?'

'Explain it, Inspector Cadover?' Lady Simney had flushed with sudden anger. 'And perhaps I am to be required to explain, too, the books on my shelves and the pictures on my walls?'

He looked slowly about the room. 'It might be useful,' he said.

And at that she looked startled. 'It is Owdon,' she snapped, 'who has suit-cases to explain. Go and ask him.'

'Will you please explain that? I don't follow you.'

She hesitated. This was something she had not meant to come out with – or not now. She had simply made a grab at it – so I judged – in order to gain time to think something out. 'I met him in the park yesterday morning,' she said. 'He was hurrying along with two suit-cases in an unmistakably furtive way. I have the impression that he was proposing to hide them near the high-road. Is Owdon, I wonder, still here? It wouldn't at all surprise me if he had made a bolt for it.'

I could see she was speaking truthfully – whatever calculations there may have been behind her truthfulness.

And I expected the chief to be a bit taken aback. For it was on Owdon's evidence that our present grasp of the affair, such as it was, turned. And preparations for a bolt made early the previous day surely argued some degree of foreknowledge and complicity which must make his whole statement worthless. But the Inspector, whatever he thought of the importance of this piece of information, was not to be drawn aside to it now. 'What we were speaking of,' he said drily, 'is this suit-case here.'

'To be sure it was.' She smiled at him. 'It belongs to a friend, a Mr Hoodless, who happened to abandon it when going abroad some years ago. I – I am keeping it for him.'

'Not Christopher Hoodless?'

She looked at him I thought with a glint of fear. But she answered steadily enough. 'Yes, Christopher Hoodless.'

'So the pictures on your walls – those charming black children – *do*, after all, link up with the suit-case? Mr Hoodless gave them to you?'

'Yes.'

'Now, Lady Simney, when Sir George shouted at you yesterday morning something about having seen your lover, might it have been Mr Hoodless that he meant?'

She caught her breath. But he gave her no time to reply. His mind had made one of its queer spurts and the result was one of the best bits of his high-speed technique.

'Yesterday's *Times*, Lady Simney. There was something in it that suddenly made you very much want the issue of the day before. That, I think, was something to do with Mr Hoodless?'

'I had no notion' – she went back to his earlier question – 'that George could be referring to Christopher.'

It was her instinct not to tell fibs. For my own part I was pleased at this, because I admired her. But it annoyed the Inspector. If a witness has something to hide (and it was difficult to feel that Nicolette Simney had not a secret of some sort) truth, skilfully deployed, is his best weapon.

'Lady Simney, you are a woman of intelligence. It is

apparent to you that reticence is pointless upon matters which the testimony of others is bound to declare. There had been, before your marriage, a close friendship between Mr Hoodless and yourself?'

'We were engaged.'

'Thank you. Now, Mr Hoodless, you say, has been abroad. That' – he glanced at the photographs of the playing children on the walls – 'would be in connexion with his work as a scientist.'

'As a configurational anthropologist.'

This additional information was no doubt of the kind which the testimony of others would be bound to declare. Even in what must have been a harassing situation Nicolette Simney apparently liked a play of subdued irony. But the Inspector was unheeding. 'I mean,' he said, 'that the nature of such work would take him to very distant parts, and that when you say he went abroad some years ago it is to be concluded that he had not been back in England since. Of late, however, you have been expecting his return.'

Lady Simney bowed. 'It has been increasingly on my mind,' she said gravely.

'And yesterday evening you found in *The Times* an announcement which seemed to suggest that he had just arrived. It was in the form of a reference to something in the issue of the previous day. You sent Owdon for that issue at once, and you were a good deal agitated.'

All this police-business is a matter of putting two and two together. And here was at least a patch of the present affair in which he had been doing that pretty rapidly. He had been handed Hoodless's name. He had known that Hoodless was an anthropologist (mere miscellaneous information can be uncommonly useful: I have often noticed this with auntie) and this had led him to infer a good deal from the photographs. In the one personally furnished room of Lady Simney's they were an assertion of something valued and held to. That gave, in fact, something very close to *lover* – and this he connected at once with what the dead man had shouted at her in the park before striking her. Then there was her statement that she had not at the time realized that it might have been Hoodless her husband was referring to. If accepted, this was a startling admission in itself. It made the reading of *The Times* of that day the likely occasion of her discovering the possibility. Her husband had seen Hoodless presumably here in the neighbourhood of Hazelwood; he had referred coarsely to their former association; he had struck her. And his death followed within a little over twelve hours.

Lady Simney had crossed to the window and was looking out over the snow. I guessed that she was squaring up to the new situation with which Inspector Cadover's penetrations had confronted her. Presently she turned round. 'And where,' she asked, 'do we go from here?'

'To the brief interval, Lady Simney, between your glancing first at *The Times* and the moment when your husband died. At eleven-forty you came out of this room and asked Owdon to fetch you the issue of the day before. Five minutes later he came back, found that you had gone to your bath, left the paper in this room, and proceeded to the study. It was empty and Owdon tidied round as usual, at the same time closing the window from the bottom. Now, we know that at about this time somebody arrived below that window and presently climbed the trellis. We know, too, that at the bottom of it again Mr Cockayne had some sort of struggle with an unidentified man at what can only have been a matter of moments after Sir George was killed. Do you think that this intruder might have been Mr Hoodless?'

There was a fraction of a second's silence – followed by a cry of horror, or of horror and passionate repudiation. 'No!' she gasped. 'No . . . it's impossible!'

'Moreover the circumstances give you yourself something under five minutes' freedom to act unobserved. Say three and a half minutes between Owdon's disappearing in quest of *The Times* and your slipping into the bath-room just before his return. Did you in that interval go to the study window yourself?'

She stared at him round-eyed and pale. 'No!' she cried again. 'No ... why ever should I do such a thing?'

There was silence. The Inspector wrote in his notebook. A coal clicked in the grate. I looked at the Papuan children absorbed in their games, and waited for what *he* was waiting for too: some further, and rash, word. But Lady Simney said nothing more. She had asked a question and left it at that, expecting an answer.

'What I have in mind, your ladyship, is no more than one of a great many hypotheses which it would be possible to form. I hope you will understand that it is my duty, in an affair so obscure as this, to think out every possible role that the persons chiefly involved could conceivably play.'

She made a gesture of impatience.

'Very well. I know nothing of your relationship with Mr Hoodless. I know nothing of his temperament. But very possibly both may be what is termed romantic. Suppose him already a little familiar with Hazelwood. And suppose that during his absence you have occasionally corresponded. He may know that your marriage has been unhappy. He may have urged you to leave your husband. He may have made you a promise.'

She looked at him a little wearily now. 'A promise?'

'Something like this: that if on returning to England he found you still with Sir George he would break in on the stroke of midnight and carry you away – carry you away from the cave of the dragon. And into Hazelwood there is one route that any dragon-killer would take – the trellis that leads straight to the study and your part of the house.'

But Lady Simney was now thoroughly nerved to cope with all this. 'You are talking a deliberate mingling of sense and nonsense,' she said. 'It is true about *The Times*. Yesterday's copy had something which implied that Mr Hoodless's return to England had been mentioned in the issue of the day before. And the news did agitate me, rather. We had been engaged, as I said.'

'You had been expecting his return round about this time?'

She hesitated. 'Yes, I had. And it did present rather a problem – but not one I want to discuss.'

'Very possibly not, Lady Simney.'

She flushed. 'But after that you talk nonsense. Of course I had no reason to suppose that he might have appeared at that very moment beneath George's study window. No rigmarole about the cave of the dragon can give the slightest colour of probability to such a suggestion. Would you dare to talk such stuff in a law court? Then why waste your time talking it to me.'

I tried to catch the chief's eye – merely to indicate the mild pleasure of a faithful but not uncritical subordinate at observing him get as good as he gave. The lady was by no means to be confused. She was still steadily admitting, or coming forward with, what must inevitably transpire sooner or later, and keeping completely close about anything else. That Hoodless had in fact been there beneath the window, however, was by no means improbable. Sir George had been a brute; he knew it; he was freshly arrived in England. This conception of a former lover as being central in the affair Inspector Cadover had arrived at with a creditable celerity. But then it was only a hypothesis. In five minutes it might vanish never to be heard of again.

And if it was not improbable that Hoodless had been there it did seem improbable that in those three or four minutes of Owdon's absence Lady Simney had effected a rendezvous with him at the window. If she spoke the truth in saying that *The Times* had given her the first inkling of his being arrived in England then the notion that he might there and then be beneath the study window was quite as lacking in colour as she had averred. If, on the other hand, she had possessed earlier knowledge that he was in the district, this travesty of a *Romeo and Juliet* meeting minutes before her husband was accustomed to come into the room, was about the last thing which it was sensible to imagine. And I could see only one conclusion. When she had sent Owdon for the previous day's *Times* she had gone direct to her bath-room to try the soothing effect of a shower. And there she had been when her husband was killed – whether by Hoodless or another. That this was how the Inspector saw it I don't know. He had crossed to the window, thrown up the sash, and was peering out and to the right. There he would see first the window of Lady Simney's bedroom, then the window of her bath-room, then the blank wall and chimney-shaft which represented the end of the study. He withdrew his head again, closed the window slowly, and looked thoughtfully at the open suit-case which had first brought Hoodless's name into the discussion. Then he glanced across the room – at some other definite object, but I wasn't quick enough to see just what. He was looking depressed. More often than not it is know-ledge rather than ignorance which has this effect on him. I glanced at Lady Simney and believed that she was puzzled. She was *looking* puzzled, though not obtrusively so.

'Lady Simney, I have one more question. You know that it was not Mr Christopher Hoodless who killed your husband?'

She brought a hand to her breast in uncontrollable agit-ation. It is a gesture one sees in the theatre. But presumably the theatre has copied it from life.

'Yes!' she cried. 'I mean, no. In your sense, no. My whole soul tells me he could not do such a thing. He *could* not strike murderously at an unsuspecting man from behind. But how can I give proof that he is innocent?'

'Ah,' said the Inspector. 'How indeed, Lady Simney?'

And he bowed and led me from the room.

6

It was dusk outside and presently we should have to be getting off to the village. That the Simney Arms would provide any very substantial comfort was something which a brief glimpse had made us doubt. However, we could hardly announce ourselves as yet another influx of uninvited guests at Hazelwood. The Australians had at least been cousins, and not policemen.

Some line on the Australian aspect of the affair was what we went after next. For my own part I would have gone for it from the first. Lady Simney didn't strike me as homicidal – and secretly, you know, I still pay a good deal of heed to these simple promptings of instinct. Moreover she herself seemed to have no Australian connexions, and far the most striking thing about her husband's death was the fact that it had followed hard upon certain mysterious disputes which the Australians' arrival had occasioned. I put this to the chief as we re-entered the study; he nodded absently and went over to the window. He flung up the sash and stuck out his head, twisting his shoulders till he was looking directly upwards. 'The trellis,' he said, 'goes up as far as the next storey.'

'You mean somebody could have come *down* it?'

I must say that I don't often play Dr Watson quite so all-out as this, but my mind had been hunting about elsewhere and I was taken by surprise. I was also a good deal disconcerted by the widening possibilities which this simple discovery revealed.

'Yes,' he said. 'My dear lad – yes. It is not an inference which is very far to seek. Perhaps you would like to comment on it in some way?'

Well, I have to put up with a little sarcasm from time to time. It generally means that he's not too pleased with the way his own nose is pointing. 'We mustn't forget that someone certainly came *up*,' I said. 'Nor the tracks in the snow. Nor young Cockayne's scuffle in the dark.'

'Very true.' He looked at me unsmilingly. 'And conceivably one person came from above and another from below. This room may have been quite a rendezvous. Anyway, the lie of the land upstairs is worth studying. But as for what you say of Lady Simney,' – he shut down the window – 'you must think again. It may not be quite true that she has no Australian connexions.'

Auntie Flo will be glad to know I tumbled to this. 'Hoodless,' I said.

'Exactly. He is an anthropologist who may well have taken Australian blacks in his stride.'

'But it doesn't seem likely that Australian blacks have anything to do with Sir George's death.'

'*Something* Australian has – or so, in our darkness, it is useful to guess. There has been some Australian mystery, and Hoodless very possibly knows Australia. I'm saying no more than that. And now let us have an Australian in.' The Inspector glanced about the study and paused. 'But wait a bit. Wasn't there something about a safe?'

I looked through Sergeant Laffer's notes. 'A wall-safe,' I said, 'behind the damaged portrait of Sir George Simney. It was found locked and has not yet been examined.' I turned the pages. 'A bunch of keys was among the articles found on the dead man.'

He had already crossed the room and given the dead man's portrait a tug. It swung on hinges – and there, sure enough, was a small safe let into the wall. 'Yes,' he called, 'it's a key, not a combination. Better get the bunch. But what about fingerprints?'

I shook my head. 'They've made a full record, of course, and it's all available for analysis. But I doubt if anything's going to appear.'

He grunted. 'If fingers only left legible prints as often as they're supposed to ... Come on, lad. Hurry up with the key.'

Without resentment, I hurried up. It appeared that he set store by the possibilities of this safe. And, indeed, he paused before it now almost dramatically. 'Do you see any reason to suppose,' he asked, 'that the secret of the affair lies here?'

'Well, sir – yes, in a way. It seems that when there was this rough house the other night the picture got smashed and the safe was revealed as a result. Everybody must have become aware of it, including the Australians. Now, there's an Australian secret, as we've said. And secrets – or the material witness to them – are frequently kept in safes.'

'So they are, lad.' He was quite genial now, and I could see that he really did regard this concealed repository with something of the confidence of a conjuror before a silk hat. 'Well, here goes. Got a torch? Just give us a little extra light.'

I shone my torch. He turned the key. The little steel shutter slid back. There can be no doubt about what we expected – about what, that is to say, the reasonable expectation was. Documents, some yellow with age, were the proper thing for this safe to hold. But what it did hold was a pair of men's boots, fairly new. There was nothing else.

This sort of thing is popularly supposed to be quite in a policeman's ordinary line of business. And, of course, we are always running up against the unexpected. But not quite like this. Those black boots appeared positively to grin at us, delighted at the effect of utter inconsequence they had achieved. I looked cautiously at the Inspector. 'Perhaps,' I asked, 'you would like me to take them round the household and see whom they fit, as I did with the things in the suit-case?'

'Of course you must do that.' Now he was looking not at the boots at all but into some speculative vacancy. 'And, of course, apply all your detective talent to them. You may find that they were worn by a swarthy man, fond of music and with a slight cast in the left eye, who has recently made a proposal of marriage.'

Just for a moment I didn't realize that he was merely making fun of me. Then I took them carefully from the safe. 'All right, sir,' I said, 'I'll have a go at it.' And I inspected them carefully. 'They are the property of someone who played football as a boy, is disregardful of both personal appearance and comfort, rides a badly neglected bicycle and is fond of gardening.' I paused. 'Moreover, I think the owner is probably left-handed.'

'Let me have a look.' He glanced at me suspiciously before taking the boots. 'Appearance and comfort, yes – they're kinked at the toes and wrinkled up inside. And the gardening's clear enough too; they've plainly been used to drive in a fork or spade – and with the *left* foot, which at least suggests left-handedness. But as for the bicycle –' He frowned. 'Yes, scratches just over the right ankle-bone such as might certainly be made by a chain – and a rusty chain rather than a well-oiled one. But the football as a boy appears to me pure fantasy.'

'It's just the way they're tied loosely together by the ends of their laces. It reminds me of what we used to do with football boots before slinging them round the neck.'

'I see. Well, nothing much of all this seems to fit the dead man. And I doubt if the boots will either. But why should he keep a pair of men's boots, whether his own or somebody else's in a concealed safe? If they had been women's shoes, now, there would be nothing odd about it at all. There's nothing commoner than the treasuring of such things as erotic symbols. They told you that in lectures, I don't doubt.'

Sometimes he likes to show that he's up in all the latest. 'Yes,' I said, 'nothing in the way of women's attire would surprise us in the least, of course. But these don't look like erotic symbols, by a long way.'

'Would you say they look like red herrings – something planted here with a deliberate meaninglessness and incongruity, the way you get things in those surrealist pictures people fancy nowadays?'

I hadn't imagined he followed art. 'No,' I replied after some thought. 'No – somehow I don't.'

'It's curious about modern painting. No understanding much of it, if you ask me.'

As you know, I try to keep wide awake when he starts talking like that. Otherwise I just get left at the post.

And I got left at the post now. 'By the way,' he said, 'apart from his being disregardful of comfort and appearance, you haven't told me much about this fellow's temperament.'

'I've told you,' I said warily, 'as much as I can infer.'

He held the boots up under my nose. 'Can't you see,' he asked, 'that he's a man of an uncommonly mistrustful nature? Make not a bad policeman, if you ask me.' He swung round, for there was the sound of somebody entering the study behind us. 'Good evening,' he said to the newcomer. 'Are you in the habit of wearing boots?'

It was Mr Hippias Simney. His glance had gone to the open safe – rather swiftly, it appeared to me – but now he halted and looked at us by no means pleasantly. 'Boots!' he said. 'What the deuce do you mean, sir?'

Inspector Cadover held out our latest discovery. 'We are interested in these,' he explained. 'They were among the objects which we found in the late Sir George's safe here. Not perhaps the most interesting objects, but certainly the oddest.'

It's wonderful with what aplomb he can tell these shocking lies – and all on the spur of the moment, too. And Hippias, I think, was disconcerted; at least he took time off to think. 'Dam' disagreeable thing, this,' he said. 'Policemen never much in my line. Don't like them pawing round a gentleman's house.'

'Sir George's death, Mr Simney, is certainly a disagreeable sequel to your arrival at Hazelwood. You must greatly regret now that what were virtually to be your kinsman's last hours should have been darkened by what appear to have been serious – even violent – disputes with yourself.'

'I certainly threw a bottle at him.' And Hippias laughed with the boisterousness of an inwardly uncertain man. 'Or perhaps I threw it at his reflection in one of those bally-fool mirrors. Missed him, anyway. Was in liquor rather, I'm afraid. Port that's actually seen Oporto treacherous, you know, after our harmless colonial brews.' He paused and gave us a calculating glance. 'Find anything in that safe about a place called Dismal Swamp? Not important, I may say, but the occasion of what little heat there was between poor old George and ourselves. He did us down in Australia a great many years ago.'

'We shall want particulars of that. And did the man Owdon do you down there too?'

Hippias looked rapidly round the study – rather as if seeking counsel from his ancestors upon the walls. 'Owdon?' he said nervously. 'Dear me, nothing of the sort. Excellent man, I believe. Most reliable. Unimpeachable and all that. Bevis most eager to keep him on.'

'I rather doubt, Mr Simney, whether Owdon is eager to keep himself on. There is some evidence that he has been proposing to make an unobtrusive departure from Hazel-wood.'

Well, at that this bluff colonial gentleman visibly paled before our eyes. 'Impossible!' he exclaimed. 'Dear fellow is held in greatest regard by us all.'

This was an odd way to speak of a man he could have known nothing of for at least sixteen years. And the Inspector took up the point at once. 'Mr Simney, there seems to have been something a good deal out of the way between Sir George and this butler of his. Moreover it is reported in the household that he was much agitated by your arrival. Can you throw any light on these matters?'

'None whatever.'

'Let me suggest certain possibilities. Owdon had some sort of hold over his late employer, possibly as a result of knowing something gravely to his discredit in Australia.'

'Quite preposterous.'

'At one time this hold was so strong as to protect the man from the consequences of – um – a serious moral lapse with some female member of the family. Sir George was not in a position to dismiss the man. But, only the other day, the situation changed. Your own arrival at Hazelwood, which I understand to have been unexpected, in some way struck at the roots of Owdon's sinister power over your kinsman. He at once became, on the contrary, alarmed for his own safety, and was driven to make plans for flight. And this situation may have produced further consequences of which we cannot yet confidently speak. Of course these are merely speculations. But have you anything to say about them?'

'Nothing whatever.'

This looked like being Hippias's formula. But the chief was pertinacious. 'As I understand the matter, Sir George – or Mr George, as he then was – went out to Australia as a young man and in the company of his younger brother?'

'Quite right. Denzell. Nice lad. Year younger than Bevis.'

'What happened to Denzell?'

'He lost his life in a sailing accident. Uncommonly sad thing.'

'Were you there?'

Hippias Simney hesitated. He had meant to say nothing at all, and now he was badly in need of more time to think. 'There?' he repeated querulously. 'All this, you know, was a deuced long time ago.'

'Come, come, sir. We know very well whether we were or were not present at a fatal accident, even if it did take place twenty or thirty years ago.'

'I didn't say I didn't know whether I was there or not. I meant that it was all far too long ago to have anything to do with this business now. Of course I was there, I remember being very much affected – very much affected, indeed.' And Hippias felt up his sleeve for a silk handkerchief, evidently feeling that the watery end of Denzell Simney might appropriately be graced with a reminiscent tear.

'And was the man Owdon there?'

Hippias shook his head decidedly. 'At that time Owdon had never been heard of.'

'Perhaps you will tell us a little more about this accident? It was on a lake – a river?'

Again Hippias hesitated. And it occurred to me that he was doing, much more clumsily, what Lady Simney had done. He was endeavouring to speak openly about matters which he knew must be somewhere on record, while keeping close on related matters which he conceived it unhealthy to reveal. 'River?' he repeated. 'Well, no. As a matter of fact, it was something that happened at sea. Out among the Islands. And certain aspects of it were – ah – kept rather quiet.'

'Um.' The Inspector's voice was ominous. 'I somehow felt that sooner or later we would come upon matters which had been kept rather quiet. But now, I think, is the time for a good clear look at them. What, exactly, were the circumstances of Mr Denzell Simney's death?'

Hippias was still standing by the open door of the study. Now he looked over his shoulder and down that crucial corridor in which Owdon (if we were to believe him) had kept guard the night before. Perhaps he was making sure that he was not overheard, but I think he was rather hoping for assistance from some mind more nimble in prevarication than his own.

'Well,' he said at last, 'I'll try.' He produced the silk handkerchief and wiped, not his eyes, but his brow. 'Only it's difficult not to convey a wrong impression. It was all a good long time ago, as I've said. And they were wilder times out there with us. People did these things without any particular feeling of being criminals, or anything of the sort.'

We looked at him with a good deal of expectation. It seemed as if in this there might be a little light at last.

'You see,' Hippias said, 'it was a matter of blackbirds.'

7

'Anthropologists and missionaries,' pursued Hippias Simney, 'have pretty well messed all that up. Government too, for that matter. Nowadays you'll find an administrator or commissioner or some other sort of superior policeman on every atoll. But in the old days it used to give a very good holiday and probably quite a handsome sum· after all expenses paid. Bevis was inquiring about buffalo hunting the other day. But for real sport I'd choose blackbirding every time.'

He looked round the study as if hoping to find a decanter which might support him through his narrative. 'No more, you know' – and his voice was at once jaunty and uneasy – 'than getting hold of a big lugger and turning it into a sort of mail-boat for the niggers. Bit crowded at times, no doubt. Nothing in the way of a games deck, and the cuisine a trifle limited during the voyage. Still, just transporting niggers about. Taking them where they're useful, that's to say.'

Inspector Cadover was leaning over a heavy, high-backed chair by the fire-place. 'In fact,' he said, 'to go blackbirding is simply to engage in the slave-trade?'

Hippias looked mildly apologetic. 'You might put it that way. All those niggers uncommonly lacking in enterprise. Home-keeping youths, as Shakespeare says, and need stirring up a bit. Point is that excellent employers – humane and that sort of thing – used to be simply crying out for them. And, mind you, we were only a little ahead of our time. Look round about you today. Ministries of Labour and Directorates of Manpower shoving people round all the time. Come to think of it, my dear fellow, you and I are treated no better than blackbirds ourselves.'

'It appears to me, Mr Simney, that some of us might very justly be treated as blackguards.'

'Come, come – I call that a bit strong.' Hippias was elaborately reasonable. 'Black sheep, if you like. Simneys are very often black sheep, of course. It's something very common in the oldest families, I think you'd find. And if you went blackbirding you were a bit of a scamp, I don't deny. As for the particular scrape we got into that time – well, we could hardly have foreseen it, could we?'

'Possibly not – nor the complications it might one day cause. But please come to the actual events.'

'To be sure.' And Hippias appeared to exchange a brief glance with one of the least engaging of his ancestors on the wall before him. 'George and Denzell, you know, came out to Australia when they were little more than lads, and before George looked like being heir to the title. They weren't altogether reliable boys, I'm afraid. There had been some troubles about banknotes, and they had done some more or less permanent injury to a lad in the village who had offended them, and there had been an affair with a girl in which they had been – um – a little too impetuous in their methods of courtship. So they were sent out with the idea of taking up land and perhaps entering Australian politics later. Gentlemen still went into our parliament in those days. But, of course, that never came off.'

'A great pity, Mr Simney. They were plainly youths admirably well-qualified to be legislators.'

Hippias, far from being offended by this heavy irony, chuckled with delight. 'Quite so. But colonial life, I'm sorry to say, is far from being what it was. Well, these lads came out when George was about nineteen and Denzell a couple of years younger. They came to Hazelwood – *our* Hazelwood, that is to say – when I was just on twenty-one myself. We got on not badly, though I'm bound to say I was a bit frightened of them.'

'Frightened of them?'

Hippias nodded. 'They were uncommon wild. I didn't mind that, and I'm sure they taught me a great deal. But I hadn't their guts, and at some of the things we did I used to get scared afterwards. I used to wonder what would happen if the troopers found out.' And Hippias Simney shook his head. 'I never did like troopers, or police, or people of that sort. Still, I did go blackbirding.'

'How long after the young men came out did this black-birding business occur?'

'I should say five or six years. But we made several expeditions before the fatal one happened. The bush, you know, gets deuced monotonous for a young chap who feels that things ought to be stirred up a bit from time to time. And a voyage over a decent stretch of the Pacific, with a slice of fun and a slice of mischief at the end of it, was an uncommon attractive thing. All we had to do was to square my father, who was naturally glad enough to get rid of us for a few months now and then.'

'Most naturally, I should imagine.'

'Well now, on this unlucky occasion we had gone up to Cairns and got hold of a lugger, and of three or four precious rascals by way of crew. We had rather a good scheme. The common thing in collecting blackbirds was simply to find a fairly large native village and begin by bargaining. Political organization, if you can call it that, appears to vary enormously among the islands, and sometimes you found a chief with whom you could do a deal and there was an end of the matter. But often dealing in a village turned out – um – a rather messy business. Moreover, you never quite knew where you were, and islands were being grabbed at that time by this government or that. You might run into a squad of Dutch or Portuguese soldiers, or – what was rather more awkward – into a gentleman in tropical whites and a topee straight from the Colonial Office. So this time we planned to pick up our black friends at sea. Only, of course, we didn't reckon on those damned anthropologists.'

'Anthropologists?' I interrupted. Not everything in police work links up as it would in some logical game, and there was probably no remote connexion here with Lady Simney's young Mr Hoodless and the beautiful photographs hanging in her room. But I was startled. 'Anthropologists, Mr Simney?' I repeated.

'Two fellows who had actually gone on this ritual trading journey in order to study it. Just fancy studying such tommyrot! Probably they were only after the women, if you ask me.' Hippias paused, perhaps dimly aware of the fatuity of this. 'Not, of course, that there are any women on these voyages. That's why we were proposing to break in on one. We were out for business, you know, and a good cheque at the end, and we thought there would be altogether less fuss that way. It's difficult to describe those voyages. Ostensibly they are a matter of trading from island to island, but really they are like a great country dance covering hundreds of miles of ocean. The goods are taken in sea-going canoes from island to island in some intricate ritual pattern, with each island sending off parties both clockwise and anti-clockwise, and in the end, and after weaving a sort of great invisible chain, everything ends up pretty well where it began. Sheer useless foolery. It was only sensible, if you ask me, to nobble some of those niggers from time to time and set them to honest work.'

'Such as you were yourself engaged in, Mr Simney.'

'Exactly so. Well, we decided to lie in wait for a couple of big sea-going canoes out on that sort of thing. And, as it happened, we made very good speed in meeting with what we wanted. There were two canoes with no end of young, able-bodied niggers. And we pinned them up against a reef and had them nicely. Nobody could have guessed what trouble was to follow. We had just got out our guns – for, of course, it was ten to one that a little wounding and maiming would be necessary before the fellows would be persuaded to come quietly – when up bobbed a couple of damned white men in the nearest canoe. I've explained what they were: bally anthropologists making the trip for learned reasons – and as high in favour with the niggers as you could imagine. Of course they knew what we were about in no time, and before you could say six one of them was on board the lugger and telling young George just what he thought of us. Well, we could either have taken a strong hand, or agreed to sheer off and no harm done – for those fellows presumably didn't know us from Adam and would have had hard work to trace us. George and I had tackled the fellow and were pretty well set to bolt for it, when up came Denzell. The anthropologist fellow took one look at him. "Denzell Simney!" he said. "I'm sorry to see you mixed up in a low game like this."

'Apparently he had been Denzell's house-master not so many years before – and a pretty pickle the recognition landed us in. Still, the situation could still have been retrieved, for once we had made a successful get-away the fact of this identification would have been hard to prove. Unfortunately, Denzell lost his head. He turned his gun on the chap and tried to shoot him – and I'm damned if he didn't miss. This, mind you, at a range of about four yards.'

Inspector Cadover had been listening to this narrative in grim silence. Now he spoke. 'Not many would-be murderers, Mr Simney, have that much luck.'

'No doubt.' Hippias was becoming increasingly agitated. 'But although Denzell didn't kill this old schoolmaster of his he did wing a nigger. The bullet got a fellow in the farther canoe and smashed his shoulder. The result was hell upon earth – or upon the Pacific Ocean. Nothing pacific about it either. The mere presence of those white men somehow got us down at the start, and correspondingly it gave the niggers the courage of demons. Their first idea seemed to be to get their two white friends out of danger – did you ever hear of anything queerer than that? – and no sooner had they stormed the lugger than they carried off the fellow who had recognized Denzell and thrust him by main force into the canoe which contained his companion. And then off that canoe went – no doubt to summon reinforcements of the black devils – and meanwhile we were left to fight it out with some thirty of the brutes armed with spears and some very nasty-looking knives. Of course there wasn't a man of us who hadn't a brace of revolvers at his belt, and we ought to have won that fight hands down. Yet, I'm ashamed to say that we didn't manage to kill one of them.'

'Fortunate again,' said Inspector Cadover. 'Quite mysteriously so.'

'It's the stark truth.' Hippias Simney was now sweating profusely. 'The first thing that happened was that Denzell went down with a spear through his thigh – he had done the shooting, so they made a dead set at him – and the next was that the devils had managed to pitch him overboard. The sharks were pretty plentiful in those waters.'

Inspector Cadover nodded, unmoved. 'Well,' he said, 'in the trade you were carrying on sharks were an obvious professional risk.'

'There was only one thing to do, and while the others fought the savages back I worked on the donkey-engine. The idea was simply to get away as fast as we could and then fight off as many of the enemy as were already on board. But when the engine started with a bit of a roar the effect was as queer as you could imagine. I suppose they believed that a demon had joined the fray, for their courage deserted them and they were overboard before you could say Jack Robinson. Which was excellent in itself.' Hippias paused. 'Unfortunately in their panicky rush to the side they carried George with them. I last saw him just where I had seen Denzell – struggling in the water. After that, it was comparatively plain sailing. The rest of us just got away as fast as we could.'

'You mean to say that you actually –'

Something that might have been a blush spread over the florid features of Hippias Simney. 'Nothing else to do,' he said. 'Those anthropologist chaps, who might a little have controlled the brutes, were still being hurried right out of the battle and had become pretty well hull-down over the horizon. A get-away was the only thing. And George did turn up again, after all. In fact, he turned up to diddle us in the matter of Dismal Swamp.'

'I can well believe it. For it seems improbable that he would return to you precisely in a grateful state of mind. You had joined with your kinsmen, Mr Simney, in a dis-reputable foray, and in a moment of danger you and your hireling companions deserted them like cravens.'

'Well' – Hippias was prepared to be reasonable – 'I did say they led me into things that rather scared me, didn't I? And I don't mind admitting that I was scared then.'

'You were demonstrably so. And would you be good enough to tell me now just what were the consequences of this blackbirding affair?'

'Well, I felt a bit bad, I'm bound to admit.'

'The legal rather than the moral consequences, Mr Simney, are what I have in mind.'

I could see that the chief didn't like Hippias at all, and that the blackbirding shocked him much less than the turn-ing tail and leaving those two young cousins floundering among savages in the water. And Hippias felt that he was distinctly not liked; he gave us a nasty look as well as a scared one before he mopped his forehead and spoke again.

'There weren't any legal consequences to speak of, I'm glad to say. If those anthropologists had traced our lugger to Cairns they might have got the whole lot of us. And if they'd managed to stir the authorities into a real rummage among the connexions of Denzell Simney I suppose it would have been the same. But somewhere or other they must have come up against good sense and the feeling that they ought to mind their own business. Nobody had been killed, you know, or nobody except George and Denzell – and George, of course, turned up after all, and diddled us nice-ly. So the affair was let die down, except that the only one of us known by name – Denzell, that is to say – was posted as wanted by the police. So, you see, the adventure hadn't ended too badly, after all. Denzell was no doubt due for from five to ten years according to the feelings of the judge, but he had got eternity anyway. And George, although he lay low for years feeling that the police might be on his track too –'

'As most certainly they ought to have been!' The chief interrupted with more emphasis than I have ever heard him use before. 'A simple inquiry into Denzell Simney's Australian connexions –'

'No doubt, Mr Inspector, no doubt.' Hippias looked momentarily complacent. 'But then all colonials are deuced easy-going, as you must have heard. And, of course, we weren't exactly nobodies in New South Wales.'

'I'm afraid,' said the chief grimly, 'you'll find it rather different here.'

'My dear man, it would be quite different at home nowadays. Only wharfies and coalminers receive the slightest consideration from an Australian government at present. But aren't we rather straying from the point?'

'I think perhaps we are. What proof was there that Denzell did not, in fact, survive?'

'I don't know that there was what you would call logical proof – although we got it admitted legally, as I'll explain. You see, my father started squaring things, and he worked out a story for me to tell, and for some other fellows to tell –'

'Your father seems to have been quite the Simney too.'

Hippias chuckled. 'Oh, quite definitely so. And he had just got up this story for having both George and Denzell legally presumed dead in some more or less respectable way, when we had word from George on the quiet that he was alive and kicking, although he had seen Denzell go down. He was going to keep out of the way for a time, but he hoped to give us the pleasure of his company at Hazelwood later. Well, we just changed the story a bit and said that Denzell was dead but that George had gone off to another part of Australia. Quite another part. And, as you know, it's a big place.'

8

Darkness had fallen over the snow-covered park outside. With Hippias Simney we were getting on famously (or rather the chief was) and vital information might at any moment spill itself all over the study carpet. Nevertheless I was beginning to have uneasy thoughts of what scraps of cold meat and rinds of cheese were likely to be left at the Simney Arms. Australia, as Hippias had just assured us, is a big place – and the human stomach is assuredly a small one. But in sheer emptiness the one can match the other very well.

The chief had turned on the lights long ago, but he was still leaning across the high-backed chair by the fire-place, with Caravaggio's Venus looking inviting above his head and two departed Simney baronets looking more than repellent on either side of her. The chief seemed prepared to stand there all night if more could be extorted from Hippias; I could see he felt that there was a good chance of getting the old rascal on the run. And Hippias had not the air of a man who feels well over the brow of the hill; I had an idea, indeed, that he felt the steepest gradient to be yet in front of him – indeed, that what he saw there was Alps on Alps arise. (See if auntie Flo knows that one.)

George was due to turn up again – Hippias had got his narrative as far as that – and I was just hoping to get at least the Dismal Swamp affair clear once for all when the study door opened and Gerard Simney, Hippias's son, came in. He took a quick look round. 'I want Lady Simney,' he said abruptly, and turned to leave the room.

But his father's eager voice restrained him – the voice of a man uncommonly anxious to find moral support. But at the same time it occurred to me that there was cunning as well as anxiety in Hippias's appeal; it was as if he had seen some positive tactical advantage in the arrival of his son. 'Looking for Nicolette?' he said. 'Deuced sensible of you, my boy. Nice woman. But don't hurry away. Have a spot. And if there's nothing to drink send for Owdon. These men – gentlemen, that is to say – and I are having a quiet crack about old colonial days.'

'To the devil with old colonial days.' Gerard Simney, although considerably more personable than his father, seemed to have something of the family violence of speech. 'The old colonial days were for the most part disgusting, so far as I can make out. But Australia has her chance now. A decent sort of social-democracy can conceivably be set going there. Spiritually and culturally it will be something thoroughly inglorious. But it will be a whole heap better than most other places.'

'Now, that's a very interesting proposition.' Hippias looked at the chief and myself with a naïve cunning. Deserves a bit of discussion to my mind. It was only a little time ago that I said to the High Commissioner –'

'Rubbish.' Gerard interrupted his parent without ceremony. 'At the present moment the subject has no interest whatever – either to these gentlemen or to ourselves. Certainly not to me. I'm looking for Nicolette.' And suddenly the young man's eye glinted at us rather wildly – and it was a glint, I realized with a start of recognition, that I had noticed somewhere about the walls of this room within the past half-hour – in fact some ancestral Simney look. 'And I want to know' – Gerard's voice rose defiantly – 'if a dead man can be a co-respondent.'

Of course this is just how it is with police work. You are getting tidily along with what looks like some principal aspect of the affair when in swims some beastly red herring and demands to be attended to. Here were the chief and I jerked some twelve thousand miles from the Pacific Ocean to Hazelwood Hall, and required to discover why Gerard

Simney should have come out with a remark so exceedingly odd. The dead man to whom he referred could hardly be other than his kinsman the late Sir George – the duration of whose acquaintance with Gerard's wife Joyleen could most conveniently be reckoned in hours. And the same reckoning held of Gerard himself and Lady Simney. That Gerard should want to part with his wife two or three glimpses of the young lady made it very possible to believe. That he should do so with a view to taking on George's widow was somewhat sudden, to say the least; nevertheless it was a rational enough scheme for a man to form. But that George and Joyleen had furthered it by posting with such celerity to an intimacy citable in a divorce court was a little startling.

And Hippias seemed to agree. 'Come, come,' he said. 'Pull yourself together, my dear boy. Poor George may have acted not quite nicely in the matter to which you refer. After all, he diddled us of Dismal Swamp, so that we knew what sort of fellow we had to deal with. But he's not yet in his grave, you know – or rather not yet in that deuced disheartening family vault. So hold off a bit, my dear chap. Plenty of time, after all. No chance of George's coming back from the grave this time, I'll be bound. And – by the way – that's just where you can help. I was telling these gentlemen – officers, that is to say – about his turning up on us again when you were a lad – time of your first riding-breeches, I think he said.'

Gerard Simney frowned impatiently. 'I was no more than a child. I scarcely remember.'

'Oh, come. You must remember a good deal. And rather a useful thing, if you ask me, to tell these – um – people from the police your own story. Independent testimony. Show I haven't been spinning them a yarn.'

It was to be observed that with Hippias the chief and myself were sinking rapidly in the social scale. Presumably this indicated that he was regaining some feeling of confidence – and indeed there was now in his eye the look of a man who sees the first thinning of the wood before him. Of this I didn't at all feel that I had the hang. . . . But now Gerard did, as he was requested, take up the tale.

'Riding-breeches I may have had, but certainly I was scarcely out of the nursery. Even there, though, it was known that our kinsman George Simney was a legend – as was his dead brother Denzell too. Long ago – indeed some years before I was born – the two of them had gone off on some queer expedition with my father here and some other men, and the result had been Denzell's death and George's going off into hiding in another part of Australia. For a time it had been believed that both brothers had died together, and then somehow my grandfather had learned about George's being alive. Something like that was the story I used to hear as a kid at Hazelwood Park.'

Inspector Cadover tapped the chair before him with a restless finger. 'May I ask if you can put a date to all this?'

'Well, I don't suppose I can have been more than eight or nine when the legendary George turned up. You may bet I stared at him! He was obviously a Simney – just as my father and grandfather were, and as I could see that I was myself. It was the first thing that made me feel the queer weight of heredity, I believe. Whether George stopped with us for long I don't remember, although it was long enough to get the information which enabled him to play the family that low trick over Dismal Swamp. He didn't feel himself on the run any longer, I believe. On the other hand I doubt whether, outside Hazelwood Park, he was yet going by his real name. George could always pick up money, it seems, and he just found it easier to be any wandering rascal than George Simney. I have a notion that we heard of him several times in an indefinite way between that last visit to us and his returning home to the baronetcy. Under one name or another I suspect there was a good deal of trouble waiting for him in various parts of Australia, but nothing against him in his own identity – or nothing serious enough to count when he had made his get-away to respectability and become a country gentleman.'

As a witness, Gerard Simney seemed to me a good deal more satisfactory than any we had encountered so far. I was prompted to put a question to him. 'And this man Owdon that George picked up in Australia,' I said. 'What do you know about him?'

'Nothing at all. There was no Owdon with him on that visit he paid us when I was a kid.' Gerard hesitated. 'One possible explanation of Owdon, however, has come into my head.'

Hippias looked up quickly. 'Explanation?' he asked. 'What do you mean by that?'

Gerard considered. 'Well, it has struck me that there is something queer in this fellow Owdon's position here. Apparently he is the father of the youth Timmy, and apparently Timmy's mother was some woman member of our family. One can't say that's not queer. And for George to keep the fellow on is queerer still. So I have a notion that Owdon may have had some hold over George.'

Hippias nodded. 'Quite so. The constable here has already mentioned some such possibility. I can't say I think much of it myself.'

'It has even occurred to me' – and Gerard glanced rather sharply at his father – 'that George's association with Owdon might go right back to that expedition on which Denzell lost his life. It may have been a more serious affair than I know of – after all, you've never told me much about it – and Owdon may have turned up on George again later and threatened disclosure. And the price of his silence may have been his butler's job.'

'But don't you think,' I asked, 'that a butler's job would be rather an odd price to ask, even if it included a chance of seducing the female members of the family? Who wants to spend his life pouring another man's wine? George was wealthy enough. A fat pension and no duties would be a much more likely demand.'

'Precisely!' Hippias spoke with emphasis. 'In fact, the blackmail theory – for that's what it amounts to – doesn't really hold water. I should judge Owdon to be a very respectable man – apart, that is to say, from the little matter of his son. Don't take me to condone fornication.'

'Respectable?' said Gerard. 'There seems to be an impression in the household that he is a retired pirate. Such a past would fit in with my suggestion well enough. But it may be a story started by the mere appearance of the man.'

'Pirate?' asked Hippias. 'Probably nothing more disreputable than a pilot. The two, you know, have been confused before now.' And in a cracked voice he began humming some stave from Gilbert and Sullivan. That was the era, I suppose, to which Hippias belongs.

Inspector Cadover had left the fire-place and was pacing slowly up and down the study. I know that prowl. It comes upon him just when he feels that a case is reaching its maximum point of complication. And certainly there was a very sufficient amount of material before us. For example, there was this young Gerard Simney. He believed that the late Sir George had achieved a sort of lightning seduction of his wife. He wanted to marry the late Sir George's widow. For all we knew so far he might have had every opportunity to climb up – or down – to the window of this room on the fatal night. In fact, he was a tip-top suspect. Ought we, then, to make a grab at him, and think about Denzell and George, and Lady Simney's Christopher Hoodless, and Hippias and Owdon, and the unaccountable boots in the safe, not now, but when we had leisure for it later on?

I looked inquiringly at the chief – and became aware that the chief had halted in his prowl and was looking at Hippias Simney thunder-struck. I think that's the right word – and certainly I had never caught Inspector Cadover with such an expression before. And now he was moving towards the door. 'Our investigations,' he said abruptly, 'will be continued tomorrow.'

It was an unexpected curtain. Shockingly puzzled, I followed him from the room.

We had to walk to the village through the darkness and the snow. He is fond of strict simplicity in matters of that sort. We walked in silence, and I'm sure the idea was that we should be thinking things out. But I have the common-place sort of mind that marches on its stomach, and I knew that no two and two would come together in it until I had despatched a decent meal. I ought therefore to have kept my mouth shut and not betrayed the fact that I wasn't revolving masterpieces of inference and deduction. But somehow I overwhelmingly wanted to ask questions – about the feather of Cuvier, for instance, although I knew it to be something I ought to look up for myself – I wanted to ask questions and peer into the chief's mind. I should have remembered that there are times when he wants to peer into mine – and that it isn't by asking questions that he does it.

I spoke into the darkness. 'What do you think, sir, of Mr Hippias Simney? It seems to me that he hasn't told us all that he knows.'

'Nobody can.'

This was not encouraging. But now I was becoming downright stupid. 'Nobody can?' I echoed.

'Nor can one tell oneself. Imagine, lad, telling yourself all you know. You could no more stand it than you could stand the pressure at the bottom of the ocean. You'd burst or crumple.'

'Yes, sir.' When the chief falls into this philosophical and psychological vein there isn't much to be said.

'Hiding from ourselves the greater part of what we know is the first tax upon such energies as we possess. We're at it even in sleep. I wonder the fellows who make you try to drink things at bedtime don't exploit that rather than the twenty-four thousand heart-beats.'

'About forty thousand, sir, if one is reckoning on eight hours' sleep or thereabouts.'

I had him there. And in the darkness I could feel him peering at me a trifle sourly. 'Sherlock Holmes,' he said, 'was among other things distinguished for this – that he guarded his memory against being burdened by useless information. As for Mr Hippias Simney, it is certainly true that he has failed to tell us all he knows. On the other hand, he has told me something he does not. Or perhaps I should say intimated. For his actual speech was singularly barren.'

'You gathered something from his manner?'

'No.'

'Neither from his speech nor his manner?'

'From neither of these.'

I felt unreasonably annoyed. After all, one's superior officer is entitled to a little mystery-mongering if it pleases him – and particularly when one has been blatantly fishing for his point of view. 'Was it something about Owdon?' I asked. 'I agree with Gerard that there is something pretty queer there.'

'It was not about Owdon. The queerness, however, I admit. Fortunately it is not, I think you will agree, a queerness of any very impenetrable sort.'

'I can't say that I see my way through it, sir.'

'You don't *see*?' Inspector Cadover had halted beside me in the darkness. 'You mean to say you don't know who this Alfred Owdon *is*?'

'No, sir. I'm afraid I don't.'

The chief moved forward again. We could now see the lights of the Simney Arms before us. When he spoke it was quite gently. 'Think of that business of the lugger and the canoes,' he said. 'Is there any real reason to suppose that only George escaped the sharks? Take it from me that Denzell got away too – and that his name has been Alfred Owdon ever since.'

9

Well, here I am in bed at the Simney Arms, and trying to think it out. I believe the chief must be right about Owdon. That he is really Denzell Simney is a hypothesis explaining a great deal.

For suppose that Denzell as well as George survived the sharks and savages during that blackbirding incident. It was Denzell whom real trouble awaited, because it was Denzell who had been identified, who had attempted to shoot one of the anthropologists, and who had actually wounded a native. Would he not, then, with a stiff prison sentence hanging over him, naturally go to ground? And, unless he was prepared to go back and face the music, would he not have to renounce his true identity for the rest of his days? That his face had suffered such shocking damage in the fracas would make this the easier, and a not inconvenient disguise would be that of his brother's man-servant.

But why, all these years later, should Denzell have been his brother's manservant *still*? Why, during a large part of his life, should he have continued to perform menial duties at Hazelwood when it might quite easily have been arranged that he should retire quietly upon some less unsuitable employment? There can be only one answer to this: the positive malice of his brother. That George had an altogether perverted sense of humour we know. It is possible then that he simply enjoyed keeping Denzell under his thumb, and that he made the continuation of these butler's offices a condition of silence. This was a state of affairs as queer as it was ugly, but it is possible enough.

And now to test the hypothesis more fully. There seems to be a general opinion at Hazelwood that Owdon is a stupid man, and yet scrutiny belies this impression. Now, if a man is a gentleman, and yet obliged to live as a servant in the house of his ancestors, it seems to me that he will be very likely to take refuge in a feigned dullness. This would always give him time to think. And how often, at least at first, Denzell Simney would stand in need of that! In time the unhappy man learnt to play his part well. His accent, for instance, is not such as would betray him. It is only his turns of expression that are occasionally not in the part. Thinking back, I can see that this is what first put the chief on the scent. 'Really, I have no idea,' the butler replied to some question of his – and, of course, when you test it on the ear, it is indefinably not a manservant's way of speaking. Indeed, I am aware now that I detected something of the same thing myself only a few minutes earlier; and I think it likely that this alien cadence must have been heard by others from time to time.

Then there is Timmy. Timmy is plainly a Simney – is the split image of Mervyn Cockayne – and this is possibly because his mother was a Simney, but quite definitely because his father the butler is one too! Does the lad know anything of this? Almost certainly not. I have an inkling that he may suspect *something* unknown in his paternity (considering Sir George's moral character, for instance, he may well wonder whether it doesn't, perhaps, lie in that quarter); but I am pretty sure he has no notion that the Hazelwood butler is a Simney too.

And so I come to the arrival of the Australians on the scene. What knowledge did they bring with them, and what knowledge did they gain on the night before Sir George's death?

The younger of them – Gerard and his wife Joyleen – almost certainly knew nothing. And, almost equally certainly, they have learnt nothing either. But Hippias is different. He knew Denzell intimately as a young man and even if (as I think likely) he really believed that Denzell had been killed years ago, it is not at all unlikely that he penetrated to the true state of affairs shortly after his arrival. Denzell himself – or Owdon, as it is perhaps less confusing to call him – may well have been apprehensive of this from the moment the Australians appeared on the doorstep – and there is, of course, a good deal of evidence that the butler was, in fact, badly shaken. Discovery after all these years might well dismay him, for it is evident that Hippias is the sort of man who would unhesitatingly exploit such a scandal for his own ends. At an ugly word from the visitor Owdon might very conceivably drop a tray of glasses, and in a moment of panic he might well drop his suit-cases in preparation for a bolt. All this fits together well enough.

But there is evidence that Sir George no less than his butler was disconcerted by some turn of events following the Australians' arrival, and that the danger he appre-hended was something much more immediate than any trouble which might be raised over the old affair of Dismal Swamp. Well, this seems to fit together not badly too. To be exposed as one who was due for a prison sentence in Australia many years ago would be unpleasant for Denzell. But to be discovered as one who had kept his younger brother in a sort of grotesque thrall would be almost equally awkward for the baronet. No wonder Sir George was a little at a stand! And no wonder, too, that the whole situation should lead to the obscure quarrel and bottle-throwing which Lady Simney witnessed in the study.

So far, so good. The initial hypothesis explains a lot. But does it explain the death of Sir George Simney – or go any way towards explaining that?

I can't see that it does. But here the chief's technique may help me out. Never, he says, try to answer the big questions till you have dealt with as many as possible of the small ones. Very well. Take the boots.

This of Owdon's being in fact Denzell Simney is a fam-ily secret. Family secrets – or the material evidences of them – often live in safes. And in Sir George's safe was a pair of boots. Could they conceivably be evidence – evidence against Denzell – in the matter of that blackbirding adventure long ago? It seems impossible that it should be so. If George, out of a nasty itch for power, had really been holding the thing over his younger brother, material evidences would be unimportant. For mere word to the police that here was a man wanted in Australia for a long-past crime would be sufficient to set going an investigation that would inevitably result in the establishing of the truth. Documents there might be – ship's papers, perhaps, or a confession signed by Denzell years before. But how a pair of boots (whether used for gardening and cycling or not) could enter into such a business I just don't see.

Here then is one matter that the hypothesis sheds no light on. Is there any other important area of the case that it leaves equally unilluminated? I believe there is.

For what of Lady Simney and her former fiancé, the young anthropologist Christopher Hoodless? That Owdon is really Denzell, or that Owdon is really the Lord High Executioner, would surely be discoveries almost equally irrelevant to the immediate marital situation at Hazelwood. And yet we have to cope with this fact: that the mysterious death of Sir George Simney followed hard upon two events. These are (1) the arrival of the Australians at Hazelwood and (2) the arrival of Christopher Hoodless in the neighbourhood, or at least in England. Perhaps the second of these circumstances is the more striking of the two. For it seems to have been only a matter of minutes after Lady Simney learnt from *The Times* that Hoodless was in England (and perhaps realized that it was to Hoodless that her husband had referred when he claimed to 'have seen her lover') that Sir George died. I can see that nothing of the significance of this has been lost on the chief, and that he has his eye on Nicolette Simney still. But it is a line of thought that takes us right away from the Owdon-Denzell approach. And indeed the tentative conclusion to which I am persuaded is this: that either one or other of those arrivals – the Australians' and Hoodless's – is coincidental. If one of them was operative in the fatality then the other is out of it, or if not out of it has certainly only a very subsidiary significance.

But here on a little reflection I see the possibility of end-less complications, and I doubt the wisdom of tackling them after much cold beef and beer, and at this last hour of the night. Still, one speculation I will jot down.

Suppose that Lady Simney had been driven beyond all bearing by her husband. Hoodless is returning and she sud-denly feels desperation come upon her. Of course there is difficulty here. A man so immoral as Sir George it would not been hard to rid oneself of in the Divorce Court – and indeed it isn't easy to see why Lady Simney didn't go about matters in that way long ago. But pass that by. Here is Hoodless returning, and at the prospect, this tor-mented lady's control snaps. What relevance might the return of the Australians have here?

One possibility is this: that Lady Simney learnt from Hippias, or perhaps even from Owdon himself, the story of her husband's dastardly dealing with his younger brother. Might this not be the last straw, so that she felt that of such a blackguard it was legitimate to be rid in any way? Moreover the arrival of the Australian cousins had brought more than commonly violent times to Hazelwood. There was bad blood over Dismal Swamp; there was a row in the very room in which Sir George was later to meet his death. Might not the lady, if sufficiently steeled to crime, regard these circumstances as likely to provide a useful element of confusion and complication? To leave the whole detestable crew of Simneys under the embarrassment of suspected murder: there might, to one stirred up to suffi-ciently ferocious feeling, be a good deal of satisfaction in that.

And yet that Nicolette Simney herself killed Sir George seems virtually impossible. There is no getting past Owdon's evidence of the empty room and empty window-embrasure – or none unless we regard him (and this, of course, is by no means ruled out) as a confederate in the crime. How then could Lady Simney succeed in attacking her husband? Only by lowering herself from her bath-room window, making her way along the terrace and climbing the trellis. But the snow on that vital stretch of terrace showed no footprints. I know that the chief in his own mind has been chewing savagely at this. He thought he had found something when he noticed that the trellis outside the study window provides a way down from the next storey as well as up from the ground. But up from the ground somebody certainly did come. Moreover from Lady Simney's bathroom there appears to be no means by which she could have gained an upper storey without coming out into the corridor and making herself visible to Owdon. The possibility of her getting down to the terrace is a different matter: a couple of lengths of the oil-silk round the shower would enable an active women to make the descent easily. And Lady Simney is accustomed to athletics, as the hockeysticks and skis in her room show. Still, the evidence of the printless snow is irrefutable. And so, I am pretty sure, is the evidence of the invisible clock which controls the affair. Between the moment of Sir George's death, and the moment of Owdon's seeing her emerge from the bath-room, the return trip by trellis, terrace and oil-silk would be impossible. Again, there is Mervyn Cockayne's scuffle with an unknown man. I believe that the chief had a good idea here, and suspected that Lady Simney took the precaution of slipping on male attire – and that here we had the explanation of the clothes which she declares belong to Hoodless. It would be rather amusing if young Cockayne's new opinion of himself as a fighter were the result of a drawn battle with a woman. But the whole notion doesn't take us far. Lady Simney, I think, cannot be fitted into the fatality except in terms of a conspiracy of which she was a member. And anything of that sort I find it hard to believe.

What happened at Hazelwood? It begins to look as if we shall have precious little to say at the inquest. And yet

I have a notion that the chief has got somewhere, or at least that he has seen or senses something that may get him there at any time. One day, and on some case, I shall be there before him. But not, I am afraid, in the Simney affair!

10

A couple of days have passed, my dear Dad, and we have not been standing still. A good deal has changed, including the weather. On our first night in this pub there was a thaw. Everything dripped and squelched; the village and the park and the great house all looked pretty drear – and it was in this rather depressing atmosphere that we were visited at the breakfast-table by the local vicar. He brought us a theory of the case – as also one or two facts that he didn't mean to bring at all. And for bagging these I really get the credit myself, as you will hear.

Mr Deamer was extremely excited. We found it hard to decide whether this was exceptional, or whether he is chronically so. But if I believed the things he believes, I am pretty sure I should be in a great fuss all the time. He appears to regard Hazelwood and an area of some five miles round as labouring beyond all other localities under the divine malediction, and himself as a sort of solitary Abdiel among the faithless. I don't know that I would myself have chosen Mr Deamer to hold such a key position. To cope with the Devil (and it is the Devil himself whom he regards as conducting operations from the neighbourhood of the Hall) I fancy that judgement as well as zeal would be desirable. And I doubt if Mr Deamer has that. Indeed, his call upon us was an error of judgment, if you ask me.

'Good morning,' said Mr Deamer. 'May I take it that you are the police-officers sent down to investigate the grievous scandals and iniquities rife at Hazelwood Hall?'

Inspector Cadover nodded. 'We are inquiring into the

violent death of Sir George Simney. I suppose that ranks as a scandal, sir, and perhaps as an iniquity too.'

Somewhat surprisingly, Mr Deamer shook his head. 'No,' he said, 'I don't think so. Sir George's life was both scandalous and iniquitous. And so, too, I have much reason to believe, are the lives of his wife and most of his relations. But his death must be otherwise regarded.' Mr Deamer paused and looked from one to the other of us with what was at once a wild and wary eye. 'Do I understand,' he asked, 'that there was a *body*?'

'Well, sir, there is to be an inquest. And I never heard of an inquest without a body – or a substantial part of one – yet.'

Mr Deamer frowned. 'Sir George Simney,' he said matter-of-factly, 'had bartered his soul to the Devil. In such cases it is unusual – altogether unusual – that there should be a body. The Devil appears at midnight, claims his own, and there is an immediate and corporeal transfer to the infernal regions.'

'Dear me!' The chief looked genuinely surprised. 'May I ask whether, in your view, many persons barter their souls to the Devil in these days?'

'Most assuredly.'

'Then surely there ought quite often to be no body? And yet one never reads or hears of such a thing from year's end to year's end.'

But Mr Deamer was by no means put to a stand. 'Every day,' he asked, 'do you not hear of persons disappearing from their home and never being seen again? These are all cases in point. A bargain has been made and the Devil has appeared to claim it. Close investigation would commonly reveal a slight smell of sulphur and brimstone at the scene of the disappearance.' Mr Deamer frowned. 'Though to be candid with you I am not quite clear about the brimstone. It is certainly something extremely unpleasant, but I cannot be confident that it gives off an odour. On the sulphur, however, I am perfectly assured.'

Inspector Cadover listened very patiently to this. I could see that for some reason he had considerable hopes of our eccentric visitor. 'What you tell us of an infernal bargain,' he said gravely, 'is very interesting indeed. I wonder if you would detail your grounds for believing in it? And may we offer you a cup of coffee?'

Mr Deamer accepted the coffee, sipped it, and appeared to go off into a brown study. Presently his lips moved. '*Sweet Helen*,' he murmured in a strange voice, '– *Sweet Helen, make me immortal with a kiss.*'

Well, I followed that one. It is what Faust says in the old play when the Devil to whom he has sold himself raises up for him Helen of Troy. And later in the play, of course, there is what Mr Deamer would call an immediate and corporeal transfer of Faust to the infernal regions. 'Do you mean,' I asked, 'that Sir George had made a bargain with the Devil to secure him various remote and impossible mistresses – paramours?'

'Yes!' Mr Deamer was suddenly violent. 'It was precisely that. It can have been nothing else. And the wretched man was snatched to his doom on the very threshold of just such an illicit enjoyment.'

It was thoroughly queer. The intensity with which the vicar of Hazelwood desired to convince himself of this tall story was as queer as anything I have ever met. And suddenly he asked a question – one altogether irrelevant to the line he had been pursuing. 'How did he die?' he demanded. 'You say there was a body. How was Simney killed?' And this fanatical clergyman glared at us with sweat pouring down his forehead.

But the chief was suddenly uncommunicative. 'I don't know about remote and impossible mistresses being summoned by the Devil,' he said. 'But perfectly ordinary ones could very well be summoned by Sir George himself up that trellis. It might well have been put there to provide him with amatory amusement without the necessity of stirring his stumps. Always provided, of course, that the mistresses were willing to present themselves. Now suppose, Mr Deamer, that there was something like that. Sir George was proposing to keep a tryst in his study with some little wanton from the neighbourhood. And some other interested party intervened and killed Sir George on the spot. That is pretty well your own story put into naturalistic terms. Does it satisfy you?'

It was at this moment that I found a question of my own to address to Mr Deamer. I had happened to walk over to the window and notice, leaning against a bench outside, an old bicycle with a decidedly rusty chain. I turned back and glanced at Mr Deamer. He was a shabby little man, plainly disregardful of both comfort and appearance. 'I think, sir,' I said, 'that you are fond of gardening?' He stared in surprise, as he well might do at so inconsequent a question. And then I risked my long shot. 'Perhaps you will tell us how you came to leave a pair of boots at the Hall on the very night that Sir George Simney was killed?'

If the Devil himself had at that moment appeared in the coffee-room of the Simney Arms and beckoned to Mr Deamer with a sinister 'Hither to me' I doubt whether the reverend gentleman would have been more upset.

'Boots?' he stammered. 'A pair of boots?'

'Certainly – and fairly new ones too. As a result of losing them you have had to put on a thoroughly well-worn pair today.'

Mr Deamer looked down at his feet, and then with his wildest glance round the room. He was engaged, I thought, in some rapid calculation – something to which persons unfortunate enough to become involved in criminal investigation are not infrequently reduced. But I had an obscure feeling that these particular calculations were something out of the way. Perhaps Mr Deamer was estimating just how much of the Hither-to-me business people so profane as ourselves would accept. It was as if, in terms of the supernatural, he had a thoroughly tall story to tell, but was rather daunted by the prospect of our blank incredulity. Perhaps he was subject to hallucinations, and really believed that the powers of darkness had robbed him of his boots as a preparatory step to providing him with cloven hooves. Be this as it may, Mr Deamer abruptly descended to a sublunary view of the matter.

'Yes, of course,' he said. 'My boots. I left them at Hazelwood.'

The chief scratched his chin, thereby indicating that it was still my ball.

'Quite so,' I pursued. 'But will you tell me how you came to leave them in Sir George's study upon the very night upon which he was killed?'

'I was tricked!' The vicar of Hazelwood was vehement. 'I was tricked by –' He hesitated and peered uncertainly into his coffee-cup.

'Perhaps by the Devil?'

'W ll – yes. Mr Deamer was almost apologetic. 'I see that I had better not obtrude upon you a point of view which you are unlikely to accept. But I am afraid it *was* the Devil. At the time, I understood it to be Miss Grace Simney.'

'You thought Miss Simney had taken your boots?'

'Dear me, no. How confusing this is! I thought it was Miss Simney who spoke to me on the telephone. She is a most devout lady and one of my truly valued parishioners. Again and again she has given information invaluable to me in my ceaseless struggles to curb the terrible immoralities and depravities which here surround us.'

'You mean that she is a great hand at smelling things out?'

'It might be put in that way. For example, she was the first to discover that both Sir George and his nephew Willoughby were intent upon seducing the blacksmith's daughter.'

'You are sure that Mr Willoughby was not intent merely upon painting her?'

Mr Deamer frowned. 'It is virtually the same thing, is it not? And, again, there is the shocking *liaison* between Lady Simney and the young man from Australia – Gerard. It was Miss Grace who immediately brought me word of that. I am very well aware that there are maiden ladies who imagine such things. But Miss Grace has always been most reliable. So when on Tuesday evening she rang up and told me of this assignation which Sir George had made with Jane Fairey –'

'Jane Fairey?'

'The blacksmith's daughter, of course! She was to climb the trellis to Sir George's study just after eleven o'clock.'

'*Eleven* o'clock?' Inspector Cadover broke in. 'The voice on the telephone said that?'

'Yes. I was greatly shocked. And I fell in with the suggestion which the D –, which the voice made, that I should keep watch and surprise the wretched girl in her intention.'

I looked at Mr Deamer with some compassion. Despite his cycling and his gardening he was a miserable wisp of a man, tormented by heaven knows what obscure fires within. 'Rather a chilly job,' I said.

'It was very cold. I stood for a long time on the terrace and nothing happened. Sometimes' – Mr Deamer hesitated – 'I felt rather ridiculous. Various images kept coming into my mind. Mr Pickwick, for instance, when he was tricked into keeping a not dissimilar vigil in the garden of a girls' school.'

The chief chuckled – but not unkindly. This, indeed, was the first human gleam we had had from our reverend visitor.

'But then there were other images too. I became convinced that I had arrived too late, and that if I wished to tax the unhappy Jane with her abominable fornication I must wait until – until –'

'Quite so,' said the chief.

'And at that a very strange urge came upon me. I must know the worst.'

'Ah,' said the chief.

'It was very dark all around. And in my mind were vivid and shocking fantasies. I determined to climb to the study and – and investigate.'

'Your impulse,' said the chief gravely, 'was not altogether out of the way.'

'But I was apprehensive of making a noise, and I distrusted myself on that trellis. I therefore removed my boots and knotted them round my neck. Doubtless it would have been more sensible to leave them on the terrace. But I was obscurely distrustful.'

'The distrustfulness,' said the chief, 'I discerned. But it was my colleague who discerned the gardening.'

Mr Deamer looked at us helplessly. 'The trellis turned out to offer no difficulty and within a minute I found myself in a window-embrasure, heavily curtained. I peered into the room. There was low light, sufficient to show me that the place was deserted.' Mr Deamer made a long pause. 'And at that,' he said in a strangled voice, 'the horror of of what I was doing came upon me.'

'Horror?' asked Inspector Cadover mildly.

'I searched my heart. And it was impure. I believed that I had come to combat sin. But I had a horrible feeling that I had really come to – to peer at it.'

The chief nodded. 'It was a situation,' he said soothingly, 'in which your judgement would naturally be strained, Mr Deamer.'

For some moments the vicar was silent. I would have said, at a guess, that he was wrestling with his conscience. But whether retroactively, so to speak, and in the matter of the peering, or whether because at this point he felt it necessary to tell us something rather less or other than the truth, it was impossible to say.

'I was horrified. My one impulse was to get down again and away. I turned and groped for the window, and as I did so the boots must have slipped from my neck. As I climbed down I was trembling all over, and when I reached the terrace I believe I went into some sort of faint or coma. When I recovered myself – and it may have been considerably later – I was still feeling very weak. And it was then, and as I was beginning to slip away from the terrace, that somebody jumped on me from behind. I found myself engaged in something like a bout of fisticuffs.'

'Had you any idea, Mr Deamer, who your assailant was?'

'None whatever. It was a mere confused scuffle in the dark. And presently I broke away and made my escape across the park.'

So here, I thought, was the antagonist a drawn fight with whom had so raised the confidence of Mervyn Cockayne! But then a more important reflection struck me. If the vicar's story was true – and I was pretty sure that a good part of it was – we were more badly off then ever for footprints in the snow. What, for instance, of Jane Fairey, the blacksmith's daughter? Either she had been transported to Sir George's study by demons through the middle air (and this, it seemed, was not a view that Mr Deamer himself would find it hard to swallow) or the whole story of the assignation was no more than a hoax. The latter was almost certainly the true explanation. It was possible, of course, that Miss Grace Simney had really telephoned and that her information had been at fault. But if this were so why had she not already come forward with facts so obviously relevant to her brother's end? It was far more likely that somebody had played a trick – a Pickwickian trick – on Mr Deamer, whose zeal in the pursuit of sexual irregularities must be very generally known. Jane Fairey's footprints, then, we had no need to sigh for.

But with *some* others we could certainly do. Deamer had come across the park, and his tracks had been clearly visible. He had climbed the trellis, peered, impinged in no other way upon the Hazelwood affair, climbed down, fainted or lurked, scuffled with young Cockayne and made off again – the tracks of what must have been his stockinged feet obscurely visible for a little way. And to this there were only Cockayne's own footprints to add. What, then, of the person who *had* impinged upon Hazelwood – and most fatally for its owner? On him – or her – there seemed to be only one possible conclusion. He had reached the study not by climbing up the trellis but by climbing *down*.

And now suppose that Mr Deamer was indeed what he professed to be: a side-show as far as the death of Sir George Simney was concerned. Suppose the bringing him to intercept Jane Fairey was a hoax. Could it be a *pure* hoax in the sense of being wholly unconnected with the fatal business of that night? Already the Hazelwood affair was pretty heavily burdened with coincidence; was it conceivable that this of Mr Deamer's vigil had nothing to do with the case? It was difficult to believe that it could be so. In what way then could the unfortunate man's fool's-errand have formed part of some other person's plan? He had been persuaded to come to the terrace and lurk beneath the study window something under an hour before Sir George died – before it was planned that Sir George should die. And – since the errand was indeed a fool's one – there would be a fair expectation that after some twenty minutes or half-an-hour of fruitless waiting he would withdraw.

Had he been brought to the terrace to seal, as it were, that particular approach, even as the butler, working in the corridor, sealed the approach from the house? It was a conceivable notion but scarcely a satisfactory one, since the probability was that after so chilly a vigil the vicar would have taken himself off again somewhat before the vital hour.

What other explanation, then, could there be? Suddenly, and as I stared at Mr Deamer's old boots, the answer came. The unfortunate man had been coaxed or conjured to Hazelwood and to that very spot on the terrace simply for the sake of the footprints he would leave in the snow. Sir George's assailant was to come from within the house, and from *above*. The coming and going of Mr Deamer was to suggest that the murderer had come from without, and from *below*.

But who put Mr Deamer's boots in Sir George Simney's safe? And why?

I doubt whether I should at all quickly have found any answer to this. But now my speculations were interrupted by the chief. He had no doubt got quite as far as I had, and his next question to our visitor was a cast back to earlier matters.

'Mr Deamer,' he said, 'I suppose it has occurred to you that Jane Fairey may really have been before her hour, and that by the time you looked into the study she and Sir George had – um – withdrawn to another apartment?'

The vicar received this warily, and I had a strong feeling that he suspected a trap.

'Yes,' he said at length. 'It is a reflection which I was bound to make.'

'Jane Fairey is a personable girl?'

'Most certainly. Her figure –' Mr Deamer checked himself. 'A good-looking girl, no doubt.'

'Such a girl would have followers, admirers, in the village? Yes? Very well. Might not one of these have detected her keeping this assignation with the squire, followed her up the trellis and concealed himself somewhere in the house?'

'It seems likely enough.'

'And then killed Sir George?'

The vicar shifted uneasily in his chair. He was without all the information which we possessed, and he was without the habit of putting such information together. He could therefore not know the difficulties this view presented. 'Yes,' he said reluctantly. 'There seems much in what you say.'

'Then, Mr Deamer, why drag in the Devil? Sir George, you declared, was carried off by the Devil when about to achieve some illicit sexual enjoyment conjured up for him by black magic. Is that sort of thing merely a fixed idea in your mind, or have you some particular ground for alleging it in this instance?'

Mr Deamer licked his lips – which were bloodless, thin and chapped. He looked round the coffee-room and fixed his eye on a steel engraving which represented (I think) Oliver Cromwell dictating a dispatch to John Milton. Then, as if there were no inspiration in this, he transferred his glance first to one and then to another more than indifferent sporting print. "It is a fixed idea,' he said in a low voice. 'Nothing more than that. My struggles against vice in this parish have been very terrible. And perhaps I am now more than a little mad. More than once I have suspected myself of being subject to hallucinations. And yet –'

'Yes, Mr Deamer?'

But the vicar of Hazelwood was soundlessly weeping. Police work has its abominable moments, without a doubt.

II

For what it was worth, we interviewed Jane Fairey. She was very composedly posed for Willoughby Simney in a room behind her father's smithy. Her figure might be described as nubile (ask auntie Flo that one) and Willoughby had persuaded her to expose rather more of it than was altogether proper in one who was not a model by profession. But I don't think that this young man dabbles in paints to any fleshly end. Whether he has real promise as a painter I have, of course, no idea. But he was genuinely absorbed in the job he was about. The sky was leaden – perhaps with a promise of fresh snow – and a dull diffused light came from the window. Through an open door flickered a red glow from Mr Fairey's forge; it played on Jane's shoulders; and I don't doubt that the result was sufficiently complex to tax whatever technique Willoughby had.

This interview, or double interview, was entirely the chief's. And it taxed his technique too.

'It must be a great adventure to you, Mr Simney,' he said, smoothly, 'to have so fine a collection of Old Masters at the Hall. There must be any amount of inspiration in that.'

Willoughby was gazing intently at what I took to be the lobe of Jane's left ear. 'Would you mind,' he asked civilly, 'going to hell out of here?'

This might be described as a straight drive to the off. But the chief fielded it smartly. 'That,' he said, 'is how your vicar regards the death of your uncle. Sir George went to hell out of here – and in the most literal way. Mr Deamer is reluctant to believe there was a body. He supposes that the only appropriate end for Sir George was to be hoisted on the back of the Devil himself and disappear through a trap. But then I suppose Mr Deamer is a little mad.'

'Mad? Nothing of the sort.' Willoughby held out a brush and appeared to measure Miss Fairey's nose. 'Wretched little man is as sane as you are.'

'Is that so, now?' The chief looked uncommonly thoughtful.

'Deamer seldom sees smoke where there's no fire. But of course this parish is pretty well fire all over. Ask Jane.'

Miss Fairey, whose fine eyes had rounded as the chief delivered himself of Mr Deamer's opinion, hitched her shift a little higher, thought better of this and let it drop again, giggled, and assumed an expression of inscrutable charm.

'Jane is very close.' Willoughby was scraping at his palette. 'To you she looks like an advertisement for soap. To me she is a girl the curve of whose chin is oddly repeated in the curve of her breast. That's why she's undressed, more or less. But it is the advertisements and the movies, and not life, that have taught her to look wanton. Jane is a good girl, and easily repelled the advances of the bad baronet. Just badger her a little, Inspector, would you? I want her sulky and not smeared with soap-box glamour.'

Miss Fairey understood enough of this to look sulky without further urging.

'All manner of lads have been after Jane,' Willoughby pursued. 'My late uncle wasn't even leading the field. Was he, Jane?'

'That 'e were not.'

These were the first words that Miss Fairey had spoken. There was no mistaking their conviction, and they settled the trellis-business for good and all. This girl had never climbed, nor thought to climb, to Sir George Simney's room. From that particular satyr the nymph had fled – nor had ever stumbled or cast a look behind. And this was enough for us. Whether Jane was indeed a good girl concerned us not at all. I am inclined to give her the benefit of the doubt.

Mr Deamer's telephone message, then, had been assuredly either mistaken or bogus – and ten to one it was the latter. But who, it occurred to me to ask myself, could sufficiently simulate Miss Grace Simney's familiar warning voice to carry conviction over the wire? With a shock I realized how strong was the pointer here. Lady Simney, a professional actress, was by far the likeliest suspect. No doubt her sister-in-law, Mrs Cockayne, was a possibility, as were Mrs Gerard Simney and various maidservants at present unknown. But none of these could have been so sure of success as the appealing Nicolette.

But the chief, as usual, was before me here. He had sat down, noticed that he cast a shadow on Jane's shoulders, thoughtfully shifted his position, and was now easily filling a pipe. 'Lady Simney, now,' he said. 'I wonder if she could be called a mischievous woman?' He turned to Willoughby. 'For instance, when young Cockayne was dropped through the window – would that appeal to her sense of fun?'

Willoughby hesitated. 'I'm damned,' he said, 'if I see why we should sit chattering about Nicolette. But she was certainly not amused. She loathes anything in the nature of a practical joke. And quite right too.'

'Can you imagine her playing rather a cruel trick on Mr Deamer?'

'Good heavens, no! Deamer dislikes her in rather an open way. But that only makes her act the perfect lady.'

'*Happen I can!*'

We swung round, startled. It was Jane Fairey who had uttered this vehement affirmation.

'After Tuesday morning I can! Didn't even treat her like dirt, he didn't. You'd notice dirt, and give yourself a shake to be rid on't. But he just looked through her when she called good morning to him.'

Inspector Cadover regarded the girl gravely. 'You mean that Mr Deamer cut Lady Simney dead?'

'Yes, did 'e – the little beast. I were standing at smithy door there and saw it myself. Mr Deamer 'e be talking to Miss Simney – Miss Grace, that is – by lich gate. And Lady Simney she passed by and called good morning to him. And Mr Deamer did nout but put his lips together and look straight through her.' Miss Fairey tossed her head. 'I'd play any cruel trick on man who did that to me.' She hesitated and looked sly. 'Though I won't say as her ladyship was up to any good that morning, either.'

'Jane,' said Willoughby, 'shut your dirty little mouth, my dear.' He picked out another brush. 'I'm not making a talkie, praise heaven.'

'I'm afraid,' said the chief, 'that Miss Fairey must continue to talk. If she doesn't do it now she must do it later.'

Jane stood up, grabbed at her shift just in time, and sat down on the table. 'Her ladyship's a good sort,' she said. 'But terrible hard, I'll say. Were she not an actress before she caught squire?'

Willoughby flung down his palette. 'Very well,' he said. 'Let's wallow.'

'Playing hide-and-seek in the park, she be, with two men at once. And then squire slapped her face for it.'

The chief nodded. 'We know he did that,' he said quietly.

'But am I to understand that you spent the morning following Lady Simney and spying on her?'

Jane Fairey nodded emphatically. 'Happen I often do,' she said. 'I do think she be a lovely lady.'

'I see.'

I rather think I saw too. Jane's mental age was round about eight, and a fascinated shadowing and watching was quite in the rural picture. I wondered if Lady Simney herself was at all aware of what rustic curiosity might achieve.

'The way she looked when Mr Deamer did that to her frightened me. I thought she were going to cry. I wanted to see her cry. So I followed without her a-knowing of it. And for a time she went dodging about as if she didn't know or care where she be going to. It be then that I saw there were a gentleman after her – the young Australian gentleman from Hall. He were a-prowling and not knowing whether to come up on her.'

Inspector Cadover frowned. 'And was Lady Simney aware of this?'

Jane Fairey paused to think. Once launched as a witness, she seemed likely to prove a fairly reliable one. 'I be sure she was. But she seemed just not to attend. Leading him on, she would be. As to whether she was really aware of the other gentleman I wouldn't like to say. Tall he was, and he just stood behind an oak tree on a rise and watched her.'

'Have you ever seen this tall gentleman before?'

Jane shook her head. 'Never!' she said. 'But I got close to him once and happen I should know him again. He were a lovely gentleman.'

Willoughby Simney uttered an exclamation of impatience and disgust, 'A lovely gentleman,' he said, 'peering at a lovely lady through a shrubbery. And my lovely but imbecile Jane peering at both of them. Good lord!'

'And then he did go off – the tall stranger. And I didn't see him again until he came from behind Sir Basil's Folly when it be all over.'

The chief looked absently at Willoughby's canvas. 'When what was all over, my good girl?'

Jane Fairey gathered her garments about her, evidently for good. 'What did happen there,' she said.

'Um. So you know about that too.'

'I can put two and two together like.'

Willoughby gave a sort of disgusted guffaw. 'Wallow, wallow, wallow,' he said.

'Now, don't you know you were talking nonsense' – the chief was severe – 'when you spoke of Lady Simney as playing hide-and-seek?'

Jane nodded sulkily. 'Happen I was.'

'The facts, were they not, were these. Lady Simney was simply taking a walk in the park; the Australian gentleman wanted to join her but was shy about doing so; and there was a stranger watching her unobserved who presently went away and – well – investigated the Folly?'

'That would be it.'

'And later the stranger emerged from behind the building in time to see Sir George strike his wife and ride away with a lady? Now please be very careful about this. Did Lady Simney see the stranger?'

'I be sure she did not. She did know there be somebody there, I think. But she did nout but walk fast away towards the Hall. And the stranger did start to follow her and then turned and went off in other direction. That be whole thing.'

Inspector Cadover nodded grimly. 'For one morning,' he said, 'I would call it quite enough. Did you see what the stranger looked like after that blow?'

'Yes,' said Jane. ''E did look like death. Somebody's death.'

12

We left the smithy – and Willoughby endeavouring to persuade Jane to undress again – and made our way past the Simney Arms and on to the only other inn in the village, the Green Cow. I had a fair idea of what Inspector Cadover was looking for. But my own mind wasn't running ahead. I was continuing to puzzle over the telephone call that decoyed Mr Deamer – and no doubt I was doing this because I wanted an explanation that would let Lady Simney out.

It wasn't easy to find. That the call had been made without any genuine belief that Jane proposed to visit the Hall I was now convinced. That it had been an ingenious trick to produce the appearance of a malefactor coming and going in the snow was pretty well a certainty too. And from this there followed the inescapable inference that Sir George Simney's death had been plotted by an inmate of the Hall who proposed to descend the trellis to the study from an upper storey.

But who could feign Miss Grace Simney's voice? Almost certainly not a man – unless (it suddenly occurred to me) conceivably Mervyn Cockayne. For this queer kid talks more often than not in an affected falsetto over which he has considerable control. It may well be that one of his private amusements has been mimicking his female relations, and that this accomplishment he exploited on Tuesday evening to a thoroughly sinister end. There was a loophole for Nicolette there. And then another loophole occurred to me. Timmy Owdon (if he was properly to be called that) is also in some ways a mimic – Mervyn's mimic. He speaks like a gentleman, and I imagine it is Mervyn he has copied. So he may have copied this particular ability too ... Even as I worked this out I saw that it was pretty feeble. The evidence, I acknowledge to myself, points back at Lady Simney every time.

We walked through slush, and all the eves were dripping. The chief paused to observe the behaviour of a robin, rather as if he were a Conservative statesman taking the air in St James's Park. Then he led the way into the Green Cow. A melancholy woman was polishing – or rather smearing – glasses in the bar. The chief nodded to her curtly. 'Is Mr Hoodless in the inn?' he asked.

'I am Mr Hoodless.'

We turned round to see a tall and uncommonly handsome man sitting on a settle near the door. There was a walking-stick in his hand. He had been idly tracing queer barbaric patterns on the sanded floor.

He bent down again, completed some intricate design, and added a spear-like flourish directed towards Inspector Cadover. 'You wouldn't recover from that one,' he said quietly.

The chief peered. 'It looks harmless enough, Mr Hoodless.'

'No doubt. But the power of such things over the human mind can be irresistible. If you stepped out one morning and found this pointing at your hut you would be dead before sunset.'

'Dear me! It must simplify homicide immensely.'

'But then among the people from whom I have come all deaths are homicide. The concept of natural death is unknown, or ignored. No man dies except by another's malevolence. Suppose that I go hunting, slip on a river-bank and am eaten by a crocodile. My friends will at once meet to decide whose magic has prompted the brute to make a snack of me. They are like' – and Christopher Hoodless smiled wearily – 'a conference of detectives. But it is only after they have decided on the guilty party that they begin to look for the clues.'

The chief frowned. 'Preposterous,' he said briefly.

'To our way of thinking, yes. But what is a clue? A cigarette-end or a couple of hairs left behind by the criminal. To the savage mind such things are instruments of power. Secure them, and you can work some counter-magic against their owner.'

'Like making a wax image,' I suggested, 'and sticking pins in it.'

'Precisely so. Absurd, is it not? And yet you will find that such queer culture-constructs often continue to exist disguised in our own society. Do you happen to know any detectives?' And Hoodless glanced with good-humoured irony from one to the other of us. But he was not really entertained, though apparently resolved to be entertaining. He struck me as a tired man.

'As you know,' said the chief, 'we are both detective-officers from Scotland Yard.'

'Witch-doctors indeed!' With a swirling motion of the ferrule of his stick Hoodless obliterated the pattern he had been tracing. 'Well now, the theory of criminology is this: you don't know your man, you hunt for clues, find them, and they lead to the guilty person. But as often as not you *do* know your man, and then you look for clues to get power over him.'

'Or her,' said the chief.

Hoodless knitted his brows and stared at the floor. Then he continued, apparently unheeding. 'With you, that power passes by the name of evidence, or proof. But the magical basis of your behaviour persists. Material traces of your enemy – a hair, a scrap of clothing – are essential to you. And what follows from this? An absurd over-estimate of the importance of such bits of rubbish for scientific criminal investigation.'

'Appleby used to say that,' I said.

'Bother Appleby.' But the chief was looking interested. 'There may be something in it, all the same. And would you say the business of believing all deaths to be homicide has left traces too?'

'I dare say it has. When we don't find sufficient colour-able murdering in real life we turn to fiction and feed our instinct that way. And, no doubt, the police are constantly seeing deaths by misadventure as more sinister than they naturally are.'

'Um. And would you be inclined to say that we see Sir George Simney's death in too sinister a light?'

Christopher Hoodless rose and glanced round the bar. 'I think,' he said, 'that we might go for a bit of a tramp?'

We tramped the park. The thaw continued. Every bough dripped and on the ground patches of grass and bare earth showed through.

'Snow,' said Hoodless. 'If I were going to kill myself and convince the police that a murder had occurred I should regard as one of my first essentials snow – with footprints suitably disposed. Footprints approaching me and footprints leaving me: what could be more irresistible to the professional mind?'

Inspector Cadover breathed heavily. 'You may not know,' he said, 'that Sir George's skull was crushed by a violent blow from behind. That such an injury should be self-inflicted is sheerly impossible.'

'From behind?' Hoodless lengthened his stride. 'Look at the kestrel.'

I caught something queer in his voice – it might have been both mockery and relief – and glanced at him. His shoulders had squared and the tired look was gone. And something prompted me to speak – though I didn't at all know how the chief would take it.

'I think you wanted information, Mr Hoodless? You wanted to know just how Sir George had been killed, and you put up quite a rigmarole to get hold of it. What Inspector Cadover has told you relieves your mind. Lady Simney had great reason to detest her husband, and you have feared that she was perhaps driven to some act of desperation. But you are convinced that she would never attack an unsuspecting man from behind and smash his skull in.'

'Either what my colleague says is true,' said the chief, 'or you have designed that we should attribute to you such processes of mind as he has distinguished. One who has felt uneasy lest another may have committed a crime must necessarily be innocent of it himself.' He paused. 'We know that an attachment at one time existed between Lady Simney and yourself. We know that her marriage was unhappy and that her husband's conduct was such as any wife might consider intolerable. During this period you have been absent abroad. Your return has coincided with Sir George's violent death – which took place, as you know, in his study on Tuesday night. Would you be good enough to give us some account of your movements since you returned to England, of the time of your arrival, and of such meetings or correspondence as you may have had with Lady Simney since that arrival?'

We had breasted a rise in the park, and the great house lay before us in the middle distance, three long lines of windows looking blankly out over the melting snow. Hoodless gazed at it sombrely. 'You are nothing if not precise,' he said. 'But why treat me in this rather hostile way? It is true that when I heard of this poor devil's being killed I feared that Nicolette might have done something fatal in the heat of a quarrel. But of course she wouldn't creep up and bash in the man's head from behind! She had stood at an altar with him, after all.'

'Um,' said Inspector Cadover.

'I don't know that I much care who did in fact kill Simney. He was a horrible man. But I realize that the truth must be found. Until that is done there will be no rest for Nicolette or anyone else.' Hoodless uttered these short sentences absently; he was still gazing fixedly at Hazelwood – as fixedly, I thought, as an abstracted eye may gaze at destiny. 'So let me tell you the whole story – or almost the whole of it – so far as it is any concern of mine. It will be more than you need know, or gather into your notebooks. Perhaps it will convince you, or be a sort of earnest of faith. I don't want you to waste time on my *alibi*. Not that I have one, likely enough.'

'We are very ready,' said the chief formally, 'to hear anything that you may think proper to communicate to us.'

Hoodless nodded, turned away from the prospect of the great house, and appeared to orientate himself anew in the park. 'This way,' he said, and set off with an oddly purposeful stride. His legs were long. We had hard work of it keeping up with him.

'I met Nicolette shortly after I took Greats and when I was just getting a first grip on my anthropology. I never went to school; my father had eccentric ideas on such things; and of that fact there were, I think, two consequences. My private tutors had been competent, but I had lacked the stimulus of competition, and for my First in Mods and Greats I had to work harder than most. I never had time to think about myself or inquire into my own nature. And the second consequence is really the same: being educated at home among my sisters, there was a lot I simply didn't know. In the way of experience and observation, that is to say. I had read all the books, I don't doubt.

'Nicolette fascinated me from the moment our eyes first met across a room. It sounds simple, does it not? And the queer thing is she found it so.'

Hoodless paused and we walked for some moments in silence. It was an odd sort of police investigation, this colloquy in the park of Hazelwood Hall. And I doubt if the chief liked it.

'Nicolette, and Nicolette alone, was perfectly real to me – unless you except one or two savage peoples whom I had not yet seen. She is very intelligent. We tired the sun with talking, and everybody came to suppose that it was quite the usual thing. There are men, you know, for whom it is as lucky and as simple as that. They find and gain, when still mere lads, the woman who is going to travel with them all the way. But with Nicolette and myself it wasn't lucky and wasn't simple. I took her in my arms in a punt, and the action seemed to plant a tiny seed of terror in my soul. The seed grew. And I ran away.'

There was another silence. We were walking towards a grove of oaks. 'Mr Hoodless,' said the chief kindly, 'I don't know that you need –'

'But I came back again. I came back from across the world and I was maturer in many ways. I had published papers and a book. And when a young man has done that' – Hoodless smiled wryly – 'he believes himself to hold the Fates fast bound in iron chains. If I wanted something I was entitled to it. And I wanted Nicolette still. To this day I torment myself hourly over the great wrong I did her in not stopping – in just not stopping to inquire.

'She was playing in Shakespeare. And in a sense I did stop. Without declaring my presence in London I saw and heard her every night. She was beautiful – I was very aware of that – and enchantingly intelligent in every line she spoke. I presented myself and we became engaged. That tree of terror had withered and I could not believe that it might germinate again at the root. But, of course, it did. A man such as I didn't, I concluded, marry, or have any issue of his natural body. He went out into the desert and rode with Arabs; he sought distant people and found his task and his solace in the mere contemplation and record of their abundant life. So I was forced to think. It was a frightful mess.

'She was divinely good. She made me believe that my work was important, and that it would always, in a way, be for her. She sent me back to it, and there was nothing but love in the good-byes we said. When I heard that she was married I think I found it in my heart to be glad. But that was before I knew what manner of man this George Simney was.' Hoodless paused and regarded us sideways and with irony as he walked. 'Do I bore you, gentlemen, with this somewhat intimate chronicle?'

Neither of us replied. Our path was leading to a little classical temple beyond the oak trees. Hoodless fixed his eye on it and walked on.

'In New Guinea I ran up against Helmholz, a fairly well-known pupil of Freud's. He was throwing a flood of light on a good deal in the cultures out there. And he took time off to throw a little on me. I am told that talk of psycho-analysis is all the go among the young. Actually the thing itself is like a long and painful illness deliberately induced. As the investigation went on I wrote letter after letter to Nicolette about it. For she would want it all, I knew – and she could take it, being that sort. Helmholz didn't regard me as being congenitally queer. My troubles were catas-trophes of the nursery, stuff that would be exquisitely pain-ful to my mother and sisters, but which any sophisticated man can face and grasp easily enough. The end was both ludicrous and disgraceful, being nothing less than a sudden, brief, and completely satisfactory love-affair with Helmholz's wife.'

Hoodless paused. I believe I was startled enough. As for the chief, he positively stumbled in his tracks.

'Quite so,' said Hoodless. 'My tragedy had ended in mere comedy. And I assure you that the wild indecency of the thing by no means escaped me. But the old boy him-self was delighted.'

'The old boy?' asked the chief.

'Helmholz. It was one of the big triumphs of his career.'

We had entered a glade and the little temple was before us. Hoodless regarded it fixedly. 'So I suppose,' he con-tinued, 'that I am not the man who should throw stones at the late Sir George Simney, or take exception to what is called an *affaire*. Still, there are limits, after all. And that brute overstepped them, if a man ever did.

'But let me go on. I stopped off writing to Nicolette. She was a married woman – though not, I knew, a happy one.

It was an ironic situation. I suppose it might be called tragic too.

'I arrive at my home-coming. I sent Nicolette no word that I was on my way. But I realized that she would possibly hear of it. For in a small and learned way I am news, and she would keep her eye on the papers for that sort of thing. Still, I hoped to get down here quietly and learn how the land lay before she did, in fact, hear. If her marriage to Simney seemed after all not so bad I would clear out for good. Well, I arrived at the Green Cow on Monday night.'

Inspector Cadover shook his head almost despondently. 'And on that same Monday night,' he said, 'several indignant Australian cousins arrived at Hazelwood and started an obscure quarrel. Fantastic questions of identity and inheritance were conceivably involved. And on the next night Sir George was murdered.'

Hoodless smiled. 'It would appear that you are confronted with an embarrassing excess of material. And you must not of course forget what happened here' – and he nodded towards the temple – 'on Tuesday morning.'

'I don't think I am likely to do that, Mr Hoodless.' And for a moment the chief glanced keenly at the tall anthropologist. 'But may we have your own account of the incident?'

'Incident is the word.' Hoodless had gone rather pale. 'I doubted if I had done right coming down, and I decided to take a walk in the park to think it over. It didn't occur to me that I might run into anybody it was awkward to meet.

'I walked through the village and came in by the west gate. That brought me up on high ground from which I had a bird's eye view of the place. And as I prowled about up there I'm bound to say I saw some uncommonly odd things.'

'Ah,' said the chief. 'So Jane Fairey wasn't the only spy at work that morning.'

'Jane Fairey? I haven't heard of her. But it's true I saw one other spy: Nicolette herself.' He smiled faintly at some reminiscence. 'But she wasn't spying when I first saw her; she was snowballing. She was pelting an oak with snowballs. And as the house seemed to be watching her in an inimical sort of way from one side it seemed to me that I might fairly keep a friendly eye on her from the other. And I was doing that when a man and a woman on horseback came up behind me and reined in within a stone's throw. I guessed that the man was Nicolette's husband, and when he gave me an angry glance I took it to be because I was, after all, trespassing. But now I think it likely that he had done a bit of guessing too, and knew me for Nicolette's former fiancé. Who the girl was I had no idea. But I had a very good understanding of the sort of way she was looking at Simney.

'I turned away, and by this time Nicolette had vanished. When I next saw her she was talking to a fellow who looked like a manservant, and who was standing in the snow between a couple of suit-cases. Well, at that I did, I think, feel a little like a spy, and I stopped giving myself the pleasure of watching Nicolette and tramped off in the other direction. But I wasn't yet through. Twice after that I came upon her. And the first time was enough to tell me that at Hazelwood things were in a precious queer way.' Hoodless paused. 'She was worming her way up a shallow snow-filled ditch towards two elderly men, total strangers to me, who were perched on shooting-sticks nearby and arguing with considerable heat.'

Inspector Cadover raised his eyebrows. 'Odd,' he said. 'In the lady of the manor, indeed, thoroughly disconcerting.'

'She must have managed to hear a good deal – but then the two men moved off. It seemed to me I had better do the same; either that or make myself known to Nicolette at once. I decided to give myself time to think things over, and I made for the village by what I thought would be the shortest route. It took me past this building. Two horses were tethered there, and so I knew that Sir George and his companion were either inside or close by. It was no business of mine, and I moved on. But when I got round to the other side I heard a twig snap and a rustling in the undergrowth. I realized that there was more spying going on, and it seemed logical to suppose that it was again Nicolette.'

The chief shook his head. 'It was the blacksmith's daughter. The girl called Jane Fairey.'

'I couldn't know that, and I was extraordinarily troubled. It occurred to me that things might have been so bad at Hazelwood that Nicolette had gone a little astray in her wits.'

'I would say that nothing' – the chief spoke rather drily – 'was farther from the truth. If it at all relieves your mind, I may tell you that I regard Lady Simney as very fully in possession of her usual marked intellectual abilities.'

Hoodless glanced at him rapidly, hesitated, and went on. 'I decided to investigate. But I had hardly got into the undergrowth when there was a sound behind me, and there was Nicolette standing about where I stand now, right in front of the temple. She had just looked at the horses and taken the situation in. She hurried forward, stopped, and suddenly the horses were rearing and plunging. And at that out came Simney and his lady friend. They mounted and made as if to ride past Nicolette. But when just up with her Simney reined in for a moment, said something, and then struck her in the face. He and the woman rode off, and I ran from behind the temple. Nicolette was walking rapidly towards the house. Something in her stride brought me to a halt. If I could have caught up with Simney it would have been another matter. But upon Nicolette hard upon that humiliation I didn't want to break. So I waited and she disappeared. I haven't seen her since.'

13

'Or communicated with her in any way?' The chief had taken a couple of strides in the melting snow and turned to face the anthropologist.

'Nor have I communicated with her.' Hoodless looked first at one and then the other of us bravely. 'I had entered that park feeling only a relationship with her; now I was in a relationship with her husband as well. It needed considering.' Hoodless paused. 'A couple of hundred years ago the solution would have been comparatively simple. But a duel would be distinctly eccentric today, nor do I suppose he was the sort of man who would have hazarded himself after that fashion. I don't know that our customs have changed for the better in these ways. Cultures in which there is some form of judicial combat usually escape a good deal of underhand violence.'

Inspector Cadover was looking appraisingly at the sinister little building called Sir Basil's Folly. 'You meditated underhand violence yourself?' he asked.

'Violence, certainly. One does in such a situation think of killing one's man. But such thoughts are atavic and one presently recognizes them as such. Sticking the Simney carving-knife, or the ancestral Hoodless stiletto, into Sir George would by no means have mended matters. I decided to sleep on my problem – and when I woke up it was to hear an excited landlord telling a group of yokels that Sir George had been murdered. All his earthly accounts were closed – my own, which was the latest opened, among them.'

We had mounted the steps of the temple as Hoodless spoke, and walked half round the little terrace before it. The chief surprised me by unceremoniously forcing a window and entering. We waited in complete silence until he came out again. 'Nicely fitted out,' he said. 'Conveniently appointed.' He frowned and added a most un-professional remark. 'Do you know, I cannot feel that society has lost much in the late Sir George?'

'I imagine,' said Hoodless, 'that, on the contrary, the gain is considerable. Still, the brains even of very bad hats should not be scattered about the carpet. If I can help clear the thing up, I will.'

Inspector Cadover brought out his pipe. 'If you don't mind,' he said, 'I'll just fumigate a little after inspecting the lovenest. And now, sir, it will be best that I put a few direct questions. Sir George has come to this violent end and Lady Simney must be presumed in considerable distress of mind. Why have you not attempted to have any communication with her?'

'I had to think things out.'

Impatiently the chief struck a match. 'That seems to be your line every time.'

Hoodless flushed. 'You don't understand. But I think you will when you have asked your remaining questions.'

'Very well. What were you doing on Tuesday, Mr Hoodless, shortly before midnight?'

'Prowling about within a stone's throw of Hazel-wood.'

We both stared at him dumbfounded. 'When you remarked that you probably had no *alibi*,' said the chief, 'it looks as if you weren't far wrong. Have you any explanation of so extraordinary a proceeding?'

'I was in love.'

There was a silence. The thing was perfectly adequate. Men do behave just so. But it took some swallowing, all the same.

'You rallied us,' said the chief, 'on the fascination' of footprints in the snow. Well, you didn't leave any.'

'I suppose I kept to the carriage sweep, which had been pretty well cleared. Why shouldn't you believe me? It would be absurd to invent such a story.'

'It would seem to be so.' The chief was cautious and

plodding. 'While you were on this prowl, then, did you see or hear anything material?'

'I certainly did. It put me in grave doubts as to how to act at the time. I was watching the house – there was, as you will have heard, a glimmer of moonlight – when I saw a dark figure apparently scaling one of the wings. I couldn't make out how it was being managed, but it appeared to be a fairly easy ascent.'

'I see.' We had turned from Sir Basil's Folly and were moving through the oak trees. 'You have quite a talent, Mr Hoodless, for failing to break new ground.'

The anthropologist laughed a trifle shortly. 'Professionally,' he said, 'I hope it is otherwise. And I don't at all know what you mean.'

'That yours, so far, is what is called corroborative evidence. But please go on.'

'What is called a cat-burglar would no doubt present just such an appearance. I wondered whether I ought to give an alarm. But to account for my presence would have been uncommonly awkward. And, after all, Sir George's spoons and forks were nothing to me.'

'To be sure they were not. Can you give us an idea of the hour, by the way?'

'I have no idea of it. I had got into the sort of state, I am afraid, at which time makes very little impression. But one very acute sense I always have – that of hearing. I doubt if, from where I was standing, any normal ear would have heard what I heard then. It was a scream – a scream of rage and terror.'

How the chief took this I don't know. For my own part I nearly jumped out of my skin. For these were the very words which Owdon – or Denzell Simney – had used to describe what he had heard from Sir George's study. This was corroborative evidence with a vengeance.

'And then the figure reappeared again and re-descended to the darkness of a terrace. I fancied I heard sounds of a scuffle. Then I heard the panting breath of somebody approaching me, and the figure of a man came into sight quite close at hand. I had just decided that it was the cat-burglar, and was wondering whether to do a rugger tackle, when he came fully into view. Three things were surprising about him and made me hold my hand.'

The village was now before us and I could see a thin wisp of blue smoke rising from the Green Cow. Dramatic sense had made Hoodless fall silent while we walked a dozen paces. 'Three things?' I asked.

'Yes. First, the cat-burglar was a clergyman. Second, he was running through the snow in his stockinged feet. And third, his face in the moonlight bore such an expression of horror and fear as I had never before seen, or seen only in New Guinea natives who believed themselves haunted by demons.'

'I see.' Inspector Cadover looked inquiringly into the bowl of his pipe. 'You might say he was like a man who had run up against the Devil?'

'Yes. Against the Devil and all his works.'

We climbed a stile and were again on the high-road. 'In the matter of those New Guinea natives,' said the chief. 'Your experience of them wouldn't, I suppose, go back twenty years or thereabouts?'

'Heavens, no. Not ten.'

'Did you ever come up against blackbirding?'

Hoodless stared in surprise. 'No,' he said, 'I never did. It's an evil that has pretty well died out. But then so have the potential blackbirds, poor devils.'

'Did you ever hear of two anthropologists who went on a trading voyage with some natives and had a brush with blackbirders?'

'Never.'

'Have you ever heard anything whatever of a family of Simneys in Australia?'

'I'm very sure I never have.'

'You say you wrote frequently to Lady Simney after her marriage. I suppose, therefore, that she wrote to you. Did she tell you anything whatever of her husband's relations or family connexions?'

'Nothing at all.'

'Would you be surprised to learn that the butler at Hazelwood is really the late Sir George's brother living under an assumed name?'

Hoodless laughed. 'I would think it a very tall story indeed. For surely –' He broke off abruptly. 'Hullo. There's something up.'

Outside the Green Cow a little knot of villagers had gathered, and in their midst was a panting youth whom I recognized as some sort of garden-boy from Hazelwood. Whatever news he brought had evidently been worth the rapid carriage, for surprise and awe were evident on the faces of those around him. The chief took one look at the scene and then pushed in without ceremony. 'Now then,' he said – and thirty years appeared to drop from him as he spoke – 'Now then, what's all this?'

The garden-boy looked at him in consternation. 'Please, sir,' he said, 'I was sent down by Sergeant Laffer to fetch you. It be Mr Owdon, sir – shot dead in his pantry.'

Well, I doubt if either of us had remotely envisaged another violent death – although such things, just like funerals, do tend to breed each other at times. We left Hoodless at his inn and hurried to Hazelwood. The chief spoke never a word on the way. But he whistled – which is a thing altogether uncommon with him, so far as I know. He whistled one tune after another in a perfunctory sort of way, and I had a strong impression that he wasn't simply seeking to soothe his own savage breast. With every fragment of tune his brow grew darker. The garden-boy, who draggled along uncertainly beside us, stared at him round-eyed.

Perhaps, I thought, we ought to have expected just this. The butler had turned ashen at the arrival of mysterious visitors out of the past. The butler had dropped trays, sneaked about with suit-cases, sagged in a nasty way at the knees. Surely conduct so conventional could only end with a pistol-shot. Perhaps he would prove to have murmured as he expired a few exquisitely enigmatic words to an under-housemaid – supposing Hazelwood to have any under-housemaids left. Perhaps a fragment of some cryptic message would be found clutched in his hand. . . .

This silly sort of reverie meant no more than that I was getting hopelessly out of my depth. From the Simneys and their obscure Australian hinterland we had been whisked to the psychopathology of Christopher Hoodless. Now we were back with that old blackbirding incident and all that had followed from it. In a sense the death of Owdon came in neatly enough on top of what we knew. He had lived for years under false colours and within the shadow of a crime. Those had returned who knew – or were about to penetrate to – his story: and now there had been a pistol-shot and he was out of the mess. The sequence was logical enough. But what of the centre of the whole affair – the violent death of his brother? Had he first attempted to stifle the past by silencing George, who had in any case treated him so vilely? And when this horrible expedient proved futile had he then in desperation taken his own life?

I couldn't see it that way. Owdon's testimony, I had firmly decided, was true so far as it went, though certainly it might have gone further. His account of Tuesday night had given us virtually our whole physical framework for the affair, and to say the least it would be tiresome to have to scrap it. But, quite apart from this, I was obstinately convinced that its essence was true. To Alfred Owdon – or Denzell Simney if one preferred to think of him that way – Sir George's death had been both unexpected and inexplicable, a mysterious catastrophe in what he knew to have been an empty room. The wretched Deamer, watched by the sombre Hoodless, had come up that trellis. But who had descended it from above? The death of Owdon brought us no nearer a solution of that.

We rounded a sweep of the drive and the great manor-house lay before us. A groom was leading a couple of horses across a paddock and near at hand a gardener placidly performed some indistinguishable task beside a lily pond. The life of the place went on, and would presumably continue to do so until impersonal economic forces strangled it. Until then the Simneys would continue their ways here. There would always be a Sir Somebody adding his portrait to that unengaging gallery in the study. Only the interspersed ladies a change of taste or humour might banish from that sinister room. . . .

Sergeant Laffer received us in the hall, a good deal awed by this second stroke of violence. He was a simple fellow and likeable; and his one tenet of faith in the affair hitherto had been that Sir George's death was to be laid to the charge of some casual marauder. He said nothing of this now but led us through green baize doors to a small apartment assigned to the butler's professional offices. Owdon lay sprawled across a table much as his master, and brother, had done. A writing-pad and fountain-pen had been pushed to one side; on the other side was a revolver which might well have fallen from his own hand. The shot had certainly been at short range and the bullet had gone in at the temple. He must have died at once.

Timmy Owdon and Mervyn Cockayne were standing silent in a corner of the room. Both were dressed in Mervyn's clothes, so that more than ever they looked like twins. But whereas Mervyn's expression displayed both shock and decent sorrow Timmy's showed tragic and stark. Years had fallen upon him like a burden; he was as one still mastering a complex and overwhelming experience. Dark circles had drawn themselves round his eyes – but his shoulders were square and his chin had tilted upwards.

We made what examination was worth making. The two lads watched us, quite silent. And then, suddenly,

Timmy turned and left the room. I was prompted to follow him. He walked to the baize doors which marked the boundary of the servants' quarters, and for a moment regarded them fixedly. He passed out into the hall and looked deliberately round. He moved to the fire-place and passed his hand over the arms of the Simneys carved above it. He crossed to a table and paused, frowning at a small bronze nymph which was its sole ornament – a vulgar little thing, and no doubt prized by Sir George on that account: Timmy took it up and pitched it into a waste-paper-basket. 'Mervyn,' he called over his shoulder, 'let's get some air.'

And he passed out into the bleak afternoon sunlight.

14

Here, then, was a second unnatural death on our hands – and of a sort that every C.I.D. man learns to detest. The revolver was Sir George's; it had been kept ready loaded in a bedroom drawer which anyone could rob; it showed the dead butler's finger-prints after a fashion which might mean nothing at all. Moreover anyone might have come in upon Owdon unobserved, and the thing had taken place at an hour when the household was dispersed and movements were difficult to check. I had an uncomfortable sense that the whole mystery was gaining on us; for example, there had been gathered for us a good deal of information about people's whereabouts at the time of the first fatality, but we had as yet made little progress in analysing this – and now here was another set of circumstances in which it looked as if similar labour would have to be undertaken. Unless something turned up almost out of hand to prove that the butler had simply taken his own life (as I, for one, was pretty sure that he had) we were faced with a tolerably formidable task.

Perhaps it is odd that, confronted by this, I should have chiefly felt the need to find out about Cuvier and his feather. But so it was, and I took myself to the library to investigate: fifteen minutes got me the facts for what they signified. It was Cuvier, it seems, who started the business of reconstructing whole prehistoric monsters from such fragments of them as archaeologists turned up. The feather told him about the wing, the wing about the thorax, and so on; presently he could describe the whole bird. And then years later somebody would dig out a skeleton of the creature in its entirety and Cuvier would be proved exactly right. No doubt it is an admirable pattern for detective investigation. But at least, I reflected rather gloomily, one has to be sure of one's feather. And where was the feather in the Hazelwood affair? Perhaps the chief knew. I was pretty sure that I did not.

But the chief, meantime, had disappeared, and inquiry revealed that he had asked his way to the music-room. I set out to find this apartment myself and was presently guided to it by strains of melody. I entered. Inspector Cadover was regaling himself with a programme of light opera on the gramophone.

Well, a quarter of an hour off to track down Cuvier was one thing; this was quite another. I suppose I gaped at him as if he were demented. And then I saw that I was not alone in this activity. No less than three ladies, sitting in a row on a window-seat, were similarly employed, *The Three Feathers*, I thought idiotically, and watched the chief irritably lift the tone-arm and remove a record.

The youngest of the ladies – it was, of course, Joyleen Simney – giggled hysterically; the chief glowered at her and turned on something from *The Yeomen of the Guard*. After a minute he removed this in turn and rummaged irresolutely in a record album. 'And where have you been?' he demanded disagreeably.

'Looking up Cuvier's feather, sir.' It always pleases me to be particularly polite when he is like this. 'I'm very sorry to have gone off duty without permission. May I help you to find a really nice piece? I believe Mrs Gerard would enjoy something from *The Bohemian Girl*.'

Joyleen giggled again. Another of the ladies – it was Mr Deamer's friend, Miss Grace – was making noises like a coffee percolator, and I couldn't decide whether she was having a quiet cry over Owdon or merely designing to express indignation at the irregular conduct of the higher constabulary. The third lady was looking rather helplessly about her. 'If my dear Mervyn were here,' she murmured vaguely, 'he would be delighted to help. He knows such a lot about music – but mostly on the heavier classical side.'

This seemed to rouse the chief momentarily from his extraordinary vagary. 'Music?' he growled at Mrs Cockayne. '*Your* concern with music is facing it. And you'd better face it now, all three of you.'

I was more startled than ever. This was not a manner which any assistant-commissioner would recommend, particularly when dealing with the propertied classes. Indeed, it is specifically condemned in the lectures, which are very strong on the dangers of Americanization.

'A short time before Sir George was killed,' said the chief, 'Mr Deamer received a telephone call from someone he believed to be Miss Grace. It had the effect of bringing him beneath the study window between eleven o'clock and midnight. Assuming that the call did, in fact, come from Hazelwood – and it will be possible to check up on that – it was almost certainly made by one of a small number of women – and by a woman with a naturally cultivated voice. Servants, it appears to me, are ruled out. Moreover this call, I am sorry to say, can scarcely have been made with other than a criminal intent. Just think it over, will you, while I try another tune.'

And, sure enough, Inspector Cadover again started up the gramophone. It almost seemed to me as if he were more genuinely concerned with his musical entertainment than with the inquiry he was sandwiching into it. This time he played, among other things, *Three Little Maids from School.* I doubt whether the three Hazelwood ladies heard it. No sooner had the music stopped than Mrs Cockayne spoke. 'It's quite absurd,' she said. 'I know nothing about it whatever. I don't like the telephone. And I don't like Mr Deamer either.'

The chief appeared to weigh this and docket it for reference. 'Mrs Simney?' he said.

Joyleen Simney tossed her head. 'Give it a go!' she said scornfully. 'Why should I telephone to some little dill I've never seen? And how could I imitate the funny way that Grace talks?' Suddenly she turned from petulance to tears. 'I don't even know,' she sobbed, 'where they keep their stupid telephone in this horrid house.'

The chief nodded gravely, as if acknowledging that there was some force in all this. 'Very well,' he said. 'The simplest explanation, after all, remains. Miss Grace sent the spurious message herself.'

There was a pause. I didn't, for my own part, expect other than a flat, and perhaps vehement, denial in this quarter also. But Miss Grace, for some reason, was struck all of a heap. She lay back on her window-seat, apparently fighting for breath, and her lips were as pale as blotting-paper. And at this the chief very seriously played another record. I began to think he was really mad. But presently he frowned, shook his head, and switched off again. 'Well?' he said.

I didn't know much about Miss Grace Simney, but had rather gathered that she was an unbalanced woman who had suffered from a morbid preoccupation with her dead brother and his morals. Was it possible, I wondered, that she was in fact some sort of maniac, and that the whole mystery would have some horrid explanation in this? She looked uncommonly queer now. And, when she spoke, what she said was uncommonly queer as well.

'George died with his sins about him,' she whispered

hoarsely. 'He died in vileness and in plotting vileness. And would you have me *not* have called Mr Deamer, who, although despised and reviled by him, was his only hope?'

Inspector Cadover was standing very still. 'Do I understand,' he said, 'that you believed – or affected to believe – in a plot to bring Jane Fairey to the study that night, and that you rang up Mr Deamer and told him so?'

Miss Grace had gone paler still; there was something in the manner of this that frightened her. '*That* night?' she faltered. 'I didn't know anything about that night. I knew only that he hoped soon to – to accomplish his vile purpose on the girl. I wanted Mr Deamer's advice – his support. But I – I didn't get through.'

'You mean that you tried to telephone him, *and failed*?'

'Yes. Nicolette's maid, Martin, was helping me to dress. There is a house telephone in my room and I asked her to put the call through that way. She did so and then left the room. But when I picked up the receiver I found there had been some hitch and the engaged signal was sounding. I felt very tired, and so I didn't try again.'

Miss Grace's voice faded out on a sigh. The chief said nothing, but put another record on the gramophone. Jaunty music filled the room. There was nothing impossible in the story Miss Grace Simney had told. But if she felt she had to lie it was obviously the best she could do, since a telephone call initiated by the maid Martin could not well be denied outright.

This was a moment at which I felt extraordinarily depressed. The chief was proceeding to badger these three women as to their whereabouts on Tuesday night, and his growing irritability suggested his sense that it was a perfectly futile task. Sir George had been killed at midnight, and some time before midnight most of the household had gone to bed. This held of the three witnesses now present. Mrs Cockayne had retired to her widowed couch shortly after eleven, and Miss Grace Simney to her virgin one some half an hour earlier. Naturally there had been no one to keep an eye on them in bed. And even if their movements had been other than they professed their stories were peculiarly easy to hold to, so that even a severe interrogation was unlikely to achieve anything. It was true that Miss Grace had told us a queer story and might fairly expect a little sharp questioning. But I certainly didn't believe that she would prove to have bashed in her brother's head from behind, and I had an uncomfortable feeling that with her the chief was doing no more than fill in time while waiting for some line to come to him.

These two women, although naturally rattled, were not bad witnesses, and I knew that in a court what they said would carry a good deal of conviction. But it was otherwise with Joyleen Simney.

Hers was the same story, for apparently at Hazelwood she had been given a room to herself at some remove from her husband's, and here she had retired and gone to sleep about eleven o'clock. Again it was an account easy to stick to. Nevertheless under the chief's questioning Joyleen was uneasy from the first. Was it simply that certain other of her Hazelwood adventures had given her a bad conscience, and that she feared lest at any moment the spotlight might be switched to Sir Basil's Folly? Or had she really been up to some mischief, relevant or otherwise, at this crucial hour?

Now with the gramophone, and now with these wretched women, the chief continued to beguile the afternoon. In desperation I took out the notes we had been given and ran over this whole *alibi* business as it affected everybody we could at present believe concerned. With what might be thought of as the outside people – Deamer and Hoodless – we had recently dealt; both told odd stories which there was no positive controverting nevertheless. And of those domiciled or visiting at Hazelwood the facts were colourless and few. The butler's routine and Lady Simney's bath had already been prominently in the picture. Bevis

Simney — Sir Bevis, as it appears he must now be called — and his son Willoughby, claimed to have been together in the latter's bedroom, smoking and talking over the day's shooting, until Willoughby emerged to investigate what proved to be the tragedy. This, I suppose, is an *alibi* of a sort, but as Sir George's death has put both father and son in the way of a baronetcy it cannot be called impressive. And no more can the only other pairing off that investigating reveals. Here again it is a matter of father and son, for Hippias and Gerard Simney declare themselves to have been playing billiards in a somewhat remote part of the house until disturbed by the general turmoil of discovery. This left Timmy Owdon, who declares himself to have been asleep throughout in his room over the stables, and Mervyn Cockayne. Mervyn has the room immediately above Sir George's bedroom. He maintains that he was restless on Tuesday night; that he looked out of his window and discerned movement on the terrace; and that he then ran downstairs and outside to engage in his notable encounter with Mr Deamer.

These, then, were the facts which I briefly chewed over to the accompaniment of the chief's inexplicable gramophone. Nobody had shaken any of them; nobody's testimony contradicted that of anyone else; no one member of the household had spotted any other on the prowl. Nor did the fact that the study might be reached by a climb from above appear at all to limit or define the issue. For the room above the study was a large untenanted bedroom; any member of the household might, as far as I could see, have reached it unobserved, climbed down and up again, and returned to base without meeting anyone. This meant that Nicolette Simney alone was positively out of it. She possessed no means of ascending to the upper storey without first emerging upon Owdon in the corridor. And, even if she had, it was just not possible for her to take such a route to the study and thence back to her bath-room in the time available to her. But anybody else might have achieved the exploit that way, and it appeared to me essential to believe that somebody had. And the telephone call designed to elicit the appearance of an attack from without must be an integral part of the plot.

I had got as far as this – and saw small prospect of getting further – when I noticed that the gramophone had abruptly stopped and that the chief was striding from the room. With no more ceremony towards the ladies than he himself had shown, I followed him into the corridor. 'Look here,' I said, 'what *is* all this, sir? Is it a variant of Sherlock Holmes's violin?'

For a moment he stared at me unheeding, and with a look in his eye that I have certainly not seen before. 'Holmes?' he echoed. 'Certainly not. Cuvier, my lad – nothing but Cuvier.'

'Cuvier?'

'That feather of his brushed against my cheek right at the beginning, and I just couldn't grasp it. But I knew' – and he grinned at me with sudden disconcerting cheerfulness – 'that I might snare it with song. Did you notice what that last record was?'

'No, I didn't.' This mystery-mongering made me feel at once excited and aggrieved. 'I was trying to get some line on the whole beastly case.'

'And were you, indeed? Now, Harold, that's very commendable. But I'm afraid you must wait till next time. The case is –'

Inspector Cadover broke off as he noticed Sergeant Laffer approach. And I saw at once that from the local officer's point of view something had gone terribly wrong. He came up to us with a face as long as a fiddle – Sherlock Holmes's or another. 'Timmy Owdon,' he said sorrowfully and in a low voice. 'He's the only one we've managed to catch tripping, after all.'

'He is?' The chief was already exultant, but this news appeared to fill him with actual glee. 'You've caught the little blighter out?'

'Yes, sir. It's the head groom's story – a most reliable man, and uncommon upset about it. Apparently on Tuesday night he woke up a little short of midnight and imagined there was a smell of burning somewhere in the stables. So he went right through them at once. And Timmy Owdon was not, as he has claimed to be, in his room. His bed had not yet been lain in.'

'Capital!' And the chief bustled me towards the hall. 'I think it gives us just what we require.'

We passed out of the house in silence. I was not only puzzled. I was more depressed than before. Timmy Owdon ought to have been nothing to me, yet I rather liked the lad. 'You were saying,' I prompted, 'that the case –'

'To be sure, Harold, the case. Now, what do you think of it?'

This wasn't what I wanted. But I came forward with the one thing clear to me. 'There are two strands to it – and they don't intertwine. In fact, one of them takes none of the strain at all.'

'That is very good, Harold, very good indeed.'

'One can approach it by way of Hoodless, or by way of the Australian cousins. It was the turning up here of one or the other that set matters moving. But between those two turnings up there is no connexion; that they happened virtually simultaneously is mere coincidence. And it follows, I think, that, although each may have some mysterious elements, only one can lead us directly to the death of Sir George. Owdon's death – if we are still to call him that – is another matter. It is almost certainly part of the Australian story, and not of Lady Simney's.'

'That is all very true. But I can't see, lad, why you should be so aggrieved about it.'

'I'm not aggrieved.' I paused on hearing the thorough peevishness in my own voice. 'Well, sir, it's like this. The Hazelwood affair is rather too full measure for my taste. Here are two mysteries, so to speak, and one of them is just something in the way, and entirely useless to us.'

The chief chuckled. 'Not a bit of it. You see, the case . . . I think you were asking me about the case?'

'Yes, sir. I was.'

'Well, the case is closed.'

'Closed!'

'Nothing mysterious remains to it. What we are now confronted with is a question of proof. And even if one of the aspects is, as you say, irrelevant, it may be possible to exploit it. In fact, I rather think I see how it can be used to force the issue. But we shall need luck as well as our usual moderate cunning.'

I looked at him dumbfounded. 'Do I understand,' I asked, 'that the whole wretched business has solved itself through the instrumentality of that indifferent old gramophone?'

He smiled cockily. Really, he might have been the youngest constable in the Force. 'In a way,' he said. 'But sister arts are involved.'

There is not much to be done with him when he is like this. We were out on the drive now and trudging towards the village. 'And may I ask,' I murmured, 'what the next step is to be?'

'Tea. A nice cup of tea, lad, at the Simney Arms. Then a sleep for me, and a couple of hours in which you can go on writing to dad and auntie Flo. And, after that, we can begin to organize the party.'

'The party?' This sort of stupid echo was about all that I could contrive.

'Certainly. We are going to give a party at Hazelwood.' He chuckled again. 'And entirely at the expense of Hazelwood's new baronet.'

Part Three: Nicolette

I

I resume the pen (as a Victorian heroine might say) aware,
Gentle Reader, that you now know quite a lot. The Hazelwood mystery is clearing up; it is realized that both George
and Denzell Simney died on the premises and that both
here and in the appearance of Christopher a good deal of
past history is involved.

Right at the beginning I let out that it wasn't I who
killed my husband, and perhaps this has been a bad failure
in technique. But then I am an amateur – and doubtless
amateur crime-writers are just as painfully incompetent as
amateur actors. But at least there was no failure in Inspector
Cadover's technique, and the only criticism I can make of
his plan is that we might – some or all of us – have simply
refused to play. Clearly when people blow out their brains
or have their heads stove in it is necessary to answer the
questions of the police. But witnesses are not, I suppose,
obliged to forgather in a large family party on the seat of
the original crime and there suffer being played off against
each other with very considerable ingenuity. It was simple
curiosity that Inspector Cadover exploited, or that and the
perennial fascination which anything with an element of
drama holds. No doubt I ought to have been quite at home
with this aspect of the thing. But I can't really pretend that
I enjoyed it. For one thing, Cadover led off with a nasty
jolt for myself.

'My first suspect,' he said blandly, 'was, of course, Lady
Simney. And this for several reasons. She had for long had
much cause to detest and fear her husband. His morals, it
appears, were bad and his manners brutal. He had actually

struck her in the face on the very day upon which he died, an action altogether out of the way, I must suppose, in the upper reaches of society.'

Inspector Cadover paused on this bit of irony or whatever it is to be called. Deliberately, I don't doubt. For it was part of his scheme to get us all thoroughly irritable and edgy.

'Again, Mr Hoodless, to whom her ladyship had at one time been engaged, was newly returned to England, and it was not impossible, despite certain indications to the contrary, that she had already known this for some days. Now, the mere fact of a former lover's returning in this way might well be sufficient to precipitate a crisis in a woman of emotional temperament. And Lady Simney, being as I understand an actress of some talent, was endowed with such a temperament as likely as not.'

There was another brief silence. I can't deny that this manner of speech got me riled at the start. As for Christopher, I could see his knuckles going white on the arms of his chair. He didn't like the good Inspector's little testimonial to my acting at all.

'There was another very obvious point. A telephone call had been sent to Mr Deamer' – and here Inspector Cadover turned to glance at our vicar, who sat fidgeting nervously in a chair near the window – 'and the effect of this call was to procure the appearance of certain evidences very misleading in the case. Mr Deamer is convinced that the speaker was Miss Grace Simney, but this suggestion Miss Grace denies. Lady Simney is the likeliest person successfully to imitate another woman's voice.

'More important than all this was the fact that Lady Simney appeared to have a conclusive *alibi*. We are always inclined, you know, to hold suspect anything obtrusive of that sort. The butler – if we are to believe him – found this room empty. He came out and thereafter had the door continuously under observation. Sir George passed him and entered. Sir George was killed. The butler rushed in, and on coming out again met Lady Simney emerging from her

bath-room. Now, you may say that it might have been possible for her to slip *out* of the room while the butler was
occupied with the body. But assuredly she had no means
of slipping *into* it – of slipping into it, that is to say, by
the door. Could she, then, have got out of the bath-room
window and along the terrace? The state of the snow
negatived this, or appeared to do so until I observed a significant fact. I think, Lady Simney, that you go in for winter
sports?'

And Inspector Cadover looked at me sharply. This was the
nasty jolt. And yet I couldn't see that it was so very effective. 'You mean,' I asked, 'that you found my skis?'

'Just that. I even found in the snow the suggestion of
such tracks as I supposed skis might leave. But inquiry convinced me that these were a mere fortuitous effect of the
wind. In point of fact skis could not be used to obviate footprints. Their tracks would be unmistakable, it seems.

'One possibility remained. If Lady Simney could not have
gone *down* from her bath-room she might have gone *up*,
climbing to the next storey and then descending to the
study window by the trellis. But I found that while anyone,
once on the upper storey, could get down to the study easily
enough, the ascent from the bath-room was impracticable
without tackle which it would have been impossible rapidly
to clear away.

'Well, every obtrusive *alibi* is not a bogus one. So much,
I said, for Lady Simney. It is necessary to step back and
take an altogether broader view of the case.'

It was clear that we were expected to settle in for a substantial evening's instruction. A fire had been lit in the
study – I can't think by whom, for it is my impression that
by now pretty nearly all the servants had quit. It flickered
on the Simneys, animate and inanimate, ranged round the
room; it cast a soft palpating warmth over the relaxed limbs
of Danae and Pasiphae on each side of the window and
threw into a darker shade Caravaggio's lurking Venus

above. Bevis had planted himself before the hearth as if to indicate that, however intrusive policemen might comport themselves, authority at Hazelwood now centred in himself. I wished him joy of it heartily, and was not without a moment's speculation as to which fashionable portrait-painter might most effectively add his heavy features to the collection of baronets about us. Perhaps Willoughby might manage it, and add a self-portrait later. But at the moment Willoughby's eye was fixed on myself and I felt fairly sure that he was speculating on what plastic properties I might present with or without a bath towel. I turned my attention back to Inspector Cadover, who also had his mind on theoretical issues.

'From the first it appeared certain that Sir George had been taken unawares from behind and deliberately killed without any sort of struggle. In other words, we were dealing with the crime of murder. It is a murderer, ladies and gentlemen, whom we have to find – and I am very sure that we have to find that murderer in this room.'

Cadover's eye was fixed on the carpet as he said this, and I think we must all have waited breathlessly to see whether he would deliberately raise them to one or other of us. And he did deliberately raise them, but only to meet the glance of his assistant, a harmless youth called Harold, much given to offering me heartening glances on the sly.

'Perhaps the majority of you had the opportunity to commit this deed, since it turned out that nothing was required except the ability to gain an empty room and climb down a trellis. It seemed to me best, therefore, to pass at least provisionally to the field of motives. But here again there proved to be much scope for speculation.

'A murder may be deliberately planned, or it may emerge as a sudden necessity imposed by some slip or miscalculation in the prosecution of a lesser crime. Take the possibilities of this latter situation first.

'What possible crime might make it thus suddenly necessary to kill Sir George? One line of thought is fairly obvious. This room is full of valuable pictures – imported, as I understand, by a whim of Sir George's, to take their place beside family portraits of somewhat lesser consideration. But would anybody, apart from a professional thief with a very specialized clientele, think to steal such pictures? Would any of you here present think to do so?'

There was a couple of second's pause during which we became aware that this was not a rhetorical question. Cadover, like a resolute teacher before his class, was determined to have an answer.

Willoughby broke the silence. 'Well, I suppose aunt Grace might. She regards this ghastly room as a sort of brothel, and I have no doubt that she would like to get at these nudes with a hatchet. I know the feeling. I have it myself at Burlington House every year.'

The feelings of Willoughby on this subject might, I suppose, be called doctrinaire. But in what he said about Grace there was a queer grain of truth – and this it was that moved me to protest.

'Willoughby's,' I said, 'is surely a most unnecessary and frivolous speculation. Even supposing Grace to have quite fanatical feelings on the matter –'

'Oh, to be sure!' And Willoughby insufferably laughed. 'Of course aunt Grace would have gone about it in quite a different way, calling upon the world to witness her righteous purge. But now, what about myself? If I –'

'Precisely so!' It was Cadover who again took the floor. 'The way in which Mr Willoughby has just dragged in his aunt suggests a temperament somewhat on the sardonic and savage side. Suppose Sir George's boorish joke' – and the Inspector made a sweeping gesture at the walls – 'had come really to irritate him supremely. He respects art, I understand; and at the same time had no great respect for his uncle. He has a taste for rather violent gestures – such as pitching sherry, for example, at his relations. So he might well have decided to do something drastic about the pictures. Perhaps he proposed to purloin the Caravaggio. It

would be a sort of knight-errantry to rescue the lady' –
and Cadover glanced upward at the Venus – 'from among
her shady Simney companions. So Mr Willoughby arranged
a little mystification and on Tuesday night climbed down
to the study by the trellis. But his uncle was in the room,
and as Mr Willoughby came through the curtains their
eyes met in that mirror' – the Inspector pointed – 'and
Mr Willoughby realized that he was detected. He relied
a good deal on his uncle's favour, and for a moment he lost
his head and struck out blindly –'

Willoughby sat back and laughed again. Then he looked
at his watch. 'And may I ask,' he said, 'if there is to be
this sort of tale of a cock and a bull about each of us in
turn? It will take rather a long time.' He paused. 'Mind
you, it would have given me a great deal of pleasure to
make off with the Caravaggio, and I can almost see myself
engineering something of the sort. But however should I
contrive a telephone call in aunt Grace's voice? And
nobody strikes out blindly when detected in a prank. Or' –
and Willoughby glanced at Mervyn – 'no grown-up does.'

'I quite agree that we are wasting time.' Bevis spoke in
his most authoritative voice. But I noticed that he had
moved away from the fire-place and sat himself down quite
unobtrusively in a corner. There was no doubt that the
police-inspector dominated the room. 'Incidentally, if
Willoughby or any one else struck out blindly he must have
had something to strike out with. Are we to suppose that
he came on this picture-stealing escapade armed with a
bludgeon?'

Inspector Cadover walked over to the window recess and
lightly touched its only ornament, a boy's bronze head set
on a marble pedestal. 'This,' he said soberly, 'was the
weapon. It was given a wipe and replaced almost immediately, but the experts tell me that there can be no doubt
about the fact. And, of course, I am bringing no accusation
against Mr Willoughby. I am merely, you will remember,
reviewing the possible motives behind one reading of the

murder, whereby we are to suppose it the sudden action of a wrong-doer detected at something else. You will all see that the point about the bludgeon is a substantial one. The fact that the weapon was simply something snatched up for the purpose powerfully suggests this reading. But it is not, of course, conclusive evidence. The criminal might, after all, be one who had deliberately formed the design of murder, and who relied upon a known object which he knew would mislead by suggesting the contrary supposition.

'Have we now exhausted the picture as a motive or magnet? Not quite. Mr Deamer, we may believe, had very much the same feeling about them as Miss Grace. Might he not have been prompted by some fanatical iconoclastic urge to destroy them? He has told a strange story of being lured here to prevent an – um – ungodly encounter, and of climbing to this room and then going away again. But what if the facts were quite otherwise, and what if he received no telephone-call at all?'

'Fiddle-faddle!' Hippias, who had been pacing nervously at the far end of the room, turned impatiently round upon Cadover. 'Never heard such bally rot. If this parson-fellow had come in on George and started arguing about his mistresses and dirty pictures and what-not the thing might be possible enough. George could be deuced irritating, and might prompt any fellow to hit out. I know' – and here Hippias laughed uneasily – 'because I pitched a bottle at him myself. Didn't find its mark, of course. Damaged his bally portrait instead. But the point is this: there's no reason whatever to suppose that the most icono-clastic clergyman would creep up behind George and bat him on the head. It isn't as if George had been a plaster saint, you know.' And Hippias glanced round the room as if calling upon us to take notice of this little joke – which was certainly a better one than he commonly contrived. 'Hasn't anyone thought to bring in a damned spot?'

Mervyn Cockayne, clinging close as he now constantly

did to Timmy, giggled shrilly. 'Out, out, damned spot,' he said, 'not in, in.' He glanced round expecting applause, much as Hippias had done. But nobody thought Mervyn funny. 'Mama –' he began – and seemed to recall that these antics now belonged to a past phase of his development. 'If you mean whiskey,' he said gloomily, 'there's some by the door.'

Silently Gerard crossed the room and poured his father's spot. Since my encounter with him in the orangery we had scarcely spoken, and I had the impression that he was being equally taciturn with everybody else. There was some pressure of thought on his forehead. It was as if he were making a final attempt to work out something that had long puzzled him. But now he did speak. 'Get on,' he said curtly to Inspector Cadover. 'Come to something, for heaven's sake, and let this damned futile curtain-raising be. Let's find out why those two men died and hang someone for it and be through with the matter.'

I must say I felt it to be a sensible speech. But it showed yet another member of the family who was considerably on edge.

'Very well.' Inspector Cadover, who sat at the centre of the long study table, took another speculative glance around us. 'We will eliminate as a motive any proposal to steal or destroy pictures. Can we find anything else which might have been the criminal's main object, and so retain the hypothesis that the killing of Sir George was unpremeditated and incidental?'

'The safe,' I said. For here again, it seemed to me, the Inspector did not design a merely rhetorical question.

'The safe, undoubtedly.' He bowed to me with a certain formal courtesy. 'And there is, of course, one special circumstance here. The safe is concealed behind Sir George's own portrait, and to some of you its very existence may have been revealed only as a consequence of the –'

'The rough house, officer.' It was Hippias who again

interrupted, and with an affectation of bluffness horridly false. 'Happened when I threw the bally bottle.'

'Quite so. There may well, then, have been a design to rob the safe. The unexpected presence of Sir George –'

Bevis stirred sharply. 'Damn it, man, there could have been nothing unexpected about my brother's presence in this room. He entered it like clockwork every night.'

'That is very good – very good indeed.' And Cadover turned upon Bevis the same sort of irony that he was wont to direct upon the attendant Harold. 'In fact, at this point we are carried right away from any unpremeditated homicide. If the safe was to be opened without great trouble, Sir George had to be present, dead or alive. And perhaps preferably dead. The key was in his pocket, and very likely nothing would have persuaded him to take it out.'

Inspector Cadover again made his slow inspection of the circle of faces around him. The action was coming to give rather the effect of a searchlight.

'Now, ladies and gentlemen, what would be in the safe? Family papers, one would say. Perhaps documents about old colonial days. Any one of a number of people might want them. Mr Hippias here, or Mr Gerard. Or the butler, Owdon.' Cadover made his longest pause yet. 'Or Timmy Owdon, the butler's son.'

2

'We all stirred uneasily – or all except Timmy himself, who stood leaning against the mantelpiece with an expression of fixed calm. Mervyn nudged him. 'Master Timmy, the butler's son,' he murmured. 'And, oh, what a happy, happy family we are!'

It was now a friendly joke; Timmy acknowledged it with a faint smile; the Inspector gave an odd, weary sigh and went on.

'But what the safe proved to contain was Mr Deamer's boots. Well, that is a bit of a surprise. But then we are not the first to be surprised in this affair. Sir George himself was uncommonly surprised – and a split second before his death.'

Inspector Cadover scratched his chin and of a sudden looked fixedly at Hippias. 'But that's not all. The surprises began on Monday night with the arrival of Sir George's Australian relatives. The butler was surprised – indeed shattered.'

Mervyn giggled. 'I would say he did the shattering. At least a dozen wine glasses went at a swoop.'

'And Sir George himself was shaken. Presently there was a row in this study. Put it like this: several angry and bewildered Simneys were faced with a thoroughly awkward situation and couldn't at all agree on what to do about it. And this is the business that must be cleared up first. I propose to do so here and now. Mr Hippias, perhaps you will be good enough to tell us what your arrival at Hazelwood revealed to you, and what you intended to do about it?'

'He intended to collect a cheque.'

Everybody stared at me, and I had a moment to wonder what had prompted me to this revelation.

'I eavesdropped,' I continued. 'On Tuesday morning I eavesdropped in the park. Bevis made Hippias a proposition. I think it was twenty thousand pounds to keep his mouth shut. Hippias didn't think much of the amount. Bevis said he thought it was handsome in view of the fact that he had to consider me as well – whatever that might mean. They walked away to beat it out. Bevis was full of fine moral feeling. Hippias was just plain unscrupulous.'

Joyleen was looking at me round-eyed. Gerard had flushed darkly – and, catching his eye, I am bound to say I felt rather a cad. But I was tired of the Simneys. Within limits, I was all for the truth.

And at least I had the satisfaction of throwing Inspector Cadover right out of his stride. He was almost as round-eyed as Joyleen. 'Do I understand,' he asked me sharply, 'that – that Sir Bevis appeared to have a *large* interest – a major *economic* interest in the suppression of whatever revelation threatened? And that the threat was – was analogous to that constituted by the possibility of your having a male child?'

'Oh, most decidedly.' Having taken on the role of a treacherous little bitch I played it whole-heartedly enough. 'Bevis was putting it on grounds of high moral tone and family shame. He is, as it happens, just that sort of humbug. But actually he was dead scared of losing something he didn't want to lose.'

'And you came in?' Inspector Cadover's reiteration appeared positively stupid. 'You and the revelation *both* came in?'

'Yes. He stood to lose equally by the revelation – Hippias's revelation – and by me.'

'If you had a son he would lose the baronetcy?'

At this point the young man called Harold exclaimed. Not articulately. What he produced was a sort of startled yelp.

Inspector Cadover's face was a study. One reads of people being dumbfounded. One seldom meets it in the flesh.

But Timmy's face was a study too. It was lit by a sort of quiet irony. Not for the first time, I was aware that he was the subtlest of the Simneys.

'I had it utterly upside down.' The Inspector's eye, still startled, circled us all. 'Had I not, Mr Bevis?'

Bevis's brow darkened. 'What the devil –'

'And you, madam' – he had turned to me – 'may I ask if you have greatly prized your position as Lady Simney?'

I shook my head. 'No, Inspector Cadover, I don't think I have.'

'It is just as well. For you have never been so. Nor will Mr Bevis ever be a baronet. In fact –'

'In fact,' said Timmy gravely, 'since my father Sir

George took his own life in his pantry six hours ago I have been Sir Timothy Simney. I welcome you all to Hazel-wood.'

Viewed as a *coup de théâtre* nothing could well have been more effective than this. It was Timmy who now stood before the fire-place, turning over a little sheaf of papers which he had drawn from his pocket. 'I am going to read you my father's last letter,' he said. 'The ink was hardly dry on it when he shot himself, and I found it when I ran into the room.' Timmy paused and looked at Cadover. 'But it appears you knew that his real name was not Alfred Owdon; that he was in fact a Simney too?'

'I did.' The police inspector had hardly yet recovered himself. 'And I supposed him to be Denzell Simney, Sir George's younger brother. But in that case Mr Bevis would have suffered no material loss by the revelation. That his younger brother Denzell was still alive would not have prevented the baronetcy coming to him should Lady Simney have no son. But if Mr Bevis was willing to pay twenty thousand pounds for silence there can be only one explanation. The secret about Owdon is very different from what I have supposed. He was not Denzell but Sir George – and a Sir George already possessed of a legitimate heir. And that heir, we must agree, has very effectively declared himself.'

Timmy smiled faintly. 'You had certainly got it mixed – which was not, perhaps, a very difficult thing to do. Uncle Bevis' – and Timmy wheeled round on his kinsman – 'is it with your permission that I read this letter?'

There was no reply. Bevis's florid face had turned pale. Timmy paused for a few moments more and then in a quiet voice read the document through. To those of us who knew nothing of that long-distant blackbirding and its consequences every sentence was illuminating. But here I need give only the latter part of the letter.

. . . We were both wild, but it was Denzell who had the very devil in him. Only the mind of a devil could have leapt, as his did, at the chance of dispossessing me – and of amusing himself by keeping me where I have been kept so long.

At first his ambition had stretched no further, I suppose, than contriving to get remittances from England. As Denzell he was dead, since to emerge would be to court a prison sentence for attempting the life of that anthropologist. After our escape we had of course separated; it seemed the safest thing to do. And when he somehow heard that I wasn't venturing to go under my own name either, and was content to pick up a living as I could, he saw his chance of continued easy money. He simply cabled home as George Simney, hinting that he had been in trouble and obliged to break with his previous Australian connexions, and that his regular remittance should be sent to him in such and such a way.

It was a queer situation. I – the real George Simney – was known to be alive; the Australian Simneys knew it; and indeed I stopped with them for a time under my own name and did myself a little good over Dismal Swamp. But mostly I was wandering about after gold, and calling myself anything that came into my head. This had its conveniences. If Brown got on the wrong side of the law (and I got on the wrong side of such law as there was on the diggings often enough) he simply disappeared and Jones took his place. And meantime Denzell, whom nobody thought of as alive, was taking advantage of the fact that somewhere there *ought* to be a George Simney, to live the life of a remittance-man comfortably enough. Mostly, I believe, he lived in Perth and was, increasingly without danger of question, George Simney to a few reputable folk bankers and the like. A certain amount of forgery and perjury was involved, and there were various chances of detection to risk every day. But on the whole it was simple enough. We had always been fairly like each other, nobody in England was interested, and the chance of exposure receded year by year.

But the day came when Fortune – ironic jade – brought us face to face. From Coolgardie I had drifted to Perth and there on the beach at Cotesloe, with nothing better to do than watch a group of bathing girls, was my brother Denzell. He had gone pretty soft and one could tell his manner of life at a glance; he was just a remittance man of the more prosperous sort. For a time he foxed with me, but presently the truth came out. Denzell had stepped into my shoes and was George Simney every time he collected his money. It didn't worry me much; indeed at the time I didn't give a damn. We were neither of us much more than rubbish on the scrap heap of society, and it seemed no matter to me which called himself what.

It wasn't much of a reunion. We had seen wild times together and been as thick as thieves, in a way. But always there had been a deep hostility between us, and at that meeting on Costesloe beach I think I had an inkling of the queer implacable hatred Denzell bore me. But it didn't seem important. England was behind us for good and no ties need ever bind us again. On that sunny beach I nodded good-bye to my brother – as I thought for ever – and left him to be George Simney and draw his monthly pittance if he cared. It didn't occur to me to reflect how near George Simney stood to fortune and a title, after all. I had two elder brothers, you know, and our father was a man as hale and hearty as myself.

Denzell was not so careless and although I said good-bye to him that day he must have been far from saying good-bye to me. I believe that in the wild years which followed he must have trailed me himself, and that somehow he must have possessed himself of sufficient money to keep others on the job as well. In Coolgardie and Broome and Wyndham he got a great deal of information. But what he really wanted he got in Sharks Bay.

Those tawny, scrawny sandhills, my dear boy, you will never see. They mark the beginnings of Australian history, for here Dampier came, searching for water, in 1692. And they nearly marked the end of Australian history for me. It is a story ugly even for those wild parts, where a gun, or a knife, or a spoonful of powdered bamboo in the porridge has often settled the possession of a little pile of honey-coloured pearls destined to be smuggled overseas in cakes of soap for the pleasure of Hindu or Chinese ladies. I need not tell it all now. Let it be sufficient that it was here, in a tumble-down pearling-pit, that I fought through half a pitch-black night with a ruffian whom I had no doubt greatly wronged. It is of this nightmare encounter, my dear lad, and not of the blackbirding affair, that my face bears such terrible evidences today. In those times, and on the fringes of that vast and empty continent, such things were hushed up often enough. And so I thought it was with this fatal fight. But Denzell knew. And not only did he know – he had collected (by what wiles and chances I need not detail) documentary evidences which would have sent me to gaol for life.

The time came when I heard of the accident – of the terrible railway smash, that is to say, in which my father and two elder brothers lost their lives. Utterly against all calculation I had entered into a fortune and become Sir George Simney. It didn't occur to me that I was up against any difficulty, for my identity could be easily established despite all the masquerading that Denzell had done. Besides, if he was inclined to kick, did I not possess the uncomfortable secret of that revolver-shot on the lugger long ago?

But it was a case of Greek meeting Greek! When I confronted

Denzell and told him I was going home to claim the title, he laid upon the table that formidable criminal dossier which he had compiled against me. 'You want to go home as master?' he said. 'By God, you shall go home as man !'. It was a wild notion, but perfectly feasible. I was unrecognizable, and after all those years not even our brother Bevis would be likely to realize that the man returning as George was really Denzell. And, in the end, it happened like that. Denzell held the stronger cards, for if it had come to exposing each other mine would have been far the heavier debt to pay. But — more important — I acknowledge that his was the stronger will; behind this queer and evil caprice of compelling his elder brother to servitude was a savage and inflexible pow-r which, in the end, I could not resist. I wanted freedom — even of a sort — and I bought it by becoming Alfred Owdon and returning to Hazelwood as an overseer of port and claret, dustpans and brooms. And so I have lived, except for a brief break-away eighteen years ago.

It was then that I married your mother, Kathleen Taylor, in the parish of Medley, Shropshire. Had she lived I believe I would have found resolution (for perhaps it required no more than that) to defy Denzell for good. But your mother died when you were born, and with that all spirit left me. I returned to Hazelwood under threat of exposure, and your early years were spent with a foster-mother in a cottage on the estate. Denzell, I suppose, was concerned not to lose sight of one who might be eleventh baronet one day.

For there was one irony in the situation which he himself, I don't doubt, appreciated to the full. The power he held over me could by no means reach beyond the grave; I had ample means of proving the truth as soon as I could afford to do so; and that moment could come when I was on my death-bed. Denzell had the strongest interest in my continuing to cling to life and judge it tolerable, and the hazards he ran in this must have been one of the pleasures of his strangely twisted nature.

The Australians came. It was a sufficient shock in itself — and then, looking out from the dining-room, I saw how Hippias's glance lit momentarily upon the supposed Sir George and then immediately passed on in search of explanation. He had recognized at once that he was in the presence of Denzell — Denzell whom he had supposed perished in that blackbirding foray so many years before. The English members of the family, you must remember, had known Denzell and myself only as boys, but Hippias had known us as young men. And later in the evening a word he spoke to me outside the study showed that he had arrived at the whole truth. For the time, I was completely unnerved. The past had claimed us and at last the truth must be told. At least, my dear Timothy, it would benefit you and bring you into your own. But for me it meant either flight or suicide. My mind was very confused. I prepared for either.

Bevis must have been told at once, and I suppose Willoughby too, and they must have learnt or conjectured your own legitimacy. There was puzzle and panic and quarrelling at Hazelwood that night. The false Sir George faced exposure; I faced exposure; Bevis and Willoughby faced the loss of the title and the estate. Only Denzell, I think, got a queer enjoyment out of knowing himself cornered. And Hippias was probably hoping to do a little by way of blackmail.

Then came this inexplicable murder. It is utterly mysterious to me – as it must be to you – and to the police I believe I have told nothing but truth in the matter, although of much I have naturally spoken not at all. Who killed Denzell, the false Sir George? No answer comes to me. Regard our strange story from whatever angle I can, I find no one whom this savage deed could benefit. I am constrained to think that it was some other of Denzell's sins that so dramatically found him out, and that only coincidence is responsible for his death's occurring at the very crisis of our particular affairs. And here I cannot do other than think of the return of Hoodless, and of his known relationship with the poor girl who has been accustomed to call herself Lady Simney.

What has happened to the documents which Denzell so long held over me I do not know. But of this I am very certain: you, my dear boy, will never be Sir Timothy until the full truth is known – and that truth, even after all these years, must mean my being dragged to Australia to stand my trial for what was done at Sharks Bay on that inky night. I am too old and too tired a man for that. There is one alternative before me, as there has always been. After what manner I have embraced it you will know before this letter reaches your hand.

Sir Timothy Simney, Bart.,   Your unhappy Father,
Hazelwood Hall.   *George Simney*

When Timmy had finished reading this extraordinary document there was a long silence. Bevis – Sir Bevis as he had appeared to be only a few minutes before – sat biting his nails, a picture of uneasy rage. Willoughby had withdrawn into the reassuring world offered by Caravaggio. Lucy, Grace and Joyleen were looking about equally bewildered; and Joyleen was alarmed as well. Hippias appeared decidedly crestfallen, perhaps because he had now lost all chance of his cheque; and Gerard, for whom I felt decidedly sorry, was staring at him in a sort of horrified astonishment. Christopher was impassive, Mr Deamer struggled with some private pandemonium, and Mervyn was still standing beside Timmy as if to offer him support. Timmy himself was very pale. And in this I don't doubt that I matched him. For one thing, it was decidedly odd to know that I had been married not to George but Denzell Simney, and that even if the marriage had been legally valid I had been plain Mrs Simney all the time.

Silence prolonged itself in that horrible study, and round the walls Simneys dead and gone appeared to sit in futile judgement upon what had been revealed. Inspector Cadover advanced before the fire-place; his expression was at once weary and severe; when he spoke his voice held a new and sombre note.

'Ladies and gentlemen, what you have just heard must appear to some of you almost incredible. But what the document reveals is, I believe, substantially true. Denzell Simney returned from Australia as George, and he compelled the real George to accompany him in the character of a servant. But the real George effected a legal marriage with one Kathleen Taylor, and I have little doubt that the son of that marriage, who has long passed as Timothy Owdon, is likely to be declared the legitimate heir. So far, this letter left by the dead man to his son may be taken at its face value. But when we come to the death of Denzell Simney in this room on Tuesday night it is a very different matter. Here, I am sorry to say, the letter is deliberately calculated to mislead. In fact' – and Inspector Cadover's brow darkened – 'it is an instrument cleverly contrived by a dead man to deflect the consequences of a crime.'

I glanced at Timmy as he stood quietly by the fire-place, and as I did so vague forebodings which had long possessed me passed into sudden acute apprehensiveness.

'Consider the facts. The Australian cousins have arrived. Sir George Simney, the pretender butler, realizes that a crisis has arrived in his affairs. While he lived he could not safely make the truth known, or claim the just rights of his son and himself. But what of communicating the secret to that son? This he must have been determined sooner or later to do. And this he now did.

'The butler's boy suddenly learnt that he was the heir to Hazelwood. He learnt that the man whom he already hated was an impostor, and one who had deeply injured his father and himself. And he learnt another thing. It was by his possession of certain documents that the impostor retained his power. And now, suddenly, the safe, the likely hiding-place of these documents, was revealed! What followed was a crime bred half of unreasoning hate and half of cunning calculation.'

There was a moment's strained silence. I heard the violent beating of my heart. Cadover's finger shot out and pointed straight at Timmy.

'One question. Where were you on Tuesday night between eleven and twelve?'

For a fraction of a second Timmy hesitated. 'I was in bed,' he said.

'That is a lie. As it happens, your bedroom was inspected by the head groom. You were not there.'

'It is not a lie.'

Cadover smiled wearily. 'Then how,' he demanded, 'do you account for that groom's evidence?'

Again Timmy hesitated. 'The man was mistaken,' he said quietly.

'You can think of nothing better than that?'

'I have nothing more to say.'

With a gesture almost as of pain, Cadover passed a hand over his brow. 'It was Timothy Simney who summoned Mr Deamer. It was Timothy Simney who climbed down the trellis and killed the man who sat at this table. To-day the wretched boy's father learnt the truth of his son's rash act. By writing the letter he did he endeavoured to give the impression that it was only after his brother's death that Timothy learnt anything about the matter. But the deception has failed and the truth is now known to us all. Timothy Simney killed his uncle.'

'No!'

We all swung round. Mr Deamer had sprung to his feet, shaking in every limb.

'No!' he shouted. 'It is false. It is as false as hell. I killed him myself.'

'And it was I who summoned Mr Deamer.' My own voice came to me as from a great distance. 'It was I who planned – well, nearly the whole thing.'

3

'I hurled the bronze head,' said Mr Deamer. 'But did not hurl it at – at the man we supposed to be Sir George.'

'Then what the deuce *did* you hurl it at?' Hippias, confident again, turned blusteringly upon the unfortunate vicar.

'I will not tell you. It would not be believed by any of you.' And Deamer looked desperately round the room. 'But I hurled the missile and then, overcome with horror and fear – fear so great that I had screamed aloud – I fled the abominable room. Nobody would divulge to me just how the unhappy man was killed, and I have been in an agony of doubt. But now I know. There can be no question of the fact. God help me! Mine was the hand that inadvertently struck him down.'

'It was a judgement.' Grace had risen hysterically to her feet. 'Mr Deamer was but the instrument of divine –'

'Silence, woman!' And Deamer turned upon my sister-in-law with a wrath which was momentarily terrible. 'You have encouraged me too long in such notions. And now I acknowledge myself guilty of spiritual pride, and veiled concupiscence, and a rash and fatal deed.'

There was silence. I found it very difficult to speak. For the man whom we had thought of as George I had, I believe, neither remorse nor compunction still. But this wretched clergyman was another matter. Simply because he had cut me in the village street, and caused me to hate him for a while, I had bound him into my plan of action against my husband. Nothing more than discomfort had been intended for him. But actually he had been led to do a deed which would remain a burden upon him for life. Little (I may repeat) did I realize what toils that walk on Tuesday morning was weaving.

And then, once more, I heard my own voice, mechanical and dull.

'You know that Mr Hoodless and I were at one time to be married, and that the engagement was broken off. He wrote to me regularly, and there came a time when he sent me certain intimate records of his life, the results of a prolonged and successful psychiatric treatment. These records fell into my husband's hands – he stole them, in fine – and he saw, just as he saw in the case of his brother the true George, that he could hold them against me. It would not, of course, be possible to publish them, but by sending them to certain of Mr Hoodless's relatives he could occasion great distress and pain. Latterly it was only because of his possession of these papers that I consented to remain at Hazelwood.'

Christopher gave a quick gasp. There was no other sound in the room as I paused to collect myself. Never before, I suppose, had I held an audience as I was holding this audience now.

'The Australians came and I realized that a crisis had come with them. Somehow my husband was cornered. I knew that if some serious disclosure obscurely faced him he would drag down with him whom he could. And I knew too that Christopher – Mr Hoodless – was due home at any time. Then came the revelation of the safe behind the portrait, and for the first time I knew where Christopher's letters must be concealed.

'The next day, when my husband struck me, and told me he had seen my lover, I knew that I could safely wait no longer, and I made my plan. I would get the letters from him by force, or he would be sorry for it.'

'Good heavens!' Hippias was staring at me in astonishment. 'Robbery under arms.'

'I proposed to myself something like that. But I knew that it was not a simple thing to achieve. My husband, who so delighted in trapping people, must be made to see or believe that he was himself effectively trapped. He must be trapped here in the study, beside the safe. He must realize that his life was in my hands. And he must realize that I could take that life in an instant without danger to myself. Only in such a situation as that would he be likely to lose his nerve and yield. So I tried –'

'Stop!' It was Timmy who interrupted me. And now he came forward and took me urgently by the hand. 'Nicolette, what nonsense is this? Do you remember once telling me that you could look after yourself? Well, I can do the same. You needn't –'

I shook my head. 'Timmy, I'm not being heroic. Everything – or nearly everything – I am going to say Inspector Cadover already knows. I don't at all understand how he came to know. But I have seen him look at – at something in this room in a way that tells me he does.'

'Music.' Cadover almost smiled. 'But please go on.'

I pressed Timmy's hand and nodded. 'My plan depended on two facts – on two facts of vision. My husband was short-sighted. And Owdon – as I must for the moment call him – had only one eye. You might say that Owdon's missing eye was the pivot of the whole scheme. It made feasible – you might say scientifically feasible – what was at first no more than a queer fantasy that drifted into my head on Monday night.

'It was when I came in upon the Simneys quarrelling. There was a whiskey-bottle on that table – a broken bottle, as you know – and all round the walls were those Simneys dead and gone. Well, I remembered a whiskey advertisement popular when I was a child. It showed a very grand gentleman sitting with a bottle of whiskey beside him, and portraits of his ancestors round about. And –'

'And the ancestors reach out of their frames and grab!' It was Mervyn, round-eyed, who supplied this inform-ation.

I nodded. 'Just that. I was going to reach out of my frame and grab – grab those letters of Christopher's which my husband had stolen from me. Of course, I couldn't be an ancestral Simney. But I could be a Venus – of sorts. Look at Caravaggio's goddess above the mantelpiece. The picture stands recessed behind those Grinling Gibbon pillars and in its own heavy chiaroscuro. I had only to get up there with the help of the high-backed chair, take the required pose, and I would virtually have vanished from this ill-lit room. My husband with his short sight would not distinguish me. Nor – what was more important – would Owdon. For it is only the fact of our having *two* eyes that enables us to discriminate between a plane surface and a body in full relief.'

Out of the corner of my eye I saw the mouth of Inspec-tor Cadover's Harold drop open; perhaps he was reflecting on what glory would have been his in the Simney affair had he pierced straight to the consequences of monocular vision.

'Of course there was a little embarrassment in being stared at even by a one-eyed man when attired as Caravaggio's Venus is. Even a strip-tease girl might feel uncomfort-able. And I must say that when, only a few minutes later, I caught Willoughby looking at me as if I *was* a work of art, I felt a decidedly macabre shiver. But the gain was immense. Once one has had a look behind the window-curtains this study holds no possible hiding-places. Owdon would be prepared to swear that he had left an empty room, and that subsequently nobody had entered by the door except my husband himself.

'And then my plan was simple. I had a revolver. With this I would descend as soon as my husband was seated and in a dozen words tell him that he was trapped. If he did not hand over the letters he would be shot. Owdon would rush in while I hid behind the opening door; while he ran to the body I would slip out to the bath-room; and seconds later I would appear again. Demonstrably it could have been only by the trellis that the assailant had come and gone, and for me to have taken that route in the time available would have been impossible. My husband had a quick enough wit and I could trust him to take the situation in at once. And there was, I reckoned, a very substantial chance that he would give in.

'Perhaps you will not believe me when I say that I meant no more than a bluff. I had no intention of killing him. Still, I had to take precautions, since it was not impossible that he would himself when cornered launch a murderous attack upon me.

'And here the snow set me a problem. I had not considered that someone might be conceived as coming down the trellis from *above*. And if I was actually driven to shoot and kill there must therefore be tracks in the snow below the window. Someone must come and go there shortly before midnight or the whole scheme would be futile. It was then that I thought of Mr Deamer, and summoned him. It never occurred to me that his zeal to reprehend Jane Fairey would bring him actually to scale the trellis and peer into the study. But that, as you know, was what he did. And so far the whole horrible business is clear enough. But why he should then have acted as it now appears he did –'

'That too is perfectly clear.' Inspector Cadover brusquely interrupted me. 'As soon as I realized about the Caravaggio the manner of your husband's death held no further mystery.'

'But how *did* you realize about the Caravaggio?' It was not, I suppose, very becoming in me to start questioning the police, but this one question I could by no means resist.

'Not through any very professional procedure.' The Inspector looked at me gravely. 'The process was rather similar to that by which you arrived at it yourself: the whiskey-bottle which recalled the advertisement. I was in this room, and something was working obscurely at the back of my mind – and then Mr Hippias broke into an air from a Gilbert and Sullivan opera. I had the baffling sensation that the truth had been tossed to me, and that I had missed it. That was why I spent a good deal of time with a gramophone this afternoon. And when I came to *Ruddigore*, sure enough, the thing fell into my lap. For there, too, ancestors come out of their frames.'

And Inspector Cadover turned to his assistant Harold. 'It wasn't a feather, after all,' he said oddly. 'It was the creature's chirp.'

'What followed,' pursued Cadover, 'is simple enough. Lady Simney stepped from before the picture, speaking some word to her husband as she did so. He looked up, and what he saw naturally produced an expression of incredulous amazement – that expression which ought from the first to have been a key to the whole affair. And it was at this moment that Mr Deamer peered into the room. What he saw seemed to confirm him in certain fantastic notions to which he was subject. Sir George Simney, he believed, had sold his soul to the Devil, and the Devil could summon him what recondite pleasures he wished for. At this very moment the thing was happening, and Caravaggio's libidinous image of Venus was being brought to life to subserve Sir George's lust. To most of you the conception must seem utterly grotesque, but you must remember that Mr Deamer has fed his imagination upon much medieval lore, in which such things are common form.

'Mr Deamer was, of course, appalled at this evidence of malign power, and he cried aloud in horror. But he acted as well. Martin Luther, you will remember, threw his ink-pot at the Devil. Mr Deamer snatched up what came first to his hand – it was the bronze head in the window embrasure – and hurled it at the phantom descending from the mantelpiece. His horror and terror must have lent him for the moment an almost preternatural strength. And it was at this moment that Lady Simney's husband sprang to his feet. The bronze caught him full on the back of the head and killed him instantly. And in the same moment Mr Deamer turned and fled.

'Lady Simney, we must believe, was utterly without any clear notion of what had occurred. But, whether her husband was alive or dead, she knew that her position was desperate. She ran to the body, picked up the bronze, wiped it, and replaced it on the pedestal. As she did so she noticed the pair of boots which Mr Deamer had let slip as he fled. She pitched them into a corner of the room, ran for the door, and concealed herself behind it as it opened when the butler burst into the room. He, of course, hurried straight to the body, and Lady Simney slipped out to her bath-room. Her plan had thus in a sense accomplished itself, but the result was very different from what she had anticipated. Her husband – by whatever mysterious agency – was mortally wounded or dead.

'And the vital letters were still in the safe. If she had reflected she would have realized that this was now of small importance, since nobody was now likely to misuse them in the way that her husband had threatened to do. She may have felt, however, that the subsequent discovery of documents of such a character might serve to bring suspic-ion upon her in regard to the tragedy. She therefore seized the first opportunity to remove them. But just how she managed it I cannot say.'

I nodded. 'Mervyn and Willoughby went into the

window embrasure to investigate. And there they fell to some sort of dispute which gave me my chance. I got the keys from the body, tiptoed across the room, opened the safe, and pitched its contents into the fire – including, I suppose, the papers about George and Sharks Bay. The flames leapt so high that I thought they would catch the attention of the lads behind the curtain. But they were quarrelling still. Suddenly my eye fell on those inexplicable boots which I had pitched into a corner. The sheer un-accountability of them scared me and I bundled them into the safe, locked it, and returned the keys. I was scarcely a moment too soon.

'But I had now only one really substantial fear. Could it conceivably have been Christopher who had killed my husband? But as soon as my panic had gone down I realized that he would never do such a thing in that way. As I knew that Mr Deamer had been below I ought, I suppose, to have suspected him. But how could I guess at his motive, and that it was really myself that he had aimed at? Later I had fears about Timmy, chiefly because of things he had said to me early that morning. And when you seemed to make out a case against him I felt, just as Mr Deamer did, that the truth must be told.'

Inspector Cadover nodded soberly. 'Thank you,' he said. 'And Sir Timothy must forgive me for forcing the issue in the way I did. It has been a perplexing affair, ladies and gentlemen, but the crime is now solved.'

'Crime?' Christopher stood up and walked to the fire-place. 'May I ask to what crime you refer?'

The Inspector scratched his chin, and I could see that he was taken aback. 'Well,' he said cautiously, 'it is very clear that more than one crime has been brought to light.'

'Mr Deamer pitched that bronze head at what he conceived to be a demon in the phantasmal form of a woman. The result was an accidental death. Does that constitute a crime?'

'The accident resulted from his being unlawfully on the premises. Therefore –'

'But was he? He was virtually invited by Lady Simney or – as he supposed – by Miss Grace Simney, a person of standing in the household. Moreover' – and Christopher faintly smiled – 'he was here to guard the morality of his parish. He was engaged in the exercise of a proper pastoral care.

'And with what other crimes are we confronted? Both George and Denzell Simney were criminals, but both are dead. Hippias Simney appears to have had some notion of blackmailing Bevis, or alternatively these two were considering entering into a conspiracy to defraud the rightful heir; but these things would be uncommonly hard to prove in court. There only remains Lady Simney, as I think we may continue to call her for the time.'

'Quite so.' Inspector Cadover looked exceedingly grim. 'Her actions are indictable, without a doubt.'

'But why?' Timmy came forward and stood beside me. 'She played a trick on Mr Deamer, and that trick had an altogether unforeseen result. She proposed to regain property of her own from her husband –'

'By threat of violence.'

'No doubt. But the thing never accomplished itself.'

'That is of scarcely any significance. She stepped from that mantelpiece armed with a revolver, and her reason for arranging that there should be footprints on the terrace outside was her expectation that her husband might, despite her innocuous intentions, after all be killed.'

Christopher nodded. 'There is a possible case, of course – and the coroner may find so. But what then? No jury on earth would convict Nicolette. Her story would gain their complete sympathy, and they would take the view that she was playing a mere intimate prank on her objectionable husband when poor Mr Deamer broke in and behaved like a lunatic.'

What Inspector Cadover replied to this I didn't catch.

For I had turned to Timmy. 'Timmy,' I whispered, 'why weren't you in your room? Was it –?'

Timmy flushed darkly and nodded. 'I was going through the house and she dodged out of her room and looked at me. You can guess how she would.'

'I certainly can.'

'She – she hadn't even anything much on. I just couldn't help it, and it turned into a long petting party in her room. It wasn't very nice.'

I looked at Joyleen; her alarm was abating and she was smoking a cigarette. 'No doubt,' I said, 'you were upset by the departure of the housemaid you used to kiss. But in future, and particularly in your new character as a dashing young baronet, I should be inclined to give Joyleen a wide berth.'

I looked at the others. Inspector Cadover was glancing irresolutely first at myself and then at Mr Deamer; I could see that he was considering whether to arrest one or other of us, or both. Harold was shutting a notebook disconsolately – but catching my eye he gave me a cautious smile. I stood up to go to Christopher. And as I did so Hippias brushed past me and took Timmy by the lapel of his coat. 'Now, look here,' he said – and his tone was at once ingratiating and aggrieved – 'about that bally low trick your father played us over Dismal Swamp . . .'

Some other Michael Innes novels published by Penguins

From *London* Far

A random scrap of Augustan poetry muttered in a tobacconist's thrusts an absent-minded scholar through a trap-door into short-lived leadership of London's greatest art racket.

Then it's a chase on the twisting trail of the Titians and Giottos – a roller-coaster ride from the highland islands of Scotland to America's rich east coast. And all the time Meredith is at grips with problems which are hardly academic.

An Awkward Lie

Hamlet, Revenge!

Money from Holme